Slightly but suddenly, like a bird which has caught movement to the side, the corpse turned its head to glare at Theophanes.

"You have come at my call," the necromancer said.

It tittered. "I have been waiting for you—sage."

Theophanes licked his lips. "Tell us what killed you and we will let you go."

"Nothing can kill *me*, sage," the corpse wheezed. "Only bodies die." It began to raise its torso from the table. "A thousand years ago I was as you are, though with power to which yours is like a candle to the sun . . . and I did not want to die. My body could rot, so long as my soul—"

"Begone!" Theophanes cried. "Begone, in the Name by which you were summoned!"

"Oh, you didn't summon me," the corpse replied.

VETTIUS AND HIS FRIENDS

DAVID DRAKE

VETTIUS AND HIS FRIENDS

A Baen Books Original

Baen Publishing Enterprises
260 Fifth Avenue
New York, N.Y. 10001

First printing, February 1989

ISBN: 0-671-69802-8

Cover art by Alan Gutierrez

Printed in the United States of America

Distributed by
SIMON & SCHUSTER
1230 Avenue of the Americas
New York, N.Y. 10020

Dedication

for Sandra Miesel
One historian to another

Acknowledgments

"The False Prophet" original to this volume.
"Black Iron" copyright 1975 by April R. Derleth and Walden W. Derleth for NAMELESS PLACES (ed. Gerald W. Page).
"The Mantichore" copyright 1978 by Andrew J. Offutt for SWORDS AGAINST DARKNESS III.
"The Shortest Way" copyright 1974 by Stuart David Schiff for WHISPERS (magazine) v 1 #3.
"From the Dark Waters" copyright 1976 by David A. Drake for WAVES OF TERROR (ed. Michel Parry).
"Nemesis Place" copyright 1978 by Ultimate Publishing Co. Inc, for FANTASTIC, April, 1978.
"Dragons' Teeth" original version copyright 1975 by Karl Edward Wagner for MIDNIGHT SUN, v 1, #2. A shorter version, copyedited by a moron, copyright 1977 by Andrew J. Offutt for SWORDS AGAINST DARKNESS. This version (based on the long version) is original to the volume.
"The Barrow Troll" copyright 1975 by Stuart David Schiff for WHISPERS (magazine) #8.
"Killer" copyright 1974 by Karl Edward Wagner for MIDNIGHT SUN, v 1, #1.
"Ranks of Bronze" copyright 1975 by UPD Inc. for GALAXY, August, 1975.
"Dreams in Amber" copyright 1985 by Stuart David Schiff for WHISPERS V (book).
"King Crocodile" copyright 1981 by Stuart David Schiff for WHISPERS III (book).

Contents

Source Materials:
By Way of Introduction

Ammianus Marcellinus, who lived in the Fourth century AD, was one of the finest of the ancient historians. For about fifteen years of his life, Ammianus was a soldier: an officer in the select body which not only guarded the emperors but also provided aides-de-camp and couriers at the very highest levels of imperial business. Thus, when he came to write, he combined his brilliant, vivid Latin style (not always the *clearest* style imaginable, I'll admit) with considerable personal knowledge of the great events of his time.

I began reading Ammianus during interrogation training at Ft. Meade in 1969 and continued while I was stationed at various places in South-East Asia. Reading difficult Latin was one of the ways I tried to stay sane when I was in the army. I didn't stay sane, of course; but I survived, and my situation certainly increased the impact Ammianus had on me.

I'd sold a couple fantasy stories to August Derleth

of Arkham House before I was drafted. When I got back to the World, I immediately wrote a piece set during the siege of Amida by the Persians in 359 AD (which Ammianus, who was present, describes with stunning effect). The story, "Black Iron," introduced a pair of friends named Vettius (a Guards officer) and Dama (a silk merchant). Mr. Derleth bought the piece—and died the day after mailing me his check.

I continued to write heroic fantasies set in the historical past, even though there was almost no market for that sub-genre in short format. I used, among others, Norse settings (one of them, "The Barrow Troll," is included here), Egyptian settings ("King Crocodile"), and various Roman settings beyond those of the Fourth century AD.

But primarily, I wrote stories about Vettius and Dama.

They weren't written for a particular market: as I said above, there *weren't* any markets that seemed likely to take them at the time, though they did all find homes eventually.

Nor did I start with a plan of the careers of the two men. The stories all involved Vettius and Dama as adults, filling in *that* bit of background and no more—the way Robert E. Howard wrote about Conan (and the way I've been doing my Hammer's Slammers stories, starting in the early '70s).

The exception is "The False Prophet," the novelet I did for this volume. It seemed like a good idea to show how Vettius and Dama met, so "The False Prophet" is the earliest in time by at least ten years. The background of this story is, in large measure, borrowed from essays by Lucian of

Samosata (with the adaptations necessary to bring it forward a couple of centuries).

There's "a bit of a story" about two of the stories included here. I wrote "Ranks of Bronze" shortly after reading Sallust's (first century BC) history of the Jugurthine War. That contained an incident described in historical present tense, which drove me to copy the technique just this once. (Sallust was a better writer than I was. Sallust was a better writer than most people.)

The published version (the version reprinted here) was edited heavily, and for the better, by Jim Baen; who liked the result well enough to ask me to base a novel on it a decade later. I used the situation to write (under the same title) a Bildungsroman, a novel describing the growth of the central character from youth to manhood. It's the book of mine in whose structure I'm the most satisfied. (Comments in reviews that "this was obviously the first book in a series" would have bothered me more if I'd had a higher opinion of reviewers to begin with.)

"Killer" started as a solo short story titled "Hunter's Moon." I did multiple drafts (still my working technique) and sent out the final without keeping a copy. The editor to whom I sent the story was in the habit, I later learned, of not returning manuscripts. Certainly he didn't return mine. (His later felony conviction involved matters not concerned with his literary affairs.)

Failing to keep a copy was remarkably stupid, even for me at the time (my head wasn't screwed on real tight for some while after I got back from Nam). I set the idea aside, because I was too angry and frustrated to recast my drafts into publishable form again.

A couple years later, a fellow in Ohio started a fanzine devoted to the work of my friend Karl Wagner. Karl wanted material besides his own to fill out the 'zine. He asked if he could rewrite "Hunter's Moon," working from my drafts. That was fine with me.

The result was a true collaboration: totally rewritten, half again as long as my version, and wearing a new title—"Killer." A British writer/anthologist (and friend of Karl's and mine: Michel Parry) gave the story professional publication after it appeared in the fanzine; and when Jim Baen suggested that Karl and I collaborate on a novel, we did so—based on this story.

Writing a new story for this volume was fun for a couple of reasons.

I chose my undergraduate double majors, history and Latin, because I loved the subjects. I still do. Latin is the only one of the many languages I've learned as an adult in which I'm still fluent. I continue to read my Martial and Ovid, Tacitus and Macrobius—and a bookcase full of others—for pleasure. It was nice to get back into aspects of those authors' world (worlds, really; "Rome" was no more a monolith than "England" is).

But it was also the world of Vettius and Dama; and that pair were friends to me at a time when there wasn't a whole lot inside my skull that was friendly. So "Hail!" guys; and I hope not "Farewell," though it may be a while before I'm with you again.

Dave Drake

The False Prophet

The big young man, grinning at Dama through the doorway of the City Prefect's private office, had the look of a killer.

Dama knew the fellow's name, Lucius Vettius—and knew that he was an officer in the imperial guard, though at the moment he wore a civilian toga.

Dama smiled back.

"The virtuous Marcus Licinius Dama!" bellowed the nomenclator in a strong Syrian accent. Why couldn't Gaius Rutilius Rutilianus—who was, by Mithra, City Prefect of Rome—buy servants who at least pronounced Latin properly?

"He didn't mention that you're only a merchant!" Menelaus whispered to Dama in amazement.

"No, he didn't," Dama agreed without amplifying his response.

The nomenclator was wearing a new tunic. So was the doorkeeper who'd let Dama and his older companion into Rutilianus's reception room with a crowd of over a hundred other favor-seekers. The tunics were best-quality Egyptian linen and represented a hefty outlay—

Even to Dama, who imported them along with the silks which were his primary stock in trade.

"His companion," cried the nomenclator, "the learned Faustus Pompeius Menelaus!" The nomenclator paused. "Known as 'The Wise.' "

Menelaus suddenly looked ten years younger. He straightened to his full height and fluffed his long gray beard.

Though Dama said nothing as the pair of them stepped into Rutilianus's private office, the nomenclator had earned himself a bonus by the degree to which his ad-libbed comment had brightened the old man's face.

Menelaus and Dama's father had remained friends throughout the latter's life. Dama stopped visiting his parent when disease and pain so wracked the older man that every conversation became a litany of insult and complaint; but Menelaus continued to come, to read aloud and to bear bitter insults because to do so was a philosopher's duty—and a friend's.

"Well, he sure looks the part, doesn't he?" quipped Caelius, one of the four civilians standing around the Prefect's couch. "Got any owls nesting in that beard, old man?"

"Looking the part's easy enough," countered Vulco. "If you want a philosopher of *real* learning, though, you'll hire Pactolides."

"I think it's unchristian to be hiring *any* sort of pagan philosopher," said Macer. "Severiana won't like it a bit."

"My wife doesn't make the decisions in *this* house," the Prefect said so forcefully that everyone listening knew that Rutilianus was as much voicing a wish as stating a fact.

The Prefect shifted his heavy body on the couch and scratched himself. Though the morning air was comfortable by most standards, Rutilianus was sweating despite having dispensed with the formality of his toga while handling this private interview.

The men were the Prefect's friends, advisors, and employees—and wore all those separate masks at the same time. Except for Vettius (who was about Dama's age), they'd accompanied Rutilianus during his governorships in Spain and North Africa. They carried out important commissions, gave confidential advice—and picked up the bits and scraps which form the perquisites of those having the ear of high office.

"Anyway," offered Sosius, "I don't think that there's anything sinful about hearing advice on living a good life, even if it does come from a pagan."

For what Dama had paid Sosius, he'd expected more enthusiastic support. Pactolides was getting much better value for his bribe to Vulco.

"Well, let's hear what he says for himself," the Prefect said, still peevish at the mention of his wife. He nodded toward Menelaus. "You *can* speak, can't you?" he demanded. "Not much use in having a personal philosopher who can't, is there?"

"Pactolides can speak like an angel," muttered Vulco. "Voice like a choirboy, that man has. . . ."

Dama prompted his friend with a tap on the shoulder. Menelaus stepped forward and bowed. "If ever there was a man who was rightly afraid when called to speak in your presence, noble Rutilianus," the old philosopher boomed, "it is I;

and I sense—" he made a light, sweeping bow to the Prefect's companions "—that those who participate in your counsels are well able to see my distress."

Menelaus was a different man as soon as he began his set oration—confident, commanding; his tones and volume pitched to blast through the chatter filling a rain-crowded basilica when he addressed his students in one corner. Dama had worried that the old man's desperate need for a job would cause him to freeze up when the opportunity was offered. He should have known better.

"—for my heart is filled with the awareness of the way you, armed like Mars himself, preserved the liberty of this Republic; and now, wearing the toga, increase its civil glory. For—"

The soldier, Vettius, crooked a finger toward Dama and nodded in the direction of the garden behind the office.

Rutilianus's other councilors looked bored—Vulco was yawning ostentatiously—but the Prefect himself listened to the panegyric with pleasure. He nodded with unconscious agreement while Menelaus continued, "—while all those who have borne the burden of your exalted prefecture are to be praised, to you especially is honor due."

Vettius, waiting at the door into the garden, crooked his finger again. Dama pursed his lips and followed, walking with small steps to disturb the gathering as little as possible—though Menelaus in full cry couldn't have been put off his stride by someone shouting *Fire!*, and the Prefect was rapt at the mellifluous description of his virtues.

The garden behind Rutilianus's house had a covered walk on three sides, providing shade at all times of the day. The open area was large enough to hold a dozen fruit trees as well as a small grape arbor and a variety of roses, exotic peonies, and other flowers.

Military equipment was stacked beside the door: a bronze helmet and body armor modeled with idealized muscles over which a pair of naiads cavorted; a swordbelt supporting the sheathed dagger and long, straight-bladed spatha of a cavalryman; and a large, circular shield in its canvas cover.

Vettius followed Dama's eyes toward the gear and volunteered, "I'm army—seconded to the City Prefect for the time being."

There were two ways for Dama to handle his response. He made the snap decision that concealing his knowledge from this big, hard-eyed soldier couldn't bring any dividends equal to getting the man's respect from the start.

"Yes," he said. "A decurion in the squadron of Domestic Horse."

Vettius was surprised enough to glance sideways to make sure that canvas still covered the gilt spikes and hearts against the blue background of his shieldface. "Right, that's me," he agreed mildly. "The Prefect's bodyguard, more or less. The name's Lucius Vettius—as I suppose you knew."

There was no question in the final clause, but Dama nodded his agreement anyway. He'd done his homework—as he always did his homework before a major sale.

This business, because it was personal and not merely a matter of money, was the most major sale of his life. . . .

"Let me hope," rolled Menelaus's voice through the open door and window of the office, "that my words today can be touched by a fraction of the felicity with which all Rome greeted the news that you had been appointed her helmsman."

"I was wondering," Vettius said, "just how much you'd paid Sosius?"

Dama prodded the inside of his cheek with his tongue.

"The reason I'm wondering," the soldier continued, "is that he's taking money from Pactolides too." He laughed. "Vulco's an unusually virtuous councilor, you know."

Dama grimaced bitterly. "Yeah," he agreed. "Vulco stays bought."

"My words are driven out under the compulsion of the virtue and benignity which I see before me . . ." Menelaus continued in an orotund voice.

"I hadn't thought," continued Dama, choosing his words carefully, "that a decurion was worth bribing. Until now that I've met you."

"I'd have taken your money," Vettius said with the same cold smile as before. "But it wouldn't've gained you anything. What I'd really like from you, Citizen Dama . . ."

Dama nodded his head upward in agreement. "Go ahead," he said.

If not money, then a woman? A *particular* woman to whom a silk merchant might have access . . . ?

". . . is information." The flat certainty with which the words came out of Vettius's mouth emphasized the size and strength of the man speaking. He had black hair and spoke with a slight tang of the Illyrian frontier.

"Go ahead," Dama repeated with outward calm.

From the office came, ". . . though I fear that by mentioning any particular excellence first, I will seem to devalue. . . ."

"I can see why the old man wants to be Rutilianus's tame philosopher," Vettius said. "It's getting harder and harder to scrape up enough pupils freelance to keep him in bread, onions, and a sop of wine. . . ."

Dama nodded.

"Thing is, I'm not quite clear what *your* part in the business might be. Citizen."

This time the soldier's smile made Dama measure in his mind the distance between him and the hilt of the sword resting against the wall. Too far, almost certainly.

And unnecessary. Almost certainly.

"Menelaus was a friend of my father's," Dama said. "A good friend. Toward the last, my father's only friend. Menelaus is too proud to take charity from me directly—but he was glad to have me stand beside him while he sought this position in the Prefect's household."

Vettius chuckled. "Stand beside him," he repeated ironically. "With a purse full of silver you hand out to anybody who might ease your buddy's road."

". . . speak of the River Tagus, red with the blood of the bandits you as Governor slaughtered there?"

"He doesn't know that," snapped Dama.

"But you do, merchant," the soldier said. "You take your family duties pretty seriously, don't you?"

"Yeah, I do," agreed Dama as simply as if he didn't know he was being mocked . . . and perhaps he was not being mocked. "Menelaus is my friend as well as my duty, but—I take all my duties seriously."

The big man smiled; this time, for a change, it gave his face a pleasant cast. "Yeah," he said. "So do I."

"I can see that," Dama agreed, feeling his body

relax for the first time since his interview with this big, deadly man began. "And it's your duty to guard Rutilianus."

"More a matter of keeping things from hitting the Prefect from somewhere he's not looking," Vettius said with a shrug. "So I like to know the people who're getting close to him."

He grinned. "Usually I don't much like what I learn. Usually."

Dama nodded toward the office, where Menelaus's measured periods had broken up into the general babble of all those in the room. "I think we'd better get back," he said. "I'm glad to have met you, Lucius Vettius."

And meant it.

The Prefect called, "Ah, Vettius," craning his neck to see over his shoulder as Dama and the soldier reentered the room. "We rather like Menelaus here, don't we, gentlemen?"

Yesyes/Wellspoken indeed/Seems solid for a pagan—

"Well, being able to spout a set speech doesn't make him learned, sir," crabbed Vulco.

He fixed Menelaus with a glare meant to be steely. Vulco's head was offset so that only one eye bore, making him look rather like an angry crow.

"Tell me, sirrah," he demanded, "who was it that Thersites fed his sons to? Quick, now—no running around to sort through your books."

The philosopher blinked in confusion. Dama thought for a moment that his friend had been caught out, but Menelaus said, "Good sir, Atreus it was who murdered the sons of his brother Thyestes and cooked them for their father."

Dama suppressed a laugh. Menelaus had paused

in order to find a way to answer the question without making his questioner look *too* much of a fool.

Vulco blinked. "Well, that seems all right," he muttered, fixing his eyes on his hands and seeming to examine his manicure.

"Yes, well," Rutilianus agreed. "But you, Lucius Vettius. What information do *you* have for us?"

Everyone else in the room looked at the tall soldier: Menelaus in surprise, the Prefect and his companions with a partially-concealed avidity for scandal; Dama with a professionally-blank expression, waiting to hear what was said before he decided how to deal with anything that needed to be countered.

Vettius glanced at Dama. "I'd suggested to his excellency," he said, "that he let me see what I could learn about the learned Menelaus."

"Of course," Rutilianus agreed, lifting his eyebrows. "After all, we need to be sure of the man who's going to be responsible for the moral training of my children."

His companions bobbed and muttered approval.

Vettius took a bi-fold notebook of waxed boards from the wallet in the bosom of his toga, but he didn't bother to open the document before he said, "Menelaus comes from Caesarea in Cappadocia where his father was one of the city councilors."

Like Dama's father.

"Was schooled in Gaza, then Athens. Returned home and taught there for most of his life. Moved to Rome about five years ago. Gives lessons in oratory and philosophy—"

"Epicurean philosophy," the subject of the discussion broke in before Dama could shush him.

"Epicurean philosophy," Vettius continued, giving Dama—rather than Menelaus—a grin that was not entirely friendly. "In the Forum of Trajan; to about a dozen pupils at any one time. Doesn't get along particularly well with the other teachers who've set up in the same area. For the past three months, he's been attacking one Pyrrhus the Prophet in his lectures, but the two haven't met face to face."

Dama was ready this time. His finger tapped Menelaus's shoulder firmly, even as the older man opened his mouth to violently—and needlessly—state his opinion of Pyrrhus.

"Well, we *know* he's a philosopher!" Caelius said. "What about his personal life?"

"He doesn't have much personal life," Vettius said. He betrayed his annoyance with a thinning of tone so slight that only Dama, of those in the office, heard and understood it. "When he's a little ahead, he buys used books. When he's behind—"

Menelaus winced and examined the floor.

"—which is usually, and now, he pawns them. Stays out of wineshops. Every few months or so he visits a whore named Drome who works the alleys behind the Beef Market.

"These aren't," Vettius added dryly, "expensive transactions."

Dama looked at the philosopher in amazement. Menelaus met his gaze sidelong and muttered, "Ah, Dama, I—thought that when I grew older, some impediments to a calm mind would cease to intrude on my life. But I'm not as old as that yet. I'm ashamed to admit."

Macer opened his mouth as if about to say something. Lucius Vettius turned toward the man and—tapped his notebook, Dama thought, with the index finger of his left hand.

Dama thought the soldier's gesture might be only an idle tic; but Macer understood something by it. The councilor's eyes bulged, and his mouth shut with an audible clop.

"Last year," Vettius continued calmly, "Menelaus moved out of his garret apartment at night, stiffing his landlord for the eight-days' rent."

"Sir!" the philosopher blurted in outrage despite Dama's restraining hand. "When I moved there in the spring, I was told the roof tiles would be replaced in a few days. Nothing had been done by winter—and my books were drenched by the first heavy rains!"

"The pair of Moors sharing the room now—" said Vettius.

"If you want to believe—" Vulco began.

"—say the landlord told them when they moved in that the roof tiles would be replaced in a few days," Vettius continued, slicing across the interruption like a sword cutting rope. "That was three months ago."

He turned to the philosopher and said coldly, "Do you have anything to add to *that*, Faustus Menelaus?"

Menelaus blinked.

Dama bowed low to the soldier and said, "My companion and I beg your pardon, sir. He did not realize that the life of an exceptionally decent and honorable man might contain, on close examination . . . incidents which look regrettable out of context."

"Well, still . . ." Rutilianus said, frowning as he shifted on his couch. "What do you fellows think?"

All four of his civilian companions opened their

mouths to speak. Macer was fractionally ahead of the others, blurting, "Well, Severiana certainly won't be pleased if an opponent of Pyrrhus the Prophet enters your household!"

"Didn't I tell you to leave my wife out of this?" Rutilianus snarled.

Macer quailed as though he'd been slapped. The other civilians froze, unwilling to offer what might not be the words the aroused Prefect wanted to hear.

Vettius looked at them with cool amusement, then back to Rutilianus. "If I may speak, sir?" he said.

"Of course, of course, Lucius," Rutilianus said, wiping his forehead with a napkin. "What do you think I should do?"

Dama squeezed Menelaus's shoulder very firmly, lest the old philosopher interrupt again—which Dama was quite sure would mean disaster. The soldier wasn't the sort of man whose warnings, voiced or implied, were to be ignored without cost.

"I can't speak to the fellow's philosophy," Vettius said.

He paused a half beat, to see if Menelaus would break in on him; and smiled when the philosopher held his peace. "But for his life—Citizen Dama stated the situation correctly. The learned Menelaus is an exceptionally decent and honorable man, fit to enter your household, sir—"

Vulco started to say something. Before the words came out, the soldier had turned and added, in a voice utterly without emotion, "—or your council. From a moral standpoint."

Vulco blanched into silence.

Dama expressionlessly watched the—almost—

exchange. This Vettius could go far in the imperial bureaucracy, with his ability to gather information and his ruthless willingness to use what he had. But the way the soldier moved, his timing—thrusting before his target was expecting it, ending a controversy before it became two-sided—those were a swordsman's virtues, not a bureaucrat's.

Dama's right palm tingled, remembering the feel of a swordhilt. In five years, he'd turned his father's modest legacy into real wealth by a willingness to go where the profits were as high as the risks. He knew swordsmen, knew killers. . . .

"Even with the . . . ?" the Prefect was saying. His eyes looked inward for a moment. "But yes, I can see that anyone's life examined closely might look—"

Rutilianus broke off abruptly as if in fear that his musings were about to enter territory he didn't care to explore.

"Well, anyway, Menelaus," he resumed, "I think we'll give you—"

"Gaius, dearie," called a silk-clad youth past the scowling nomenclator, "there's somebody here you just *have* to see."

Rutilianus looked up with a frown that softened when he saw the youth—the boy, really—who was speaking. "I'm busy, now, Ganymede. Can't it wait. . . ?"

"Not an eensie minute," Ganymede said firmly, lifting his pert nose so that he looked down at the Prefect past chubby cheeks.

"Oh, send him in, then," Rutilianus agreed with a sigh.

The nomenclator, his voice pitched a half-step up with scandal and outrage, announced, "The honorable Gnaeus Aelius Acer . . ." he paused ". . . emissary of Pyrrhus the Prophet."

"*That* charlatan!" Menelaus snapped.

"It ill behooves a pagan to criticize a Christian, you!" Macer retorted.

"Pyrrhus is no Christian!" said Menelaus. "That's as much a sham as his claim to know the future and—"

Dama laid a finger across his friend's lips.

A young man whose dress and bearing marked his good family was being ushered in by the nomenclator.

Rutilianus glanced from the newcomer to Menelaus and remarked in a distant tone, "A word of advice, good philosopher: my wife believes Pyrrhus to be a Christian. A belief in which I choose to concur."

He turned to the newcomer and said, "Greetings, Gnaeus Acer. It's been too long since you or your father have graced us with your company."

Instead of responding with a moment of smalltalk, Acer said, "Pyrrhus to Gaius Rutilianus, greetings. There is—"

There was a glaze over the young man's eyes and his voice seemed leaden. He did not look at the Prefect as his tongue broke into sing-song to continue:

"—one before you
"With whose beard he cloaks for boys his lust.
"Cast him from you hastily
"And spurn him in the dust."

Pyrrhus's messenger fell silent. "I think there's a mistake—" Dama began while his mind raced, searching for a diplomatic way to deny the absurd accusation.

Menelaus was neither interested in nor capable

of diplomacy. "That's doggeral," he said, speaking directly to the Prefect. "And it's twaddle. I've never touched a boy carnally in my life."

After a pause just too short for anyone else to interject a comment, the philosopher added, "I can't claim that as a virtue. Because frankly, I've never been tempted in that direction."

"Vettius?" the Prefect asked, his eyes narrowing with supposition.

The soldier shrugged. "I can't prove an absence," he said—his tone denying the possibility implicit in the words. "But if the learned Menelaus had tastes in that direction, *some* neighbor or slave would surely have mentioned it."

"In his wallet—" Acer broke in unexpectedly.

"—the debaucher keeps

"A letter to the boy with whom he sleeps."

"That," shouted Menelaus, "is a lie as false and black as the heart of the charlatan whose words this poor deluded lad is speaking!"

Vettius reached toward the bosom of the philosopher's toga.

Menelaus raised a hand to fend off what he saw as an assault on his sense of propriety. Dama caught the philosopher's arm and said, "Let him search you now. That will demonstrate the lie to all these gentlemen."

Vettius removed a cracked leather purse whose corners had been restitched so often that its capacity was reduced by a third. He thumbed up the flap—the tie-strings had rotted off a decade before—and emptied it, item by item, into his left palm.

A stylus. A pair of onions.

"I, ah," Menelaus muttered, "keep my lunch. . . ."

Dama patted him to silence.

A half-crust of bread, chewed rather than torn from a larger piece. The lips of Rutilianus and his companions curled.

A tablet, closed so that the two boards protected the writing on their waxed inner sides. All eyes turned to the philosopher.

All eyes save those of Gnaeus Acer, who stood as quietly as a resting sheep.

"My notebook," explained Menelaus. "I jot down ideas for my lectures. And sometimes appointments."

Vettius dumped back the remainder of the wallet's contents and opened the tablet.

"It's in Greek," he commented. He shifted so that light from the garden door threw shadows across the marks scored into the wax and made them legible.

"Yes, I take my notes—" the philosopher began.

" 'Menelaus to his beloved Kurnos,' " Vettius said, translating the lines rather than reading them in their original. " 'Kurnos, don't drive me under the yoke against my will—don't goad my love too much.' "

"What!" said Dama.

"*Oh* . . . !" murmured several of the others in the room.

" 'I won't invite you to the party,' " the soldier continued, raising his voice to a level sufficient to bark commands across the battlefield, " 'nor forbid you. When you're present, I'm distressed—but when you go away, I still love you.' "

"Why, that's not my notebook!" Menelaus cried. "Nor my words. Why, it's just a quotation from the ancient poet Theognis!"

Dama started to extend a hand to the notebook. He caught himself before he thought the gesture was visible, but the soldier had seen and understood. Vettius handed the tablet to Dama open.

Pyrrhus's messenger should have been smiling—should have shown *some* expression. Gnaeus Acer's face remained as soft and bland as butter. He turned to leave the office as emotionlessly as he'd arrived.

Menelaus reached for Acer's arm. Dama blocked the older man with his body. "Control yourself!" he snarled under his breath.

The message on the tablet couldn't have been written by the old philosopher . . . but the forgery was very good.

Too good for Dama to see any difference between Menelaus's hand and that of the forger.

"Lies don't change the truth!" Menelaus shouted to the back of Gnaeus Acer. "Tell your master! The truth will find him yet!"

"Citizen Menelaus," the Prefect said through pursed lips, "you'd better—" his mind flashed him a series of pictures: Menelaus brawling with Pyrrhus's messenger in the waiting room "—step into the garden for a moment while we discuss matters. And your friend—"

"Sir," Vettius interjected, "I think it might be desirable to have Citizen Dama present to hear the discussions."

"We don't owe an explanation to some itinerant pederast, surely?" said Caelius.

Rutilianus looked at him. "No," he said. "I don't owe anyone an explanation, Caelius. But my friend Lucius is correct that sometimes giving an explanation can save later awkwardness—even in matters as trivial as these."

For the first time, Dama could see that Rutilianus

had reached high office for better reason than the fact that he had the right ancestors.

A momentary tremor shook Menelaus's body. The philosopher straightened, calm but looking older than Dama had ever seen him before.

He bowed to the Prefect and said, "Noble Rutilianus, your graciousness will overlook my outburst; but I assure you I will never forgive my own conduct, which was so unworthy of a philosopher and a guest in your house."

Menelaus strode out the door to the garden, holding his head high as though he were unaware of Caelius's giggles and the smug certainty in the eyes of Vulco.

"Citizen Dama, do you have anything to add?" the Prefect said—a judge now, rather than the head of a wealthy household.

"There is no possibility that the accusation is true," Dama said, choosing his words and knowing that there were no words in any language that would achieve his aim. "I say that as a man who has known Menelaus since I was old enough to have memory."

"And the letter he'd written?" Macer demanded. "I suppose *that's* innocent?"

Dama looked at his accuser. "I can't explain the letter," he said. "Except to point out that Pyrrhus knew about it, even though Menelaus himself obviously had no idea what was written on the tablet."

Caelius snickered again.

"Lucius Vettius, what do you say?" Rutilianus asked from his couch. He wiped his face with a napkin, dabbing precisely instead of sweeping the cloth promiscuously over his skin.

"In my opinion," the soldier said, "the old man

didn't know what was on the tablet. And he isn't interested in boys. In my opinion."

"So you would recommend that I employ the learned Menelaus to teach my sons proper morality?" Rutilianus said.

For a moment, Dama thought—hoped—prayed—

The big soldier looked at Dama, not the Prefect, and said, "No, I can't recommend that. There're scores of philosophers in Rome who'd be glad of the position. There's no reason at all for you to take a needless risk."

And of course, Vettius was quite right. A merchant like Dama could well appreciate the balance of risk against return.

Pyrrhus the Prophet understood the principles also.

"Yes, too bad," Rutilianus said. "Well-spoken old fellow, too. But—" his eyes traced past the nomenclator as if hoping for another glimpse of the boy Ganymede "—some of those perverts are just too good at concealing it. Can't take the risk, can we?"

He looked around the room as his smiling civilian advisors chorused agreement. Vettius watched Dama with an expression of regret, but he had no reason to be ashamed of what he'd said. Even Dama agreed with the assessment.

The wheezing gasp from the garden was loud enough for everyone in the office to hear, but only Vettius and Dama understood what it meant.

Sosius was between Vettius and the garden door for an instant. The soldier stiff-armed him into a wall, because that was faster than words and there wasn't a lot of time when—

Vettius and Dama crashed into the garden together. The merchant had picked up a half step by not having to clear his own path.

—men were dying.

It looked for a moment as though the old philosopher were trying to lean his forehead against the wall of the house. He'd rested the pommel of Vettius's sword at an angle against the stucco and was thrusting his body against it. The gasp had come when—

Menelaus vomited blood and toppled sideways before Dama could catch him.

—the swordpoint broke the resisting skin beneath Menelaus's breastbone and slid swiftly upward through the old man's lungs, stomach and heart.

Vettius grabbed Menelaus's limp wrist to prevent the man from flopping on his back. The swordpoint stuck a finger's breadth out from between Menelaus's shoulder blades. It would grate on the stone if he were allowed to lie naturally.

Dama reached beneath the old man's neck and took the weight of his torso. Vettius glanced across at him, then eased back—putting his own big form between the scene and the excited civilians spilling from the office to gape at it.

"You didn't have to do that, old friend," Dama whispered. "There were other households . . ."

But no households who wouldn't have heard the story of what had happened here—or a similar story, similarly told by an emissary of Pyrrhus the Prophet. Menelaus had known that . . . and Menelaus hadn't been willing to accept open charity from his friend.

The old man did not speak. A trail of sluggish blood dribbled from the corner of his mouth. His eyes blinked once in the sunlight, twice—

Then they stayed open and began to glaze.

Dama gripped the spatha's hilt. One edge of the blade was embedded in Menelaus's vertabrae. He levered the weapon, hearing bone crack as the steel came free.

"Get back!" the merchant snarled to whoever it was whose motion blurred closer through the film of tears. He drew the blade out, feeling his friend's body spasm beneath his supporting arm.

He smelled the wastes that the corpse voided after mind and soul were gone. Menelaus wore a new toga. Dama'd provided it "as a loan for the interview with Rutilianus."

Dama stood up. He caught a fold of his own garment in his left hand and scrubbed the steel with it, trusting the thickness of the wool to protect his flesh from the edge that had just killed the man he had known and respected as long as he had memory.

Known and respected and loved.

And when the blade was clean, he handed the sword pommel-first to Lucius Vettius.

There were seats and tables in the side-room of the tavern, but Vettius found the merchant hunched over the masonry bar in the front. The bartender, ladling soup from one of the kettles cemented into the counter, watched hopefully when the soldier surveyed the room from the doorway, then strode over to Dama.

The little fella had been there for a couple hours. Not making trouble. Not even drinking *that* heavy . . .

But there was a look in his eyes that the bartender had seen in other quiet men at the start of a real bad night.

"I thought you might've gone home," Vettius said as he leaned his broad left palm on the bar between his torso and Dama's.

"I didn't," the merchant said. "Go away."

He swigged down the last of his wine and thrust the bronze cup, chained to the counter, toward the bartender. "Another."

The tavern was named *At the Sign of Venus.* While he waited for the bartender to fill the cup—and while he pointedly ignored Dama's curt demand to *him*—Vettius examined the statue on the street end of the counter.

The two-foot high terracotta piece had given the place its name. It showed Venus tying her sandal, while her free hand rested on the head of Priapus's cock to balance her. Priapus's body had been left the natural russet color of the coarse pottery, but Venus was painted white, with blue for her jewelry and the string bra and briefs she wore. The color was worn off her right breast, the one nearer the street.

Dama took a drink from the refilled cup. "Menelaus had been staying with me the past few days," he said into the wine. "So I didn't go back to my apartment."

The bartender was keeping down at the other end of the counter, which was just as it should be. "One for me," Vettius called. The man nodded and ladled wine into another cup, then mixed it with twice the volume of heated water before handing it to the soldier.

"Sorry about your friend," Vettius said in what could have been mistaken for a light tone.

"Sorry about your sword," Dama muttered, then took a long drink from his cup.

The soldier shrugged. "It's had blood on it before," he said. After a moment, he added, "Any ideas about how Pyrrhus switched the notebook in your friend's purse?"

Like everyone else in the tavern, the two men wore only tunics and sandals. For centuries, togas had been relegated to formal wear: for court appearances, say; or for dancing attendance on a wealthy patron like Gaius Rutilius Rutilianus.

Dama must have sent his toga home with the slaves who'd accompanied him and Menelaus to the interview. The garment would have to be washed before it could be worn again, of course. . . .

"It wouldn't have been hard," the merchant said, putting his cup down and meeting Vettius's eyes for the first time since walking behind his friend's corpse past the gawping servants and favor-seekers in the reception hall. "In the street, easily enough. Or perhaps a servant."

He looked down at the wine, then drank again. "A servant of mine, that would probably make it."

Vettius drank also. "You know," he said, as if idly, "I don't much like being made a fool of with the Prefect."

"*You're* still alive," Dama snapped.

Vettius looked at the smaller man without expression. The bartender, who'd seen *that* sort of look before also, signaled urgently toward a pair of husky waiters; but the soldier said only, "Yeah. We are alive, aren't we?"

Dama met the soldier's eyes. "Sorry," he said. "That was out of line."

"Been a rough day for a lot of people," said Vettius with a dismissive shrug. "For . . . just about everybody except Pyrrhus, I'd say. Know anything about that gentleman?"

The merchant chuckled. "I know what I've heard

from Menelaus," he said. "Mostly that Pyrrhus isn't a gentleman. He's a priest from somewhere in the East—I've heard Edessa, but I've heard other places. Came here to Rome, found an old temple that was falling down and made it his church."

Dama sipped wine and rolled it around his mouth as if trying to clear away the taste of something. Maybe he was. He'd felt no twinge at mentioning Menelaus's name, even though his friend's body was still in the process of being laid out.

Menelaus had always wanted to be cremated. He said that the newer fashion of inhumation came from—he'd glance around, to make sure he wasn't being overheard by those who might take violent offense—mystical nonsense about resurrection of the body.

Vettius looked past Dama toward the bartender. "You there," he called, fishing silver from his wallet. "Sausage rolls for me and my friend."

To the merchant he added, as blandly as though they *were* old friends, "There's something about a snake?"

"Yes . . ." Dama said, marshalling his recollections. "He claims to have one of the bronze serpents that Christ set up in the wilderness to drive away a plague. Something like that. He claims it talks, gives prophecies."

"Does it?"

Dama snorted. "I can make a snake talk—to fools—if there's enough money in it. And there's money in this one, believe me."

He bit into a steaming sausage roll. It was juicy; good materials well-prepared, and the wine was better than decent as well. It was a nice tavern, a reasonable place to stop.

Besides being the place nearest to the Prefect's doorway where Dama could get a drink.

He poured a little wine onto the terrazzo floor. The drops felt cool when they splashed his sandaled feet. Vettius cocked an eyebrow at him.

"An offering to a friend," Dama said curtly.

"One kind of offering," the soldier answered. "Not necessarily the kind that does the most good."

Dama had been thinking the same thing. That was why he didn't mind talking about his friend after all. . . .

For a moment, the two men eyed one another coldly. Then Vettius went on, "Happen to know where this temple Pyrrhus lives in might be?"

Dama hadn't mentioned that Pyrrhus lived *in* his church. It didn't surprise him that the soldier already knew, nor that Lucius Vettius probably knew other things about the Prophet.

"As it happens," the merchant said aloud, "I do. It's in the Ninth District, pretty near the Portico of Pompey. And—"

He popped the remainder of his sausage roll into his mouth and chewed it slowly while Vettius waited for the conclusion of the sentence.

An open investigation of Pyrrhus would guarantee the soldier an immediate posting to whichever frontier looked most miserable on the day Rutilianus's wife learned what he was doing to her darling.

You know, I don't much like being made a fool of with the Prefect.

Vettius wasn't going to get support through his normal channels; but it might be that he could find someone useful who took a personal interest in the matter. . . .

Dama washed down the roll with the last of his wine. "And since it's a Sunday," he resumed, "they'll be having an open ceremony." He squinted past Venus and the smirking Priapus to observe the sun's angle. "We'll have plenty of time to get there, I should think."

He brought a silver coin from his purse, checked the weight of it with his finger, and added a bronze piece before slapping the money onto the counter. "To cover the wine," Dama called to the bartender. "Mine and my friend's both."

The two men shouldered their way into the crowded street, moving together as though they were a practiced team.

They heard the drum even before they turned the corner and saw the edges of a crowd which Vettius's trained eye estimated to contain over a thousand souls. Dusk would linger for another half hour, but torches were already flaring in the hands of attendants on the raised base of a small temple flanked by three-story apartment buildings.

"Are we late?" the soldier asked.

Dama dipped his chin in negation. "They want places near the front, and a lot of them can't afford to buy their way up."

His eyes narrowed as he surveyed the expensively-dyed cloaks and the jewelry winking in ears and coiffures of matrons waiting close to the temple—the church—steps. "On the other hand," he added, "a lot of them *can* afford to pay."

The crowd completely blocked the street, but that didn't appear to concern either the civic authorities or the local inhabitants. Vettius followed the merchant's eyes and muttered, "Pyrrhus himself owns the building across the street. He uses it to house his staff and put up wealthy pilgrims."

A flutist, playing a counterpoint on the double

tubes of his instrument, joined the drummer and torch-bearers on the porch. Two of the attendants at the back of the crowd, identifiable by their bleached tunics and batons of tough rootwood, moved purposefully toward Vettius and Dama.

The merchant had two silver denarii folded in his palm. "We've come to worship with the holy Pyrrhus," he explained, moving his hand over that of one of the attendants. The exchange was expert, a maneuver both parties had practiced often in the past.

"Yes," said the attendant. "If you have a request for guidance from the holy Pyrrhus, give it on a sealed tablet to the servants at the front."

Dama nodded and reached for another coin. "Not now," said the attendant. "You will be granted an opportunity to make a gift directly to the divinity."

"Ah . . ." said Vettius. "I don't have a tablet of my own. Could—"

The other attendant, the silent one, was already handing Vettius an ordinary tablet of waxed boards. He carried a dozen similar ones in a large scrip.

"Come," said—ordered—the first attendant. His baton, a dangerous weapon as well as a staff of office, thrust through the crowd like the bronze ram of a warship cleaving choppy waves.

There were loud complaints from earlier—and poorer—worshippers, but no one attempted physical opposition to the Prophet's servant. Vettius gripped Dama's shoulder from behind as they followed, lest the pressure of the crowd separate them beyond any cure short of open violence.

"Pyrrhus's boys aren't very talkative," Vettius whispered in the smaller man's ear. "Drugs, perhaps?"

Dama shrugged. Though the attendant before them had a cultured accent, he was as devoid of small-talk and emotion as the messenger who brought deadly lies about Menelaus to the Prefect. Drugs were a possible cause; but the merchant already knew a number of men—and a greater number of women—for whom religious ecstasy of one sort or another had utterly displaced all other passions.

Pyrrhus's converted temple was unimposing. A building, twenty feet wide and possibly thirty feet high to the roof-peak, stood on a stepped base of coarse volcanic rock. Two pillars, and pilasters formed by extensions of the sidewalls, supported the pediment. That triangular area was ornamented with a painting on boards showing a human-faced serpent twined around a tau cross.

The temple had originally been dedicated to Asklepios, the healing god who'd lived part of his life as a snake. The current decoration was quite in keeping with the building's pagan use.

There were six attendants on the temple porch now. The newcomers—one of them was Gnaeus Acer—clashed bronze rattles at a consistent rhythm; not the same rhythm for both men, nor in either case quite the rhythm that the staring-eyed drummer stroked from his own instrument.

The guide slid Vettius and Dama to within a row of the front of the crowd. Most of the worshipers still ahead of them were wealthy matrons, but a few were country folk. Vettius thought he also saw the flash of a toga carrying a senator's broad russet stripe. More attendants, some of them carrying horn-lensed lanterns rather than batons, formed a line at the base of the steps.

Dama had paid silver for a second-rank location. The first rank almost certainly went for gold.

The merchant had opened a blank notebook and

was hunching to write within the strait confines of the crowd. The tablet Vettius had been given looked normal enough at a glance: a pair of four-by five-inch boards hinged so that they could cover one another. One of the boards was waxed within a raised margin of wood that, when the tablet was closed, protected words written on the soft surface. A cord attached to the back could be tied or sealed to the front board to hold the tablet shut.

Dama finished what he was doing, grinned, and took the tablet from Vettius. "Shield me," he whispered.

Vettius obediently shifted his body, though the two of them were probably the only members of the crowd who weren't focused entirely on their own affairs.

Dama had been scribbling with a bone stylus. Now, using the stylus tip, he pressed on what seemed to be a tiny knot through the wooden edge of the tablet supplied to Vettius. The knot slipped out into his waiting palm. A quick tug started the waxed wooden back sliding away from the margin of what had seemed a solid piece.

"Pyrrhus the Prophet has strange powers indeed," Vettius said as he fitted the tablet back together again. "Let me borrow your stylus."

He wrote quickly, cutting the wax with large, square letters; not a calligrapher's hand, but one which could write battlefield orders that were perfectly clear.

"What are you asking?" Dama whispered.

"Whether Amasius will die so that I get promoted to Legate of the Domestic Horse," the soldier replied. He slapped that tablet closed. "I suppose the attendants seal these for us?"

"Ah . . ." said Dama with a worried expression.

"That might not be a tactful question to have asked . . . ah, if the information gets into the wrong hands, you know."

"Sure wouldn't be," Vettius agreed, "if I'd signed 'Decurion Vettius' instead of 'Section Leader Lycorides.' "

He chuckled. "You know," he added, "Lycorides is about dumb enough not to figure how a question like that opens you up to blackmail."

He grinned at the pediment of the church and said, "Pyrrhus would figure it out, though. Wouldn't he?"

Dama watched a heavy-set woman in the front rank wave her ivory tablet at an attendant. She wore a heavy cross on a gold chain, and the silk band which bound her hair was embroidered with the Chi-Rho symbol. Menelaus may not have thought Pyrrhus was a Christian; but, as the Prefect had retorted, there were Christians who felt otherwise.

"Hercules!" Vettius swore under his breath. "That's Severiana—the Prefect's wife!"

He snorted. "And Ganymede. That boy gets around."

"Want to duck back now and let me cover?" the merchant offered.

Vettius grimaced. "They won't recognize me," he said in the tone of one praying as well as assessing the situation.

An attendant leaned toward Dama past the veiled matron and her daughter in the front rank who were reciting prayers aloud in Massiliot Greek.

"If you have petitions for advice from the Prophet," the man said, "hand them in now."

As the attendant spoke, he rolled a lump of wax between his thumb and forefinger, holding it over the peak of the lantern he carried in his other hand. Prayers chirped to a halt as the women edged back from the lantern's hissing metal frame.

Dama held out his closed notebook with the cord looped over the front board. The attendant covered the loop with wax, into which Dama then firmly pressed his carnelian seal ring. The process of sealing Vettius's tablet was identical, except that the soldier wore a signet of gilt bronze.

"What're you asking?" Vettius whispered under cover of the music from the porch and the prayers which the women resumed as soon as the attendant made his way into the church with the tablets.

"I'm asking about the health of my wife and three children back in Gades."

"You're not from Spain, are you?" the soldier asked—reflexively checking the file of data in his mind.

"Never been there," Dama agreed. "Never married, either."

The door of the church opened to pass an attendant with small cymbals. He raised them but didn't move until the door shut behind him.

The music stopped. The crowd's murmuring stilled to a collective intake of breath.

The cymbals crashed together. A tall, lean man stood on the porch in front of the attendants.

"Mithra!" the merchant blurted—too quietly to be overheard, but still a stupid thing to say here.

Dama understood about talking snakes and ways to read sealed tablets; but he didn't have the faintest notion of how Pyrrhus had appeared out of thin air that way.

"I welcome you," Pyrrhus cried in a voice that pierced without seeming especially loud, "in the name of Christ and of Glaukon, the Servant of God."

Vettius narrowed his eyes.

Dama, though he was uncertain whether the soldier's ignorance was real or just pretense, leaned even closer than the press demanded and whispered, "That's the name of his snake. The bronze one."

"Welcome Pyrrhus!" the crowd boomed. "Prophet of God!"

A double *crack!* startled both men but disturbed few if any of the other worshipers. The torch-bearing attendants had uncoiled short whips with poppers. They lashed the air to put an emphatic period to the sequence of statement and response.

Pyrrhus spread his arms as though thrusting open a double door. "May all enemies of God and his servants be far from these proceedings," he cried.

"May all enemies of Pyrrhus and Glaukon be far from these proceedings!" responded the crowd.

Crackcrack!

"God bless the Emperors and their servants on Earth," Pyrrhus said. Pyrrhus *ordered*, it seemed to Vettius; though the object of the order was a deity.

"Not taking any chances with a treason trial, is he?" the soldier muttered.

"God bless Pyrrhus and Glaukon, his servants!" responded the crowd joyously.

The merchant nodded. Those around them were too lost in the quivering ambiance of the event to notice the carping. "What I want to know," he whispered back, "is how long does this go on?"

"Pyrrhus! Liar!" a man screamed from near the

front of the gathering. The crowd recoiled as though the cry were a stone flung in their midst.

"Two months ago, you told me my brother'd been drowned in a shipwreck!" the man shouted into the pause his accusation blew in the proceedings.

The accuser was short and already balding, despite being within a few years of Vettius's twenty-five; but his features were probably handsome enough at times when rage didn't distort them.

"Blasphemer!" somebody cried; but most of the crowd poised, waiting for Pyrrhus to respond. The attendants were as motionless as statues.

"His ship was driven ashore in Malta, but he's fine!" the man continued desperately. "He's home again, and I've married his *widow*! What am I supposed to do, you lying bastard!"

Pyrrhus brought his hands together. Dama expected a clap of sound, but there was none, only the Prophet's piercing voice crying, "Evil are they who evil speak of God! Cast them from your midst with stone and rod!"

What—

"You've ruined my—" the man began.

—doggeral, Dama thought, and then a portly matron next to the accuser slashed a line of blood across his forehead with the pin of the gold-and-garnet clasp fastening her cloak. The victim screamed and stumbled back, into the clumsy punch of a frail-looking man twice his age.

The crowd gave a collective snarl like that of dogs ringing a boar, then surged forward together.

The paving stones were solidly set in concrete, but several of the infuriated worshipers found chunks of building material of a size to swing and hurl. Those crude weapons were more danger to the rest of the crowd than to the intended victim—

knocked onto all fours and crawling past embroidered sandals, cleated boots, and bare soles, all kicking at him with murderous intent.

Vettius started to move toward the core of violence with a purposeful look in his eye. The merchant, to whom public order was a benefit rather than a duty, gripped the bigger man's arm. Vettius jerked his arm loose.

Tried to jerk his arm loose. Dama's small frame belied his strength; but much more surprising was his willingness to oppose the soldier whom he knew was still much stronger—as well as being on the edge of a killing rage.

The shock brought Vettius back to present awareness. The accuser would probably survive the inept battering; and one man—even a man as strong and determined as Lucius Vettius—could do little to change the present odds.

The mob jostled them as if they were rocks in a surf of anger. "Two months ago," Dama said, with his lips close to the soldier's ear, "he'd have been one of those kicking. That's not why we're here."

The victim reached the back of the crowd and staggered to his feet again. A few eager fanatics followed some way into the darkness; but Pyrrhus spread his arms on the porch of the church, calming the crowd the way a teacher can appear and quiet a schoolroom.

Whips cracked the worshipers to attention.

"Brothers and sisters in God," the Prophet called, clearly audible despite the panting and foot-shuffling that filled the street even after the murderous cries had abated. "Pray now for the Republic and the Emperors. May they seek proper guidance in the time of testing that is on them!"

"What's that mean?" Dama whispered.

The soldier shrugged. "There's nothing special *I* know about," he muttered. "Of course, it's the sort of thing you could say anytime in the past couple centuries and be more right than wrong."

Pyrrhus's long prayer gave no more information as to the nature of the 'testing' than had been offered at the start, but the sentences rambled through shadowy threats and prophetic thickets barbed with words in unknown languages. On occasion—random occasions, it seemed to Vettius—the Prophet lowered his arms and the crowd shouted, "Amen!" After the first time, the soldier and merchant joined in with feigned enthusiasm.

Despite his intention to listen carefully—and his absolute need to stay awake if he were to survive the night—Vettius was startled out of a fog when Pyrrhus cried, "Depart now, in the love of God and his servants Pyrrhus and Glaukon!"

"God bless Pyrrhus, the servant of God!" boomed the crowd, as though the meaningless, meandering prayer had brought the worshipers to some sort of joyous epiphany.

Whips cracked. The musicians behind Pyrrhus clashed out a concentus like that with which they had heralded the Prophet's appearance—

Pyrrhus was gone, as suddenly and inexplicably as he'd appeared.

The crowd shook itself around the blinking amazement of Vettius and Dama. "I don't see . . ." the merchant muttered. The torches trailed sparks and pitchy smoke up past the pediment, but there was no fog or haze sufficient to hide a man vanishing from a few feet away.

"Is this all—" Vettius began.

"Patience," said Dama.

The attendants—who hadn't moved during the

near riot—formed a double line up the stepped base of the building to where the drummer opened the door. Worshipers from the front of the crowd, those who'd paid for their places and could afford to pay more for a personal prophecy, advanced between the guiding lines.

Vettius's face twisted in a moue as he and Dama joined the line. *He* shouldn't have to be counseled in patience by a silk merchant. . . .

The private worshipers passed one by one through the door, watched by the attendants. A man a couple places in front of Vettius wore an expensive brocade cloak, but his cheeks were scarred and one ear had been chewed down to a nub. As he stepped forward, one of the attendants put out a hand in bar and said, "No weapons. You have a—"

"Hey!" the man snarled. "You leave me—"

The attendant on the other side reached under the cloak and plucked out a dagger with a wicked point and a long, double-edged blade.

The pair of women nearest the incident squealed in horror, while Vettius poised to react if necessary. The man grabbed the hand of the attendant holding his dagger and said, "Hey! That's for personal reasons, see?"

The first attendant clubbed the loaded butt of his whip across the back of the man's neck. The fellow slumped like an empty wineskin. Two of the musicians laid down their instruments and dragged him toward the side of the building. Twittering, the women stepped past where he'd fallen.

Vettius glanced at Dama.

"I'm clean," the merchant murmured past the ghost of a humorless smile. He knew, as Vettius did, that the man being dragged away was as likely dead as merely unconscious.

That, along with what happened to the fellow who'd married his brother's wife, provided the night's second demonstration of how Pyrrhus kept himself safe. The Prophet might sound like a dim-witted charlatan, and his attendants might look as though they were sleep-walking most of the time; but he and they were ruthlessly competent where it counted.

As he passed inside the church, Dama glanced at the door leaves. He hoped to see some sign—a false panel; a sheet of mirror-polished metal; *something*—to suggest the illusion by which Pyrrhus came and left the porch. The outer surface of the wooden leaves had been covered with vermillion leather, but the inside showed the cracks and warping of age.

These were the same doors that had been in place when the building was an abandoned temple. There were no tricks in them.

A crosswall divided the interior of the church into two square rooms. The broad doorway between them was open, but the select group of worshipers halted in the first, the anteroom.

Crosswise in the center of the inner room, Pyrrhus the Prophet lay on a stone dais as though he were a corpse prepared for burial. His head rested on a raised portion of the stone, crudely carved to the shape of an open-jawed snake.

Behind the Prophet, against the back wall where the cult statue of Asklepios once stood, was a tau cross around which twined a metal-scaled serpent. The creature's humanoid head draped artistically over the crossbar.

Pairs of triple-wick lamps rested on stands in

both rooms, but their light was muted to shadow by the high, black beams supporting the roof. A row of louvered clerestory windows had been added just beneath the eaves when the building was refurbished, but even during daylight they would have affected ventilation more than lighting.

Vettius estimated that forty or fifty people were allowed to enter before attendants closed the doors again and barred them. The anteroom was comfortably large enough to hold that number, but the worshipers—he and Dama as surely as the rest—all crowded toward the center where they could look through the doorway into the sanctum.

Bronze scales jingled a soft susurus as the serpent lifted its head from the bar. "God bless Pyrrhus his servant!" rasped the creature in a voice like a wind-swung gate.

Vettius grabbed for the sword he wasn't carrying tonight. He noticed with surprise that Dama's arm had curved in a similar motion. Not the sort of reflex he'd have expected in a merchant . . . but Vettius had already decided that the little Cappadocian wasn't the sort of merchant one usually met.

"God bless Glaukon and Pyrrhus, his servants," responded the crowd, the words muzzed by a harshly-echoing space intended for visual rather than acoustic worship.

"Mithra!" Dama said silently, a hand covering his lips as they mimed the pagan syllables.

He knew the serpent was moved by threads invisible in the gloom. He knew one of Pyrrhus's confederates spoke the greeting through a hole in the back wall which the bronze simulacrum covered.

But the serpent's creaking, rasping voice frightened him like nothing had since—

Like nothing ever had before.

Goods of various types were disposed around the walls of the anteroom. Sealed amphoras—sharp-ended jars that might contain anything from wine to pickled fish—leaned in clusters against three of the four corners. From wooden racks along the sidewalls hung bunches of leeks, turnips, radishes—and a pair of dead chickens. In the fourth corner was a stack of figured drinking-bowls (high-quality ware still packed in scrap papyrus to protect the designs from chipping during transit) and a wicker basket of new linen tunics.

For a moment, Vettius couldn't imagine why the church was used for storage of this sort. Then he noticed that each item was tagged: they were worshipers' gifts in kind, being consecrated by the Prophet's presence before they were distributed. Given the number of attendants Pyrrhus employed in his operation, such gifts would be immediately useful.

Pyrrhus sat up slowly on the couch, deliberately emphasizing his resemblance to a corpse rising from its bier. His features had a waxy stillness, and the only color on his skin was the yellow tinge cast by the lamp flames.

"Greetings, brothers and sisters in God," he said. His quiet, piercing voice seemed not to be reflected by the stone.

"Greetings, Pyrrhus, Prophet of God," the crowd and echoes yammered.

A pile of tablets stood beside the couch, skewed and colorful with the wax that sealed each one. Pyrrhus took the notebook on top and held it for a moment in both hands. His fingers were thin and exceptionally long, at variance with his slightly pudgy face.

"Klea, daughter of Menandros," he said. The elder of the two praying women who'd stood in front of Vettius during the open service gasped with delight. She stepped through the doorway, knelt, and took the tablet from the Prophet's hands.

"Remarriage," Pyrrhus said in the sing-song with which he delivered his 'verses,' "is not for you but faith. You may take the veil for me in death."

"Oh, Prophet," the woman mumbled as she got to her feet. For a moment it looked as though she were going to attempt to kiss Pyrrhus.

"God has looked with favor on you, daughter," the Prophet said in a distant, cutting voice that brought the suppliant back to a sense of propriety. "He will accept your sacrifice."

From the bosom of the stola she wore, Klea took a purse and thrust it deep within the maw of the stone serpent-head which had served Pyrrhus as a pillow. The coins clinked—gold, Dama thought; certainly not mere bronze—beneath the floor. The bench served as a lid for Pyrrhus's treasury, probably a design feature left from the days the building was a temple.

"Oh, Master," the woman said as she walked back to her place in the anteroom.

Tears ran down her cheeks, but even Vettius's experience at sizing up women's emotions didn't permit him to be sure of the reason. Perhaps Klea cried because she'd been denied remarriage during life . . . but it was equally likely that she'd been overcome with joy at the prospect of joining Pyrrhus after death.

The Prophet took another from the stack of tablets. "Hestiaia, daughter of Mimnermos," he called, and the younger of the pair of women stepped forward to receive her prophecy.

Pyrrhus worked through the series of requests tablet by tablet. A few of the responses were in absolute gibberish—which appeared to awe and impress the recipients—and even when the doggeral could be understood, it was generally susceptible to a variety of meanings. Dama began to suspect that the man who'd been stoned and kicked from the gathering outside had chosen the interpretation he himself desired to an ambiguous answer about his brother's fate.

A man was told that his wife was unfaithful. No one but the woman herself could know with certainty if the oracle were false.

A woman was told that the thief who took her necklace was the slave she trusted absolutely. She would go through her household with scourge and thumbscrew . . . and if she found nothing, then wasn't her suspicion of this one or that proof her trust hadn't been complete after all?

"Severiana, daughter of Marcus Severianus," the Prophet called. Vettius stiffened as the Prefect's simpering wife joined Pyrrhus in the sanctum.

"Daughter," said Pyrrhus in his clanging verse, "blessed of God art thee. Thy rank and power increased shall be. Thy husband's works grow anyhow. And morrow night I'll dine with thou."

Dama thought: Pyrrhus's accent was flawless, unlike that of the Prefect's nomenclator; but in his verse he butchered Latin worse than ever an Irish beggar did. . . .

Vettius thought: Castor and Pollux! Bad enough that the Prefect's wife was involved with this vicious phony. But if Pyrrhus got close to Rutilianus himself, he could do real harm to the whole Republic. . . .

"Oh beloved Prophet!" Severiana gurgled as she

fed the stone serpent a purse that hit with a heavier *clank!* than most of the previous offerings. "Oh, we'll be so honored by your presence!"

"Section Leader Lycorides!" Pyrrhus called.

Vettius stepped forward, hunching slightly and averting his face as he passed Severiana. The timing was terrible—but the Prefect's wife was so lost in joy at the news that she wouldn't have recognized her husband, much less one of his flunkies.

Though Pyrrhus's thin figure towered over the previous suppliants who faced him one-on-one, Vettius was used to being the biggest man in any room. It hadn't occurred to him that he too would have to tilt his head up to meet the Prophet's eyes.

Pyrrhus's irises were a black so deep they could scarcely be distinguished from his pupils; the weight of their stare gouged at Vettius like cleated boots.

For a moment the soldier froze. He *knew* that what he faced was no charlatan, no mere trickster preying on the religiously gullible. The power of Pyrrhus's eyes, the inhuman perfection of his bearded, patriarchal face—

Pyrrhus was not merely a prophet; he was a *god.*

Pyrrhus opened his mouth and said, "Evil done requited is to men. Each and every bao nhieu tien."

The illusion vanished in the bath of nonsense syllables. Vettius faced a tall charlatan who had designs on the official whom it was Vettius's duty to protect.

Rutilianus would be protected. Never fear.

"God has looked with favor on you, son," Pyrrhus prodded. "He will accept your sacrifice."

Vettius shrugged himself to full alertness and

felt within his purse. He hadn't thought to bundle a few coins in a twist of papyrus beforehand, so now he had to figure desperately as he leaned toward the opening to the treasury. He didn't see any way that Pyrrhus could tell if he flung in a couple bits of bronze instead of real payment, but. . . .

Vettius dropped three denarii and a Trapezuntine obol, all silver, into the stone maw. He couldn't take the chance that Pyrrhus or a confederate *would* know what he had done—and at best expose him in front of Severiana.

He stepped back into place.

"Marcus Dama!" the Prophet called, to the surprise of Vettius who'd expected Dama to use a false name. Diffidently lowering his eyes, the little man took the notebook Pyrrhus returned to him.

"God grants us troubling things to learn," the Prophet sing-songed. "Sorrows both and joys wait your return."

A safe enough answer—if the petitioner told you he'd left his wife and three minor children behind in Spain months before. Dama kept his eyes low as he paid his offering and pattered back to Vettius's side.

There were half a dozen further responses before Pyrrhus raised his arms as he had before making an utterance from the porch. "The blessings of God upon you!" he cried.

A single tablet remained on the floor beside the stone bench. Vettius remembered the well-dressed thug who'd tried to carry in a dagger. . . .

"God's blessings on his servants Pyrrhus and Glaukon!" responded that majority of the crowd which knew the liturgy.

"Depart in peace . . ." rasped the bronze serpent from its cross, drawing out the Latin sibilants and chilling Dama's bones again.

The doors creaked open and the worshipers began to leave. Most of them appeared to be in a state of somnolent ecstasy. A pair of attendants collected the tablets which had been supplied to petitioners who didn't bring their own; with enough leisure, even the devoutest believer might have noticed the way the waxed surface could be slid from beneath the sealed cover panel.

The air outside was thick with dust and the odors of slum tenements. Dama had never smelled anything so refreshing as the first breath that filled his lungs beyond the walls of Pyrrhus's church.

Almost all of those who'd attended the private service left in sedan chairs.

Vettius and Dama instead walked a block in silence to a set of bollards protecting an entrance to the Julian Mall. They paused, each lost for a moment in a landscape of memories. No one lurked nearby in the moonlight, and the rumble of goods wagons and construction vehicles—banned from the streets by day—kept their words from being overheard at any distance.

"A slick operation," Vettius said.

The merchant lifted his chin in agreement but then added, "His clientele makes it easy, though. They come wanting to be fooled."

"I'm not sure how . . ." Vettius said.

For a moment, his tongue paused over concluding the question the way he'd started it: *I'm not sure how Pyrrhus managed to appear and disappear that way*. But though he knew that was just a trick, the way some sort of trick inspired awe when Pyrrhus stared into the soldier's eyes . . . neither of those were things that Vettius wanted to discuss just now.

". . . he knew what your question was," Vettius's tongue concluded. "Is the tablet still sealed?"

"Sealed again, I should guess," Dama said mildly as he held the document up to the full moon. "They could've copied my seal impression in quick-drying plaster, but I suspect—yes, there."

His fingertip traced a slight irregularity in the seal's edge. "They used a hot needle to cut the wax and then reseal it after they'd read the message."

He looked at his companion with an expression the bigger man couldn't read. "Pyrrhus has an exceptional memory," he said, "to keep the tablets and responses in proper order. He doesn't give himself much time to study."

Vettius gestured absently in agreement. The soldier's mind considered various ways, more or less dangerous, to broach the next subject.

Three wagons carrying column bases crashed and rumbled past, drawn by teams of mules with cursing drivers. The loads might be headed toward a construction site within the city—but more likely they were going to the harbor and a ship that would carry them to Constantinople or Milan.

Rome was no longer a primary capital of the empire. It was easier to transport art than to create it, so Rome's new imperial offspring were devouring the city which gave them birth. All things die, even cities.

Even empires . . . but Lucius Vettius didn't permit himself to think about *that*.

"It doesn't appear that he's doing anything illegal," the soldier said carefully. "There's no law against lying to people, even if they decide to give you money for nothing."

"Or lying about people," Dama said—'agreed' would imply there was some emotion in his voice, and there was none. "Lying about philosophers who tell people you're a charlatan, for instance."

"I thought he might skirt treason," Vettius went on, looking out over the street beyond. "It's easy to say the wrong thing, you know. . . . But if Pyrrhus told any lies—" with the next words, Vettius would come dangerously close to treason himself; but perhaps his risk would draw the response he wanted from the merchant "—it was in the way he praised everything to do with the government."

"There was the—riot, I suppose you could call it," Dama suggested as his fingers played idly with the seal of his tablet.

"Incited by the victim," the soldier said flatly. "And some of those taking part were—very influential folk, I'd estimate. There won't be a prosecution on that basis."

"Yeah," the merchant agreed. "That's the way I see it too. So I suppose we'd better go home."

Vettius nodded upward in agreement.

He'd have to go the next step alone. Too bad, but the civilian had already involved himself more than could have been expected. Dama would go back and make still more money, while Lucius Vettius carried out what he saw as a duty—

Knowing that he faced court martial and execution if his superiors learned of it.

"Good to have met you, Marcus Dama," he muttered as he strode away through a break in traffic.

There was a crackle of sound behind him. He

glanced over his shoulder. Dama was walking toward his apartment in the opposite direction.

But at the base of the stone bollard lay the splintered fragments of the tablet the merchant had been holding.

The crews of two sedan chairs were dicing noisily—and illegally—beside the bench on which Vettius waited, watching the entrance to Pyrrhus's church through slitted eyes. Business in the small neighborhood bath house was slack enough this evening that the doorkeeper left his kiosk and seated himself beside the soldier.

"Haven't seen you around here before," the doorkeeper opened.

Vettius opened his eyes wide enough to frown at the man. "You likely won't see me again," he said. "Which is too bad for you, given what I've paid you to mind your own business."

Unabashed, the doorkeeper chewed one bulb from the bunch of shallots he was holding, then offered the bunch to the soldier. His teeth were yellow and irregular, but they looked as strong as a mule's.

"Venus!" cried one of the chairmen as his dice came up all sixes. "How's *that*, you Moorish fuzzbrain?"

"No thanks," said Vettius, turning his gaze back down the street.

The well-dressed, heavily-veiled woman who'd arrived at the church about an hour before was leaving again. She was the second person to be admitted for a private consultation, but a dozen other—obviously less wealthy—suppliants had been turned away during the time the soldier had been watching.

He'd been watching, from one location or another in the neighborhood, since dawn.

"I like to keep track of what's going on around here," the doorkeeper continued. He ate another shallot and belched. "Maybe I could help you with what you're looking for?"

Vettius clenched his great, calloused hands, only partly as a conscious attempt on his part to warn this nuisance away. "Right now," he said in a husky voice, "I'm looking for a little peace and—"

"Hey there!" one of the chairmen shouted in Greek as the players sprang apart. One reached for the stakes, another kicked him, and a third slipped a short, single-edged knife from its hiding place in the sash that bound his tunic.

Vettius and the doorkeeper both leaped to their feet. The soldier didn't want to get involved, but if a brawl broke out, it was likely to explode into him.

At the very best, that would disclose the fact that he was hiding his long cavalryman's sword beneath his cloak.

The pair of plump shopowners who'd hired the sedan chairs came out the door, rosy from the steam room and their massages. The chairmen sorted themselves at once into groups beside the poles of their vehicles. The foreman of one chair glanced at the other, nodded, and scooped up the stakes for division later.

Vettius settled back on the bench. Down the street, a quartet of porters were carrying a heavy chest up the steps of the church. Attendants opened the doors for the men.

Early in the morning, the goods Vettius had seen in the building's anteroom had been dispersed, mostly across the street to the apartment house which Pyrrhus owned. Since then, there had been a constant stream of offerings. All except the brace of live sheep were taken inside.

Pyrrhus had not come out all day.

"A bad lot, those chairmen," the doorkeeper resumed, dusting his hands together as though he'd settled the squabble himself. The hollow stems of his shallots flopped like an uncouth decoration from the bosom of his tunic. "I'm always worried that—"

Vettius took the collar of the man's garment between the thumb and forefinger of his left hand He lifted the cloth slightly. "If you do not leave me alone," he said in a low voice, "you will have something to worry about. For a short time."

Half a dozen men, householders and slaves, left the bath caroling an obscene round. One of them was trying to bounce a hard leather ball as he walked, but it caromed wildly across the street.

The doorkeeper scurried back to his kiosk as soon as Vettius released him.

Three attendants, the full number of those who'd been in the church with Pyrrhus, came out and stood on the porch. Vettius held very still. It was nearly dusk—time and past time that the Prophet go to dinner.

If he was going.

Pyrrhus could lie and bilk and slander for the next fifty years until he died on a pinnacle of wealth and sin, and that'd still be fine with Lucius Vettius. There were too many crooked bastards in the world for Vettius to worry about one more or less of 'em. . . .

Or so he'd learned to tell himself, when anger threatened to build into a murderous rage that was safe to release only on a battlefield.

Vettius wasn't just a soldier any more: he was an agent of the civil government whose duties required him to protect and advise the City Prefect. If Pyrrhus kept clear of Rutilianus, then Pyrrhus had nothing to fear from Lucius Vettius.

But if Pyrrhus chose to make Rutilianus his business, then. . . .

A sedan chair carried by four of Pyrrhus's attendants trotted to the church steps from the apartment across the street. A dozen more of the Prophet's men in gleaming tunics accompanied the vehicle. Several of them carried lanterns for the walk back, though the tallow candles within were unlighted at the moment.

Pyrrhus strode from the church and entered the sedan chair. He looked inhumanly tall and thin, even wrapped in the formal bulk of a toga. It was a conjuring trick itself to watch the Prophet fold his length and fit it within the sedan, then disappear behind black curtains embroidered with a serpent on a cross.

Three attendants remained on the porch. The remainder accompanied the sedan chair as it headed northeast, in the direction of the Prefect's dwelling. The attendants' batons guaranteed the vehicle clear passage, no matter how congested the streets nearer the city center became.

Vettius sighed. Well, he had his excuse, now. But the next—hours, days, years; he didn't know how long it'd take him to find something on this 'Prophet' that'd stick. . . .

The remainder of the soldier's life might be simpler if he didn't start at all. But he was going to start, by burglarizing Pyrrhus's church and private dwelling while the Prophet was at dinner. And if that didn't turn up evidence of a crime against the State, there were other things to try. . . .

A hunter learns to wait. It would be dead dark soon, when the sun set and the moon was still two hours beneath the horizon. Time then to move to the back of the church which he'd reconnoitered by the first light of dawn.

Men left the bath house, laughing and chatting as they headed for their dinners. Vettius watched the three attendants, as motionless as statues on the church porch; as motionless as he was himself.

And he waited.

When Vettius was halfway up the back wall of the church, a patrol of the Watch sauntered by in the street fronting the building.

Watch patrols were primarily fire wardens, but the State equipped them with helmets and spears to deal with any other troubles they might come across. This group was dragging the ferules of its spears along the pavement with a tremendous racket, making sure it *didn't* come across such troubles . . . but Vettius still paused and waited for the clatter to trail off in the direction of the Theater of Balbus.

Back here, nobody'd bothered to cover the building's brick fabric with marble, and the mortar between courses probably hadn't been renewed in the centuries since the structure was raised as a temple. The warehouse whose blind sidewall adjoined the back of the church two feet away was also brick. It provided a similarly easy grip for the cleats of Vettius's tight-laced boots.

Step by step, steadying himself with his fingertips, the soldier mounted to the clerestory windows beneath the transom of the church. Each was about three feet long but only eight inches high, and their wooden sashes were only lightly pinned to the bricks.

Vettius loosened a window with the point of his sword, then twisted the sash outward so that the brickwork continued to grip one end. If matters went well, he'd be able to hide all signs of his entry when he left.

He hung his cloak over the end of the window he'd swung clear. He'd need the garment to conceal his sword on the way back.

The long spatha was a terrible tool for the present use. He'd brought it rather than a sturdy dagger or simply a prybar because—

Because he was still afraid of whatever he thought he'd seen in Pyrrhus's eyes the night before. The sword couldn't help that, but it made Vettius *feel* more comfortable.

There was a faint glow from within the building; one lamp wick had been left burning to light the Prophet's return home.

Vettius uncoiled his silken line. He'd thought he might need the small grapnel on one end to climb to the window, but the condition of the adjoining walls made the hooks as unnecessary as the dark lantern he'd carried in case the church was unlighted. Looping the cord around an end-frame of the window next to the one he'd removed, he dropped both ends so that they dangled to the floor of Pyrrhus's sanctum.

He had no real choice but to slide head-first through the tight opening. He gripped the doubled cord in both hands to keep from plunging thirty feet to the stone floor.

His right hand continued to hold the hilt of his naked sword as well. Scabbarded, the weapon might've slipped out when he twisted through the window; or so he told himself.

Pyrrhus's bronze serpent gaped only a few feet from Vettius as he descended the cord, hand over hand. The damned thing was larger than it had looked from below, eighteen—no, probably twenty feet long when you considered the way its coils wrapped the cross. Shadows from the lamplight below drew the creature's flaring nostrils into demonic horns.

At close view, the bronze head looked much less human than it had from the anteroom. There were six vertical tubes in each eye. They lighted red and green in alternation.

Vettius's hobnails sparked as he dropped the last yard to the floor. The impact felt good.

Except for Pyrrhus's absence, the sanctum looked just as it had when the soldier saw it the night before. He went first to the couch that covered the Prophet's strongbox. It was solid marble, attached to the floor by bronze pivots. Vettius expected a lock of some sort, but only weight prevented the stone from being lifted. So. . . .

He sheathed his sword and gripped the edge of the couch with both hands. Raising the stone would require the strength of three or four normal men, but—

The marble pivoted upward, growling like a sleeping dog.

The cavity beneath was empty.

Vettius vented his breath explosively. He almost let the lid crash back in disgust, but the stone might have broken and the noise would probably alert the attendants.

Grunting—angry and without the hope of immediate triumph to drive him—Vettius lowered by main strength the weight that enthusiasm had lifted.

He breathed heavily and massaged his palms against his thigh muscles for a minute thereafter. Score one for the Prophet.

Vettius didn't know precisely what he'd expected to find in the crypt, but there *had* to be some dark secret within this building or Pyrrhus wouldn't have lived in it alone. Something so secret that Pyrrhus didn't dare trust it even to his attendants. . . .

Perhaps there was a list of high government personnel who were clients of Pyrrhus—or who supplied him with secret information. The emperors were—rightly—terrified of conspiracies. A list like that, brought to the attention of the right parties, would guarantee mass arrests and condemnations.

With, very probably, a promotion for the decurion who uncovered the plot.

If necessary, Vettius could create such a document himself; but he'd rather find the real one, since something of the sort *must* exist.

The bronze lamp had been manufactured especially for Pyrrhus. Counterweighting the spouts holding the three wicks was a handle shaped like a cross. A human-headed serpent coiled about it.

Vettius grimaced at the feel of the object as he took it from its stand. He prowled the sanctum, holding the light close to the walls.

If there was a hiding place concealed within the bricks, Vettius certainly couldn't find it. The room was large and clean, but it was as barren as a prison cell.

There was a faint odor that the soldier didn't much like, now that he'd settled down enough to notice it.

He looked up at the serpent, Glaukon. Lamplight broke the creature's coils into bronze highlights that swept from pools of shadow like great fish surfacing. Pyrrhus might have hidden a papyrus scroll in the creature's hollow interior, but—

Vettius walked through the internal doorway, stepping carefully so that the click of his hobnails wouldn't alarm the attendants outside. He'd check the other room before dealing with Glaukon.

He didn't much like snakes.

The anteroom had a more comfortable feel than the sanctum, perhaps because the goods stored around the walls gave it the look of a large household's pantry. Vettius swept the lamp close to the top of each amphora, checking the tags scratched on the clay seals. Thasian wine from the shipowner Glirius. Lucanian wine from the Lady Antonilla. Dates from—Vettius chuckled grimly: my, a Senator. Gaius Cornelius Metellus Libo.

A brace of rabbits; a wicker basket of thrushes sent live, warbling hopefully when Vettius brought the lamp close.

In the corner where the stacks of figured bowls had been, Vettius found the large chest he'd watched the porters stagger in with that evening. The label read: *A gift of P. Severius Auctus, purveyor of fine woolens.*

A small pot of dormice preserved in honey. Bunches and baskets of fresh vegetables.

The same sort of goods as had been here the night before. No strongbox, no sign of a cubbyhole hidden in the walls.

Which left Vettius with no better choice than to try that damned bronze serpent after—

Outside the front doors, the pins of a key scraped the lock's faceplate.

Bloody buggering Zeus! Pyrrhus should've been gone for hours yet!

Vettius set down the lamp with reflexive care and ran for the sanctum. Behind him, the key squealed as it levered the iron dead-bolts from their sockets in both doorframes.

He'd be able to get out of the building safely enough, though a few of the attendants would probably fling their cudgels at him while he squirmed through the window. The narrow alley would be suicide, though. They'd've blocked both ends by the time he got to the ground, and there wasn't room enough to swing his spatha. He'd go up instead, over the triple-vaulted roof of the warehouse and down—

The door opened. "Wait here," called the penetrating, echoless voice of Pyrrhus to his attendants.

Vettius's silken rope lay on the floor in a tangle of loose coils. It couldn't have slipped from the window by itself, but. . . .

The door closed; the bolts screeched home again.

Vettius spun, drawing his sword.

"Beware, Pyrrhus!" cried the bronze serpent. "Intruder! Intruder!"

Vettius shifted his weight like a dancer. Faint lamplight shimmered on the blade of his spatha arcing upward. Glaukon squirmed higher on the cross. Its somewhat-human face waved at the tip of the bar, inches from where the rope had hung. The creature's teeth glittered in wicked glee.

A chip of wood flew from the cross as Vettius's sword bit as high as he could reach; a hand's breadth beneath Glaukon's quivering tail.

"Come to me, Decurion Lucius Vettius," Pyrrhus commanded from the anteroom.

He couldn't know.

The flickering lamplight in the other room was scarcely enough to illuminate the Prophet's toga and the soft sheen of his beard. Vettius was a figure in shadow, only a dim threat with a sword even when he spun again to confront Pyrrhus.

Pyrrhus couldn't know. But he knew.

"Put your sword down, Lucius Vettius," the Prophet said. For a moment, neither man moved; then Pyrrhus stepped forward—

No, that wasn't what happened. Pyrrhus stepped *away* from himself, one Pyrrhus walking and the other standing rigid at the door. There was something wrong about the motionless figure; but the light was dim, the closer form hid the further . . .

And Vettius couldn't focus on anything but the eyes of the man walking toward him. They were red, glowing brighter with every step, and they were drawing Vettius's soul from his trembling body.

"You are the perfect catch, Lucius Vettius," Pyrrhus said. His lips didn't move. "Better than you can imagine. In ten years, in twenty . . . there will be no one in this Empire whom you will not know if you wish to, whom you cannot sway if you wish to. On behalf of Pyrrhus the Prophet. Or whatever I call myself then.

"Put your sword down, Lucius Vettius."

The hilt of Vettius's sword was hot, as hot and glowing as the eyes of the approaching Pyrrhus. He couldn't hold the blade steady; light trembled along its sharp double edges like raindrops on a willow leaf.

But it didn't fall from his hand.

Pyrrhus stepped through the doorway between the rooms. His shoulder brushed the jamb, brushed through it—form and stuccoed brickwork merging, separating; the figure stepping onward.

"I will have this empire," Pyrrhus said. "And I will have this world."

Vettius stared down a black tunnel. At the end of the tunnel glared Pyrrhus's eyes, orange-hot and the size of the universe. They came nearer yet.

"And when I return to those who drove me out, when I return to those who would have *slain* me, Lucius Vettius," said the voice that echoed within the soldier's skull, "they will bow! For mine will be the power of a whole world forged to my design. . . .

"*Put down your sword!*"

Vettius screamed and swung his blade in a jerky, autonomic motion with nothing of his skill or years of practice to guide it. Steel cut the glowing eyes like lightning blasting the white heart of a swordsmith's forge—

The eyes gripped Vettius's eyes again. The Prophet's laughter hissed and bubbled through the soldier's mind.

"You are mine, Lucius Vettius," the voice said caressingly. "You have been mine since you met my gaze last night. Did you think you could hide your heart from me?"

Vettius's legs took a wooden, stumbling step forward; another step, following the eyes as they retreated toward the figure standing by the outer door. The figure of Pyrrhus *also*, or perhaps the only figure that was really Pyrrhus. The soldier now understood how the Prophet had appeared and vanished on the church porch the night before, but that no longer mattered.

Nothing mattered but the eyes.

"I brought you here tonight," said the voice.

"No . . ." Vettius whispered, but he wasn't sure either that he spoke the word or that it was true. He had no power over his thoughts or his movements.

"You will be my emperor," the voice said. "In time. In no time at all, for me. With my knowledge, and with the weapons I teach you to build, you will conquer your world for me."

The glowing eyes shrank to normal size in the sockets of the thing that called itself Pyrrhus. The bearded phantasm moved backward one step more and merged with the figure that had not moved since entering the church.

"And then . . ." said the figure as all semblance of Pyrrhus drained away like frost in the sunshine, ". . . I will return home."

The toga was gone; the beard, the pudgy human cheeks. What remained was naked, bone-thin and scaly. Membranes flickered across the slit-pupiled eyes, cleaning their surfaces; then the reptilian eyes began to carve their path into Vettius's mind with surgical precision.

He heard the creak of hinges, a lid rising, but the sound was as faint and meaningless as a seagull's cry against the thunder of surf.

"Pyrrhus!" shrieked the bronze serpent. "Intruder! Guards! Guards! *Guards!*"

Vettius awakened, gasping and shaking himself. He felt as though he'd been buried in sand, a weight that burned and crushed every fiber of his body.

But it hadn't been his body that was being squeezed out of existence.

The chest—*A gift of P. Severius Auctus, purveyor of fine woolens*—was open. Dama was climbing out of it, as stiff as was to be expected when even a small man closed himself in so strait a compass. He'd shrugged aside the bolt of cloth that covered him within the chest, and he held the scabbard of an infantry sword in his left hand.

His right drew the short, heavy blade with a musical *sring!*

"Guards!" Glaukon shouted again.

The serpent had left its perch. It was slithering in long curves toward Dama.

Pyrrhus reached for the door-latch with one reptilian hand; Vettius swung at him off-balance. He missed, but the spatha's tip struck just above the lock plate and splintered its way deep into the age-cracked wood.

Pyrrhus hissed like tallow on a grill. He leaped toward the center of the room as the soldier tugged his weapon free and turned to finish the matter.

Glaukon struck like a cobra at Dama. The merchant, moving with a reflexive skill that would have impressed Vettius if he'd had time to think, blocked the bronze fangs with the scabbard in his left hand. Instead of a clack as the teeth met, light crackled like miniature lightning.

Dama swore in Greek and thrust with his sword at the creature's head. Glaukon recoiled in a smooth curve. The serpent's teeth had burned deep gouges into the scabbard's iron chape.

Vettius pivoted on the ball of his left foot, bringing his blade around in a whistling arc that would—

Pyrrhus's eyes blazed into the soldier's. "Put down your sword, Lucius Vettius," rang the voice in his mind. Vettius held as rigid as a gnat in amber.

There were shouts from outside. Someone knocked, then hammered the butt of his baton on the weakened panel. Splinters of gray wood began to crack off the inside.

Glaukon was twenty feet of shimmering coils, with death in its humanoid jaws. Dama feinted. Glaukon quivered, then struck in earnest as the merchant shifted in the direction of Pyrrhus who was poising in the center of the anteroom as his eyes gripped Vettius.

Dama jumped back, almost stumbling over the chest in which he'd hidden. He was safe, but the hem of his tunic smoldered where the teeth had caught it.

Put—

Several batons were pounding together on the door. The upper half of a board flew into the room. An attendant reached through the leather facing and fumbled with the lock mechanism.

—down your sword, Lucius Vettius.

Dama's sword dipped, snagged the bolt of cloth that had covered him, and flipped it over the head of the bronze serpent. Wool screamed and humped as Glaukon tried to withdraw from it.

Dama smiled with cold assurance and stabbed where the cloth peaked, extending his whole body in line with the blow. The sharp wedge of steel sheared cloth, bronze, and whatever filled the space within Glaukon's metal skull.

The door burst inward. Pyrrhus sprang toward the opening like a chariot when the bars come down at the Circus. Vettius, freed by the eyes and all deadly instinct, slashed the splay-limbed figure as it leaped past.

The spatha sliced *in* above the chin, shattering pointed, reptilian teeth. *Down* through the sinuous neck. *Out*, breaking the collar bone on the way.

The blood that sprayed from the screaming monster was green in the lamplight.

Attendants hurled themselves out of the doorway with bawls of fear as the creature that had ruled them bolted through. Pyrrhus's domination drained with every spurt from his/its severed arteries. Men—men once more, not the Prophet's automatons—hurled away their cudgels and lanterns in their haste to flee. Some of the running forms were stripping off splattered tunics.

The point of Dama's sword was warped and blackened. The merchant flung his ruined weapon away as he and Vettius slipped past the splintered remnants of the door. Behind them, in the center of a mat of charred wool, the serpent Glaukon vomited green flames and gobbets of bronze.

Pyrrhus lay sprawled in a green pool at the bottom of the steps. The thin, scaly limbs twitched until Vettius, running past, drove his spatha through the base of the creature's domed skull.

The soldier was panting, more from relief than exertion. "Where did he come from?" he muttered.

"Doesn't matter." Dama was panting also. "*He* didn't expect more of his kind to show up."

"I thought he was a phony. The tablets—"

They swung past the bollards where they'd talked the previous evening. Dama slowed to a walk, since they were clear of the immediate incident. "He was a charlatan where it was easier to be a charlatan. That's all."

Vettius put his hand on the smaller man's shoulder and guided him to the shadow of a shuttered booth. "Why didn't you tell me you were coming back tonight?" the soldier demanded.

Dama looked at him. "It was personal," he said. Their faces were expressionless blurs. "I didn't think somebody in the Prefect's office ought to be involved."

Vettius sheathed his blade and slid the scabbard parallel to his left leg. If the gods were good, the weapon might pass unnoticed on his way home in the cloud-swept moonlight. "I was already involved," he said.

The merchant turned and met Vettius's eyes. "Menelaus was my friend," he replied, almost too softly to be heard. "Lucius Vettius, I didn't come here with a sword tonight to *talk* to my friend's killer."

In the near distance, the night rang with cries of horror. The Watch had discovered the corpse of Pyrrhus the Prophet.

Black Iron

Vettius's markers were of green tourmaline that glinted cruelly in the lamplight. The pieces had been carven by a Persian. Though as smoothly finished as anything Dama had seen in the West, the heads had a rudeness, a fierceness of line that he disliked. Living near the frontier had shaken him, he thought with a sigh.

The soldier moved, taking one of Dama's pieces. The slim Cappadocian countered with a neat double capture.

"God rot your eyes!" Vettius exploded, banging his big hand down on the game board. "I should know better than to play robbers with a merchant. By the Bull's blood, you're all thieves anyway. Doris, bring us some cups!"

The little slave pattered in with a pair of chalices. As she left the room Vettius slapped her on the flank and said, "Don't come back till you're called for."

The girl smiled without turning around.

"Little slut," the soldier said affectionately. Then, to Dama, "How do you want your wine?"

"One to three, as always," the blond merchant replied.

"I thought maybe your balls had come down since I saw you last," Vettius said, shaking his head. "Well, here's your wine; water it yourself."

He filled his own cup with the resin-thickened wine and slurped half of it. "You know," he said reflectively, "when I was on Naxos three years ago I made a special trip to a vineyard to get a drink of this before they added the pitch to preserve it in transport."

Vettius paused. "Well," Dama pressed him, "how was it?"

"Thin as piss," the soldier admitted. "I'd rather drink Egyptian beer."

He began to laugh and Dama joined him half-heartedly. At last Vettius wiped the tears from his eyes and gulped the rest of his wine. When he had refilled his cup he rocked back on his stool and gazed shrewdly at his friend. "You brought a bolt of cloth with you tonight," he said.

"That's right," Dama agreed with a thin smile. "It's a piece of silk brocade, much heavier than what we usually see here."

Vettius smiled back at him, showing his teeth like a bear snarling. "So I'm a silk fancier now?" he asked. "Come on, nobody will come until I call for them. What do you have under the silk that you didn't want my servants to see?"

Dama unrolled the silk without answering. The lustrous cloth had been wound around a sword whose hilt gleamed richly above a pair of laths bound over the blade. He tugged at the hilt and the laths fell away to reveal a slim blade, longer than that of a military sword. The gray steel was marked like wind-rippled water.

"Do you believe that metal can be enchanted?" Dama asked.

"Stick to your silk, merchant," the soldier replied with a chuckle and took the sword from Dama. He whipped the blade twice through the air.

"Oh, yes," he went on, "it's been a long time since I saw one of these."

Setting the point against the wall, the big soldier leaned his weight against it. The blade bowed almost double. The point shifted very slightly and the steel sprang straight, skidding along the stone. The sword blurred, humming a low note that made both men's bowels quiver.

"Thought the way it bends was magical, hey?"

Dama nodded. "I thought it might be."

"Well, that's reasonable," Vettius said. "It doesn't act much like a piece of steel, does it? Just the way it's tempered, though. You know about that?"

"I think I know how this blade was tempered," the merchant answered.

"Yeah, run it through a plump slave's butt a few times to quench it," Vettius said offhandedly. His fierce smile returned. "Not very . . . civilized, shall we say? But not magic."

"Not magic?" Dama repeated with an odd inflection. "Then let me tell you the rest of the story."

Vettius raised his cup in silent consent.

"I was in Amida . . ." the merchant began, and his mind drifted back to the fear and mud-brick houses overlooking the Tigris.

"We knew that Shapur was coming, of course; that Spring, next Spring—soon at least. He'd made peace with the Chionitae and they'd joined him as allies against Rome. Still, I had a caravan due any day and I didn't trust anyone else to bring it home to Antioch. It was a gamble and at the time it seemed worth it."

Dama snorted to himself, "Well, I guess it could have been worse.

"Aside from waiting to see whether my people would arrive before the Persians did, there was nothing to do in Amida but bake in the dust. It had never been a big place and now, with the shanties outside the wall abandoned and the whole countryside squeezed in on top of the garrison, there wasn't room to spit."

The merchant took a deep draught of his wine as he remembered. Vettius poured him more straight from the jar. "Mithra! There were two regiments of Gaulish foot there, half dead with the heat and crazy from being cooped up. That was later, though, after the gates were shut.

"Wealth has its advantages and I'd gotten a whole house for my crew. I put animals on the ground floor and the men on the second; that left me the roof to myself. There was a breeze up there sometimes.

"The place next door was owned by a smith named Khusraw and I could see over his wall into the courtyard where his forge was set up. He claimed to be Armenian but there was talk of him really being a Persian himself. It didn't matter, not while he was turning weapons out and we needed them so bad."

"He made this?" Vettius asked, tapping the sword with his fingernail. The steel moaned softly.

Dama nodded absently, his eyes fixed on a scene in the past. "I watched him while he worked at night; the hammer ringing would have kept me awake anyway. At night he sang. He'd stand there singing with the hearth glaring off him, tall and stringy and as old as the world. He had a little slave to help him, pumping on the bellows. You've seen a charcoal hearth glow under a bellows?"

Vettius nodded. "Like a drop of sun."

Dama raised his eyebrows. "Perhaps," he said, sipping at his thick wine, "but I don't find it a clean light. It made everything look so strange, so flat, that it was hours before I realized that the plate Khusraw was forging must have weighed as much as I did."

"Siege armor?" the soldier suggested.

"Not siege armor," Dama replied. "There were other plates too, some of them that he welded into tubes, singing all the time."

The blond Cappadocian paused to finish his wine. He held out the cup to his host with a wan smile. "You may as well fill it again. I'm sweating it out faster than I drink it."

He wiped his brow with a napkin and continued. "It was a funny household in other ways. Khusraw, his wife, and his son—a boy about eight or ten. You can't really say with Persians. Those three and one slave boy I never heard to speak. No other servants in the house even though the woman looked like she was about to drop quints.

"I saw her close one day, trying to buy a sword for my foreman, seeing the way things were tending. Her belly looked wrong. It didn't shift like it ought to when she moved and she didn't seem to be carrying as much weight as if she were really pregnant. Padded or not, there was something strange about her.

"As for my own problem, that was decided the

morning the Persians appeared. Oh, I know, you've fought them; but Lucius, you can't imagine what they looked like stretched all across the horizon with the sun dazzling on their spearpoints and armor. Mithra! Even so, it didn't seem too bad at first. The walls were strong and we were sure we could hold out until Ursicinius relieved us."

Vettius made a guttural sound and stared at the table. Dama laid his hand on the big soldier's forearm and said, "Lucius, you know I meant nothing against you or the army."

Vettius looked up with a ghost of his old smile, "Yeah, I know you didn't. No reason for me to be sensitive, anyhow. I didn't give the orders.

"Or refuse to give them," he added bitterly after a moment's reflection. "Have some more wine and go on with your story."

Dama drank and set his cup down empty. "Until things got really serious I spent most nights on my roof. Khusraw was working on a sword, now, and I forgot about the other stuff he had been forging. But every time he had the metal beaten out into a flat blade he folded it back in on itself and started over."

The soldier nodded in understanding, running his finger along the water-marked blade. The merchant shrugged.

"Very late one night I awakened. Khusraw stood beside the forge and that evil white light flared over the courtyard every time the bellows pulsed. Tied to the anvil was a half-filled grain sack. The only noise, though, was the thump of the bellows and perhaps a whisper of the words Khusraw was chanting, and I couldn't figure out what had awakened me. Then another moan came from the house. That sound I knew—Khusraw's wife was in labor and I thought I'd been wrong about her belly being padded.

"Out in the courtyard the smith laid one hand on the grain sack. With the other, all wrapped in hides, he took the blade out of the hearth. The slave let the bellows stop and for an instant I could see both pairs of eyes reflecting the orange steel of the sword. Then Khusraw stabbed it through the sack. There was a terrible scream—"

"I'll bet there was!" Vettius interjected, his eyes glittering like citrines.

"—and inside the house the woman screamed too. Khusraw drew the blade out, half quenched and barely visible, then plunged it back in. There was no scream but his wife's, this time. The slave had fallen to his knees and was making gabbling noises. When the smith drove the sword into the sack a third time, the woman bawled in the last agony of birthing and there was a crash of metal so loud I thought a Persian catapult had hit Khusraw's house. He ran inside shouting, 'My son! My son!' leaving the sword to lie crossways through that sack."

Dama paused. Vettius tossed him a fresh napkin and poured out more wine. "His own son," the soldier mused. "Strange. Maybe Romulus really did sacrifice his brother to make his city great the way the old legends say."

The merchant gave him a strange smile and continued. "That was the last night I spent in the house. Our garrison was too worn down to hold out any longer and every able man in the city had to help on the walls.

"Seventy-three days," Dama said, shaking his head. "It doesn't sound like much to hold out, does it? Not in so strong a city. But there were so many Persians . . .

"No matter. The end came when a section of wall collapsed. The Persians didn't bring it down, we did ourselves—built it too high and it toppled. We tried to mass in the breach as the Persians poured through."

Dama paused with a wry grin. "Oh, you should have liked that, Lucius; the dust was sticky with blood. The armory had been buried when the wall fell and because the Persians were pushing us back, whenever a man lost his weapon he was out of the fight. I dodged out of the melee when my sword shattered on a shield boss. Then, when I had caught my breath I ran to Khusraw's shop, thinking he might still have some weapons I could carry back to the fighting.

"The front of the shop was empty, so I burst into the back. The smith was alone, holding a slender box open on his lap. When he saw me he slammed the lid shut, but I'd already caught the glint of steel inside. 'Give me the sword!' I said. 'No!' he cried, 'it's for my son to carry to King Shapur.' I grabbed the box, then, and knocked him down with my free hand. There was no time to talk and gods! but I was afraid.

"I tore the box open and drew this sword while Khusraw shouted something I didn't understand. Something clanged in the inner room. I turned to see the door swing open, and then I knew what the smith had made of his forgings.

"It was about a man's height, but from the way the ground shook there must have been twenty manloads of iron in it. I took a step back and the thing followed me. Even with the weight I might have thought it was a man in armor, but the eyes!

They were little balls of cloudy orange. No one could have seen out through them, but they swiveled as I moved.

"I cut at the head of the . . . the iron man. The sword bounced off. As sharp as the blade was, it only scratched the thing. Khusraw was backed against the wall to my left. He began to cackle, but I couldn't take my eyes off his creation long enough to deal with him.

"I thrust at the thing's throat. The point caught where the neck joined that black iron skull, but I didn't have enough strength to ram it home. Before I could recover, the iron man closed its hand over the blade. I yanked back and the sword shrieked out of its grip, slicing the metal fingers as neatly as it would have flesh."

Dama laughed grimly and tossed down his wine. "I've mentioned how Khusraw was giggling at me? Well, he stopped then. He shouted, 'Son!' and jumped at me, just as his toy tried to smash me with its fist. I ducked and the steel hand caught Khusraw on the temple and slammed him into the wall. I tried to dodge through the door then, but my boot slipped in the blood. I scrambled clear of the thing's foot, but it had me backed against the wall.

"I thrust again, at the face this time. The tip skidded into an eye socket without penetrating, and the weight of the iron drove the hilt against the wall behind me. The blade bent but the very weight on it held the hilt firm. Then, as the thing reached for my head, the sword point shifted and the blade sprang straight, driving itself through the skull. The remaining eye went black and the thing crashed to the floor.

"There wasn't time to think then. I tugged the

sword free and ran into the street to find the Persians had . . . well, the rest doesn't matter, I suppose. I was one of the lucky ones who slipped out of the city that night."

The soldier sighted down the length of the blade. "So your smith put his own son's soul in the sword and it wrecked his machine for him," he said at last.

The slender merchant ran a hand through his blond hair, the tension gone from him now that he had finished his story. "No, I don't think so," he said quietly. "You're forgetting Khusraw's wife."

"Her pregnancy?" the soldier asked in bewilderment.

"She wasn't pregnant," Dama explained, "she was just a vehicle. The smith had his materials, a soul and a body. Somehow his wife's pretense of labor allowed him to join them. The thing was alive, an automaton."

Vettius shook his head. "What you're calling an automaton—there must have been a dwarf inside with some very clever machinery."

Dama smiled gently. "There was no man inside. Lucius, when I pulled that sword free it was as clean as you see it now; no blood, no brains sticking to it."

The soldier looked from his friend to the sword. The blade had a faint green cast to it now as it caught the reflection of the gaming pieces so finely carven by some Persian craftsman.

The Manitchore

"You've led me to a death pit, merchant," said the black-robed necromancer as he grimly surveyed their destination.

"You wouldn't feel safe with anything but death around you, Theophanes," Dama said in agreement. He gripped the saddle with his hands and tried to shake cramps from the day's ride out of his leg muscles. "I've kept my part of the bargain. You wanted a place where the government wasn't looking over your shoulder, an oasis that neither Rome nor Shapur held. Here it is."

Harness creaked as Hlodovech shifted his overburdened horse a little closer to Theophanes and the merchant who had guided them. Though the necromancer always gave Hlodovech orders in German, a word like "death" or "kill" in any language made the huge bodyguard restive. He was seven feet tall, gaunt enough to appear frail until a closer look focused on wrists as thick as Dama's thighs and the muscles that corded gracelessly without any subcutaneous fat to blur their outlines. Except for the red woolen scarf knotted at his throat, Hlodovech was dressed in uncured hides which might have been responsible for the miasma of decay around him. A violet tinge lurked beneath his pallor. The same cast in his irises made his direct gaze a startling thing.

Dama's horse sidled away from the German. Dama jerked savagely on the reins, angry that the beast's action might be taken as a sign of the rider's fear. That fear was very real, but the Cappadocian had kept it strictly under control throughout the twenty hard days of riding from Antioch. "Shall we go down?" he asked in a voice that the evening wind whipped over the sand.

"You chose the spot, merchant," sneered Theophanes. "Don't you like the view?"

The western sun threw their shadows down the long slope of the dune toward the oasis and the abandoned inn. Sand had lapped over the north wall of the courtyard surrounding the low building. Three date palms still grew around a well-curb in the rear, but a questing thumb of sand had tilted one tree into a failed diagonal. Still, the trees were the only signs of life in a landscape that was more dead than the leagues of sand around it.

Behind the three Europeans, one of the mule drivers called in harsh Armenian, "Well, do they move us bleeding on, or do we unsaddle the bleeding mules?"

A caravan leader again, Dama's face hardened and he turned back toward the long worm of men and laden animals. "Move them in," he ordered his chief driver, a scrag-bearded patriarch named Vonones. The Armenian bobbed his head twice and shouted his fellow-countrymen on. As Dama watched them file past, he noted without humor that the muleteers were swinging wide to avoid Hlodovech. The slight merchant did not bother speaking again before he prodded his gelding into line behind the mules.

The courtyard gate was as high as the eight-foot sandstone wall in which it was set. The heavy wood had been pared into ridges by decades of blowing sand. The same grit had peened the bright metal of the hinges into rigid units so that the gate, swung back against the outside wall at some time in the far past, was a decoration rather than a closure. Dama was between the gateposts when the angry babble broke out in front of the inn. He kicked his horse into a trot, then swore and clutched a handful of mane as the acceleration proved more than his numbed thighs could brace against. Theophanes and the German galloped past him to reach the crowd of muleteers first.

The Armenians split apart, less at the threat of the hooves sparking on the flagstones than from the presence of the riders. Vonones alone stood his ground in the arch of the inn's main door. He had flung the panel open, but his flowing robes shielded the portal as effectively as a curtain. "Did you think you'd bed us down in a grave?" he demanded to the face of the necromancer leaning from his saddle. The driver stepped sideways to display what lay just within the palm-beamed hall.

Dama had reined up and dismounted. Now he pressed between the two horsemen and said irritably, "What's the matter, Vonones? Old as you are, haven't you seen a damned skeleton before?"

Due to the desert air it was almost a mummy instead. The ligaments were dry and shrunken, but they still articulated the bones. An amber translucence, skin and flesh merged into a substance like crisp horn, was spread thinly over the whole.

Taken aback at the commonplace taunt, Vonones first sputtered, then said, "Bones, bodies . . . but this isn't—you know it's not right, it doesn't *feel* right, sir."

"Balls," Dama said. He walked into the room without looking back at his audience. His water bag hung from his shoulder, a porous goatskin bladder made clammy by the evaporation that cooled the liquid within. Now he unslung it and raised it over the corpse with both hands. "This gift of life I offer to the spirit of the one who waits us here," he said in Armenian, loud enough that all could hear him. "May he be kindly disposed toward us for this gift and for the burial we will give his body."

The Cappadocian's strong, stubby fingers worked the wooden stopper out and spilled a quick gush of water on the corpse. The fluid was red in the sun's last rays. It splashed across the grinning rictus, upturned as though to gulp it down. Then Vonones gasped and Dama, looking down in feigned piety, snarled out a curse. The body had been preserved only by the dryness. It was melting away from the libation like a pearl in acid. The cancerous disintegration proceeded as quickly as a man could draw a breath. The bones themselves pattered on the stone floor and lay in a loose jumble, still mocking.

"Pitch camp in the damned courtyard, then!" Dama roared to Vonones's back as the driver bolted out to join his men.

Theophanes dismounted, his smile approaching a smirk. "Stable the horses in the back," he directed his dank-haired bodyguard. To Dama he added, "Your plan to convince the drivers that there's no reason here to fear the . . . supernatural . . . seems to have worked the reverse."

"I know," the merchant agreed, keeping his anger in check. When Theophanes bent down to finger the detached skull Dama added, "They're raised to believe the dead come back, that a place itself can be good or bad. They're not fools, they're uneducated."

"*I*'m not uneducated, little man," said the necromancer with a hinted rasp in his voice, "and I believe those things."

Dama stared at him, his face twisting with the words he had waited to use. "*They* aren't fools, I said."

Theophanes's expression crystalized. His fingers tightened in reflex on the skull they held staring back at him; they lacked the strength to crumble it. The necromancer was a full head taller than Dama but even thinner than his guide. His face, at first as stiff and brown as a varnished finial, suddenly crinkled in a parody of humor. "You're very bold with Hlodovech gone, aren't you?" he remarked.

"Hlodovech? I'll worry about him when I have to," the Cappadocian said with partial truth. He set his waterbag on the heavy table, the only piece of wooden furniture in a room marked otherwise by stone side-benches and a large fireplace on the eastern wall. Those, and the bones still strewn in the doorway. "I'll tell you something about your bodyguard," Dama went on. "I don't know if I could take him myself—"

"You, merchant?" Theophanes sneered.

"Me." The short sword belted to Dama's right

thigh nodded a hair as the small man shifted his weight. It was a service weapon and its hilt was worn. "I don't know that I could, but I've known people who could eat him alive. He doesn't have the spark. He's big, but he's flat—just so much meat. You'll need him for something more than bluffing one of these days, and he won't come through."

"Hlodovech?" the necromancer said with almost a giggle. "Oh, no one will eat *him* alive, I assure you. And he's perfectly loyal to me, utterly so—though you doubt my art, don't you, merchant?"

"All I know about your art is that when the emperor's pagan-hunters clamped down on Antioch, you didn't vanish in a puff of smoke," Dama said. "You paid me in good gold to take you to a place where you could be safe."

The room darkened as Hlodovech stepped through the door, its only source of illumination. The bones scrunched unnoticed beneath his boots. "Light us a lamp," Theophanes demanded irritably. The swift tropic darkness had thickened and pooled by the time Hlodovech had filled a flat clay lamp and replaced the crumbled wick. The smoky yellow glow when it ignited was as brilliant as a sunrise by contrast. In it the necromancer's eyes suddenly narrowed to see charcoal scribblings on the wall, hidden until Dama had closed the door against the growing chill. "What's that?" Theophanes asked sharply.

"Umm," the merchant puzzled, moving to avoid shadowing the words. "It's the script the Indian priests use. I haven't seen much of it, but it's a lot like the common writing and—"

"I know what language it is, you idiot," snapped the Greek as he lifted the lamp closer to the plastered wall, "but what's it doing here?" Dama's eyes chilled and he looked around quickly. He said nothing. The necromancer's face screwed up as he mouthed the syllables to himself. Then, translating into Greek, he read, " 'I am the mantichore. While here, worship life; lest I, who am death, shall find you.' "

" 'Mantichora' means 'manslayer,' " the Cappadocian put in, surprised at Theophanes's sudden tenseness. There was an edge to Hlodovech as well that had not been present ever before.

"The mantichore," Theophanes repeated. "My studies in the lore of priests and sages have gone a little deeper, I think, than anything to be expected of . . . a merchant, shall we say, who trades gold for cloth and pottery with similar human dregs across the sea." Theophanes slitted his eyes, making his dense, black eyebrows crawl. "A thing with the body of a great cat," he said, "and the face of a man; a thing with a scorpion's tail and a deadly barb—the mantichore."

Dama's laughter was loud and genuine. It bounced off his companions as if from a wall. "Oh, my!" he exclaimed. "Theophanes, you'd raise a pyramid to have a place to crack pistachios on. Do the Indian priests maunder about some fanciful animal? Fine. But I dare say that when they talk about 'mantichores' they mean the same thing a soldier does, or a peasant, or—if you like—a silk merchant. They mean a man who kills another man. Once in a while they may be talking about a killer tiger, and maybe that's where your ridiculous animal came from, but mostly just a man. That poor bastard on the floor"—his finger traced the strinkle of bones—"killed somebody and ran. He ended up here, maybe starving; and because he wrote poetic nonsense on the wall, you're dreaming up a myth that would make Athanasius gulp."

Theophanes shrugged and gave the elaborately false smile of an adult asked by a child to praise his drawing. "Hlodovech, bring in my apparatus," he ordered. Switching back to Greek as the servant went out he said, "Whatever makes you happy to believe, little man. After you've watched my . . . researches, I'll ask you again. But I'm surprised that even senses as dulled by trade as yours are able to ignore the, the pressure, the power that gathers around this inn. The Armenians feel it."

Dama snorted. "Back home the Armenians'll show you a cave that goes all the way down to where Hades holds the dead in bondage. And they'll swear to it." He sat down on a stone bench, crossing an ankle over a knee and beginning to massage suppleness back into the thigh. "I'll tell you what," he added. "I'll promise to believe in your man-cat-insect if you'll tell me what it eats around here. Maybe it's a ghost mantichore and it scares twits to death? Though our little friend on the floor there seems to have died as calm as an archbishop."

He was chuckling and still kneading his muscles when Hlodovech banged open the door and strode in, a 300-pound wooden pack under each arm. "There," Theophanes said, pointing to a corner. His servant set the pack frames down gently and without apparent effort, then went out for another load. Theophanes smiled sidelong at the Cappadocian. "Yes," he said, "Hlodovech is strong, isn't he? Which is almost as important to me as his perfect—I'm not using the term lightly, you know—his perfect loyalty toward me." Without further comment, he unstrapped one of the cases and began carefully to check the delicate paraphernalia within.

As Hlodovech opened the door with his third load, angry shouts billowed in with the sand. Dama was on his feet in an instant. His sword was free and bright in his hand. "Somebody's shouting 'Murder!' " he explained as he darted past the bodyguard.

There was no moon and the stars, though they jeweled the heavens, did nothing to light the compound. The drivers had pitched a pair of tents at the northwest corner of the wall, out of the wind. The sullen flames of a dung fire waved there, but the shout came from the row of stalls where torches now flared angrily. Dama slowed to a walk as he approached the clustered muleteers, shouting, "All right, what's happened?" Torchlight was glinting on hook-bladed knives; Dama did not care to be stabbed for moving suddenly into a keyed-up mob.

But the Armenians parted before the assurance of his tone. "See for yourself," whined Vonones, gesturing with his torch.

The muleteers had dumped the packs without ceremony in the courtyard but they had lodged the beasts properly in the old stables along the east wall, fifty paces from the rear of the inn. Now seven of the mules lay crumpled in their stalls. Across the nearest, a stiff-legged bay whose eyes had started from the impact that dished its skull, lay one of the drivers face upward. He was not visibly marked except by the blood that had spewed from his open mouth to stain his beard and robes.

The Cappadocian knelt, cursing as his shoulder bumped the stall divider. He took the driver's hand. "It's as warm as mine," he said. "Come on, did anybody hear something?"

"He went off to piss," Vonones said. "I took everyone with me to search when I noticed he hadn't come back." He paused, his lips struggling. "You brought us here to die," he said. "We won't stay."

"Of course you won't," Dama agreed. "Tomorrow I'll go back with you like we planned, so Theophanes can have his solitude. But we're not leaving now, unless you want to kill the rest of the mules; and in this dark—how do you know something isn't coming along with you, hey?"

The truth of his words forced silence over the drivers. Into it Dama ordered, "Now, two of you grab your buddy here. We'll haul him into the building where there's room and no damned wind, and we'll see what really did happen to him."

The nearest Armenians shied back from Dama's glance. "Oh, for the love of the crucified God," the Cappadocian muttered, standing up again in the narrow confines of the stall.

"Hlodovech," the necromancer ordered from the darkness. The gaunt German stepped forward, his appearance making the drivers spring away from him like heat from a flame. Dama pressed aside, allowing Hlodovech to slide his great pale hands beneath the body and lift it lightly as a straw dummy.

Vonones groaned and turned away. His torch wavered in the breeze as he led his countrymen back to their tents. Dama followed Hlodovech and his burden toward the inn. Last of all was Theophanes, his expression liquid with tension and the thrill of the hunt. Dama looked back at him from the door of the inn. "This much I'll give your 'wisdom,' " he said. "Something here caved in the heads of those mules, and it isn't something I care to share a small oasis with. Want to come back with us tomorrow?"

Theophanes did not bother to answer.

Hlodovech laid the body on the trestle table and stepped back. "Stand outside the door and keep the others away," his master directed. "I don't want to be disturbed in this." The German obeyed silently and, as the eddies of the closing door died away, Theophanes lit another lamp for additional light.

Dama drew a flat knife from the folds of his leggings and ran it down the front of the muleteer's tunic. The cloth parted easily before the wire edge, but only to display another garment beneath: dirtier, greasier, and much more worn. The Cappadocian grinned. "Bastard didn't change clothes, just put more on top when all the rest wore through somewhere."

Theophanes glanced up from the tracery of glass rods he was fitting together. "Don't damage the body any further," he directed. "I'm going to have a difficult enough time as it is."

Dama grunted. The next layer slit as easily as the first, but the third and fourth were gummed together with blood. The merchant wiped the blade and stropped it twice on his palm. This time it ripped the cloth down to the driver's ruined chest.

The necromancer left his own operations to survey the corpse. "Looks as though someone hit him with a quarryman's maul, doesn't it?" Dama suggested. He gestured, using the knife as a pointer but not quite touching it to the body. "The breastbone is loose and five ribs on each side got crushed against his spine. A big cat might have hit him like that, you're right . . . but just maybe, a man could be that strong too."

"I understand you, merchant," said Theophanes, coupling a final tube into his construct by means of a pair of silver clamps. "If you're just trying to irritate me with nonsense, you're a fool—by now it should be obvious to anyone that my art is our only hope of escaping here alive. If you really believe what you suggest, you're even more a fool. Hlodovech is *mine*, wholly. He has no existence apart from me."

Dama was briefly silent, watching the necromancer work. He had created a lattice of tubes, its base a hollow oval the length of a tall man. From that rose the real framework, joined at twelve nexi. The clear tubes suggested the facets of a cabochon-cut gem; the framework as a whole was reminiscent rather of a skeletal coffin. "What are you going to do with that?" the Cappadocian asked finally.

"Give me a hand and I'll show you," Theophanes replied. Over the trill of the wind was the thin sound of the Armenians singing some hymn against darkness. "This has to be set over the body," he explained. "Don't let any part of it touch the corpse."

The glass webbing was heavier than its shimmering delicacy had led Dama to expect, but the two men had little difficulty in arranging it to the necromancer's grunted satisfaction. "Now . . ." Theophanes said, and he threaded a bead into the socket near the victim's head. At first Dama thought it was of blue glass, but a closer glance revealed it as a clear bulb filled with something else to give it color.

Theophanes blew out one lamp and raised the remaining one. "Do you know what my art really is?" he asked. He held the lamp so that its flame wrapped the bead and threw the Armenian's shadow on the far wall as a blotch that leaped and fell.

"Supposedly, you speak to dead men," said Dama, his eyes as bright as the flames.

"No, I speak to corpses," Theophanes corrected flatly. "Dead bodies, not dead men. Men have souls—though I will not pretend to define them with the precision of one of the Emperor's ranting priests. What I have my dealings with assuredly lacks . . . something . . . though still my questions receive answers that no living man could give."

He cackled suddenly. "No living man but me."

The heated glass bulb spewed its contents out into the lattice. The tubes glowed a fiery azure. Theophanes snuffed his lamp with a quick gesture but the room still burned sickly in the lighted tracery.

Dama was rigid against the stone wall. He had not drawn his sword, but the room was full of the presence of evil lunging at its halter. Theophanes stood with his hands high, crying words into the blue-lit night. The seething tubes trembled at the impact of his voice.

Slightly but suddenly, like a bird which has caught movement to the side, the corpse turned its head to glare at Theophanes. The necromancer broke off his incantation and knelt, sagging a little and bracing his left hand against the table top in exhaustion. He gave a giggle of relief and said to Dama, "It's so . . . easy, here. The power is all about. Hours, days sometimes, I used to spend in Antioch and on the Rhine. . . ." He recollected himself and stood, once again an imposing figure with a nose hooked like an owl's beak. "You have come at my call," he said in Armenian to the corpse.

It tittered. The sound came from its throat. The shattered chest inflated like a bladder, then slowly collapsed to force out uninflected words. "I have been waiting for you—sage," the corpse said.

Theophanes's face tensed, less at the veiled impudence of the words than at the language in which they were spoken. Dama could follow them, too. While not quite the trade dialect, the spoken version was far simplified from written Sanskrit. "Manslayer," the merchant whispered, and now his sword slipped free into his hand.

The necromancer licked his lips. Still speaking in Armenian, the language native to the muleteer in life and the only one of which his dead body should have retained command, he said, "Tell us what killed you. Tell us what killed you and we will let you go."

"Nothing can kill *me*, sage," the corpse wheezed. "Only bodies die." It began to raise its torso from the table with the jerky stiffness of a lifting drawbridge. "A thousand years ago I was as you are, though with power to which yours is like a candle to the sun . . . and I did not want to die. My body could rot, so long as my soul—"

"Begone!" Theophanes cried in a voice that rose on the last syllable. He pointed his index finger as if it were a thin, crooked wand. "Begone, in the Name by which you were summoned!"

"Oh, you didn't summon me," the corpse said. It touched the lattice which surrounded it. The pop of the spark was visible even through the sapphire glow. "I was here, *sage*, brought three hundred years ago by a priest-king who knew enough to purge his own land of . . . me. Not quite enough to save himself, as it turned out. And now you have brought me another home."

It started to lift the cage away from its crushed body. Theophanes screamed and threw his arms in front of his face. Dama's sword arced to the point where the corpse-hand gripped the juncture of three tubes. Glass and fingers leapt into the air. The gas in the lattice puffed, faded, then blossomed into white fire that left a vacuum of light behind it.

Dama fumbled flint and steel from his pouch, cursing at the pain crinkling across the back of his seared right hand. With a flaring twist of lint he relit the hanging lamp. The corpse was sprawled face down, half off the table. Only a seepage of blood beaded on its severed phalanges.

Outside, shrieks of pain and terror exploded from the drivers' tents. Dama grasped the necromancer by the forearms and shook him savagely. "What happened?" he demanded. "By the crucified God, what *happened*?"

Theophanes freed himself with a backward step. His eyes were dilated with fear, and when he ran a hand across his face it was as if to wipe away the images he had seen. "That body was a wrecked one," the necromancer said in a husky whisper. "Only in the Frame of Orestes could it be controlled. He—the waiting thing, the mantichore—couldn't animate it himself; he had no mouth to shape the words. But the power, the incredible power he had to take over a body that I had brought to life! Oh, I was so wrong—deathless and living to kill by whatever flesh it can take control of . . . manslayer indeed!"

Dama flung open the outer door. As he had expected, Hlodovech was gone. The tents of the Armenians were down. In the ember-glow of the fire the merchant could see two figures remaining, fleeing and pursuing. They merged with a scream that was as brief as it was ghastly. There could be no mistaking the gaunt silhouette that rose from its victim and began hulking back toward the inn.

The Cappadocian ducked within and slammed the door. With a strength that belied his slender frame, he began to skid the table to brace the latch. The corpse rolled at the jostling and fell to the floor among the litter of glass shards. "Tell me about Hlodovech," Dama panted as he worked. "He's another one, isn't he?"

"He hanged himself," Theophanes said with a shrug. The necromancer was unharmed but had the stunned emptiness of a fish gasping its life away on a wharf. "I was there. You can still see the mark when his scarf slips." He blinked with returned animation. "But not him. For a decade Hlodovech has been mine. His whole existence has been my will, my safety. Nothing can displace my control of him now, not an Indian magician whose body was dust a thousand years."

Gasping for breath, Dama retrieved his sword from where it had fallen. There was a nick in one of the edges, but the blade was still serviceable. "You fool," he said quietly. "It happened almost as soon as we got here; and you didn't even know it."

A fist crashed on the door. Dama threw his weight against the table. It trembled but did not slide. There was a second blow. The panel itself burst inward.

Dama backed away, watching Hlodovech clear his path of the splintered wood. With a quick gesture of his broad hands, the German threw the table upside down and out of his way. A knife slash had laid open his face so that his whole right cheek flapped against his neck scarf. The edges of the cut were bloodless. Hlodovech's silver-wrapped swordhilt still projected from the scabbard behind his back, disdained by a killer soul whose bloodlust went beyond satisfaction by steel. Dama drew free his dagger as he wondered how many seconds he had yet to live.

Theophanes stepped in front of his bodyguard, denying the new Hell-light in the corpse's eyes. "I command you to stop!" he said. "You are my servant, my creation—*mine.*"

Hlodovech paused and a tremble ran through the knotted muscles. As if avoiding a stone pillar instead of a man half his own bulk, the stark killer circled to the left, keeping his eyes fixed on Dama. No one spoke. Theophanes knelt and began to weep softly. Hlodovech spread his gore-smeared arms and shuffled a step closer. The merchant's shoulder rubbed the wall beside the cold fireplace.

But Hlodovech's brief hesitation had hinted to Dama at least a chance of safety. His left wrist snapped his knife toward the necromancer's chest.

Hlodovech's corpse began two actions, an inhumanly-quick lunge sideways to snatch the thrown dagger, and a forward thrust that would have speared a hand through the trapped Cappadocian. Neither motion was completed. Ten years' conditioning fought a will that had resisted dissolution—though not madness—for a millenium. Something non-physical ripped within the gaunt corpse as guardian and crazed slayer fought for its possession. There was a slurping sound as the whole left side of the body liquesced and drained out of its garments. The right side fell, for a moment to twitch and shudder in a stinking pool. Then it, too, slumped away, leaving yellowing bones that glinted where they showed through interstices of the rawhide clothing.

Theophanes lay on his back. The knife jutted up beside his breastbone, hilt and a sliver of blade visible above the black robe. His left hand clenched and reopened, black with the fluid spreading slowly across the floor. "Mine," he whispered hoarsely in German, but his eyes were beginning to glaze.

The Shortest Way

The dingy relay station squatted beside the road. It had a cast-off, abandoned look about it, though light seeped through chinks in the stone where mortar had crumbled. Broken roofslates showed dark in the moonlight like missing teeth. To the rear bulked the stables where relays for the post riders stamped and nickered in their filthy stalls, and the odor of horse droppings thickened the muggy night.

The three riders slowed as they approached.

"Hold up," Vettius ordered. "We'll get a meal here and ask directions."

Harpago cantered a little further before halting. He was aristocrat enough to argue with a superior officer and young enough to think it worthwhile. "If we don't keep moving, sir, we'll never get to Aurelia before daybreak."

"We'll never get there at all if we keep wandering in these damned Dalmatian hills," Vettius retorted as he dismounted. His side hurt. Perhaps he had gotten too old for this business. At sunup he had strapped his round shield tightly to his back to keep it from slamming during the long ride. All day it had rubbed against his cuirass, and by now it had left a sore the size of his hand.

The shield itself galled him less than what it represented. A sunburst whose rays divided ten hearts spaced around the rim had been nielloed onto the thin bronze facing: the arms of the Household Cavalry. Leading a troop of the emperor's bodyguards should have climaxed Vettius's career, but he had quickly discovered his job was really that of special staff with little opportunity for fighting. He was sent to gather information for the emperor where the stakes were high and the secret police untrustworthy. There was danger in probing the ulcers of a dying empire, but Vettius found no excitement in it; only disgust.

Dama chuckled with relief to be out of his saddle again. He used his tunic to fan the sweat from his legs, looking inconsequential beside the two powerful soldiers. Though he was a civilian, a sword slapped against his thigh. In the backcountry, weapons were the mark of caution rather than belligerence. He nodded toward the still silent building, his blond hair gleaming as bright in the moonlight as the bronze helmets of his two companions. "If it weren't for the light, I'd say the place was empty."

The door of the station creaked open, making answer needless. The man who stood on the threshold was as old and gnarled as the pines that straggled up the slopes of the valley. He faced them with wordless hostility. The last regular courier had passed, and he had been dozing off when this new party arrived. Like many petty officeholders, the stationmaster reveled in his authority—but did not care to be reminded of the duties that went with his position.

Vettius strode forward holding out a scroll of parchment. "Food for us," he directed, "and you can give our horses some grain while we eat."

"All right for you and the other," the stationmaster rasped. "The civilian finds his own meal."

"Government service," Harpago muttered. He spat.

Vettius began kneading one wrist with his other hand. The little merchant touched his friend's elbow, but Vettius shook him away. "I'll take care of it my own way," he said. His temper had worn thin on the grueling ride, and the stationmaster's sneering slovenliness gouged at his nerves.

"Old man," he continued in a restrained voice, "my authority is for food and accommodations for me and my staff. The civilian is with me as part of my staff. Do you dispute the emperor's authority?"

The stationmaster reared back his head to look the soldier in the eyes. "Even the emperor can't afford to feed every starving thief who comes along," he began.

Vettius slapped him to the ground. "Will you call my friend a thief again?" he grated.

The old man's eyes narrowed in hatred as he sullenly dabbed at his bleeding lip, but he shook his head, cowering before the soldier. "I didn't mean it that way."

"Then take care of those horses—and be thankful I don't have you rub them down with your tongue." Vettius stamped angrily into the station, Harpago and Dama behind him.

"Food!" Vettius snapped. A dumpy peasant woman scurried to open a cupboard.

"I could have paid something, Lucius," the merchant suggested as they seated themselves at the trestle table. "After all, I came because I thought I could set up some business of my own here."

"And I brought you because I need your contacts," his friend replied. "The traders here won't tell me if they think the governor really is trying to raise money for a rebellion."

He paused, massaging the inside of his thighs where they ached from holding him into his stirrupless saddle since early dawn. "Besides," he added quietly, "it's been a long day—too long to be put upon by some lazy bureaucrat."

Dama sighed as the serving woman set down barley bread and cheese. "Not much of a meal anyway, is it?" he said. "I thought the empire fed its post couriers better than this, even in the back country."

"And I thought we were going to get directions here," Harpago complained. "If we don't get to Aurelia before the fair ends we'll find all the merchants scattered—and then how are we going to learn anything?"

"We'll find a way," Vettius assured him sourly. He took a gulp of the wine the woman had poured him, then slammed the wooden cup back on the table. "Gods! that's bad."

"Local vintage," Dama agreed. "Maybe I should try to sell some decent wine here instead of silk."

The older soldier swigged some more wine and grimaced wryly. "Old man!" he shouted. After a moment the stationmaster came to the door. He limped slightly and his swollen lip was a blotch of color against his tight face.

The soldier ignored the anger in the old man's eyes. "How far is it to Aurelia?" he demanded.

"By which road?" the other growled.

Vettius touched the pommel of his spatha so that the long straight blade rattled against the bench. "By the shortest way," he said testily.

"You have to . . ." the stationmaster began, then paused. He seemed to consider the matter carefully before he started again. "The shortest way, you say. Well, there's a road just past the station. If you turn north on it, it's only about twenty miles. But you'll have to look well, because nobody's been over that road for fifty years and the beginning is all grown over with trees."

The serving woman suddenly chattered something in her own language. The man snarled back at her and she fell silent.

"Could you catch any of that?" Vettius asked Dama under his breath.

The little Cappadocian shrugged. "She said something about bandits. He told her to be quiet. But I don't really know the language, you know."

"Bandits we can take care of," Harpago muttered, one finger tracing a dent in the helmet he had rested on the table.

"How else can we get to Aurelia?" Vettius questioned, half squinting as if to measure the stationmaster for a cross.

"You can keep on into Pasini, then turn back west on the Salvium road," the other replied without meeting the officer's eyes. "It's several times as long."

"Then we go by the straight route?" Vettius said, looking at his companions questioningly.

Harpago rose and reslung his shield.

"Why not?" Dama agreed.

The stationmaster watched them mount and ride off. His gnarled face writhed in terrible glee.

* * *

"What did they do, tear the whole road up?" Harpago asked. Even with the stationmaster's warning they had almost ridden past the junction. The surfacing flags and concrete certainly had been taken up. Seeds had lodged in the road metal beneath. They had grown to sizable trees by now, so that the only sign of the narrow road was a relative absence of undergrowth.

"The locals must have torn up this branch because it wasn't used much and they were tired of the labor taxes to repair it," Vettius surmised. "They probably used the stone to fill holes on one of the main roads."

"But if this leads to the district market town, it should have gotten quite a lot of use," Dama argued.

"At least it'll guide us to where we're going," Harpago put in, plunging into the trees.

The pines grew close together and their branches frequently interlocked; riding through them was difficult. Vettius began to wonder if they should stop and turn back, but after a hundred yards or so the torn up section gave way to regular road.

Dama paused, looking back in puzzlement as his fingers combed pine straw out of his hair. "You know," he said, "I think they planted those trees on the roadbed when they tore up the surface."

"Why should they do that?" Vettius snorted.

"Well, look around," his friend pointed out. "The road is cracked here, too, but there aren't any trees growing in it. Besides, the trees don't grow as thickly anywhere else around here as they do on that patch of road. Somebody planted them to block it off completely."

The soldier snorted again, but he turned in his

saddle. Dama had a point, he realized. In fact, the pines might even be growing in crude rows. "Odd," he admitted at last.

"Sir!" called Harpago, who had ridden far ahead. "Are you coming?"

Vettius raised an eyebrow. Dama laughed and slapped his horse's flank. "He's young; he'll learn."

"Sorry if I seem to push," the adjutant apologized as they trotted onward, "but I don't like wasting time on this stretch of road. It's too dark for me."

"Dark?" Vettius echoed in amazement. For the first time he took more than cursory notice of their surroundings. The swampy gully to the left of the road had once been a drainage ditch. Long abandonment had left it choked with reeds, while occasional willows sprouted languidly from its edge. On the right, ragged forest climbed the slope of the valley. Scrub pine struggled through densely interwoven underbrush to form a stark, desolate landscape.

But dark? The moonlight washed the broken pavement into a metal serpent twisting through the forest. The trees were too stunted to overshadow the road, and the paving stones gleamed against the contrast of frequent cracks and potholes. Even the scabbed boles of the pines showed silver scales where the moon touched them.

"I wouldn't call it dark," Vettius concluded aloud, "though you could hide a regiment in those thickets."

"No, he's right," Dama disagreed unexpectedly. "It does seem dark, and I can't figure out why."

"Don't tell me both of you are getting nervous of shadows," jeered Vettius.

"I just wonder why they blocked off this road,"

the merchant replied vaguely. "From the look of the job it must have taken most of the district. Wonder what that stationmaster sent us into. . . ?"

Miles clattered gloomily by under their horses' hooves. It was fell, waste land, a wretched paradigm for much of the empire in these latter days. This twisting valley could never have been much different, though. The humid bottoms had never been tilled; perhaps a few hunters had taken deer among its drooping pines. For the others who had come this way—lone travellers, donkey caravans, troops in glittering armor—the valley was only an incident of passage.

Now even the road was crumbling. Although only a short distance had been systematically destroyed, nature and time had taken a hand with the remainder. The flags had humped and split as water seepage froze in the winter, and one great section had fallen into the gully whose spring torrents had undercut it. They led their horses over the rubble while the pines drank their curses.

The usual nightbirds were hushed or absent.

Even Vettius began to feel uneasy. The moonlight weighed on his shoulders like a palpable force, crushing him down in his saddle. The moon was straight overhead now. Occasional streaks of light pierced the groping branches to paint the dark trunks with swordblades.

It *was* dark now. No white face would gleam from the forest edge to warn of the bandit arrow to follow in an instant. Was it fear of bandits that made him so tense? In twenty years service he had ridden point in tighter places!

Letting his horse pick its own way over the broken road, Vettius scanned the forest. He took off his helmet and the tight leather cap that cushioned it. The air felt good, a prickly coolness that persisted even after he put the helmet back on, but there was no relief from the ominous tension. Grunting, he tried to hike his shield a little higher on his back.

Dama chuckled in vindication. "Nervous, Lucius?" he asked.

Vettius shrugged. "The woman at the station said there were bandits."

"On an abandoned piece of road like this?" Dama laughed bitterly. "I wish she were here now. I'd find out for sure what she did say. Do you suppose she knew any Greek besides 'food' and 'wine'?"

"No, she was too ugly for other refreshment," Vettius said. His forced laughter bellowed through the trees.

After a short silence, Harpago said, "Well, at least we should be almost to Aurelia by now."

"Look where the moon is, boy," Vettius scoffed. "We've only been riding for two hours or so."

"Oh, surely it's been longer than that," the younger man insisted, looking at the sky in amazement.

"Well, it hasn't," his commander stated flatly.

"Shall we rest the horses for a moment?" Dama suggested. "That pool seems to be spring fed, and I'm a little thirsty."

"Good idea," Vettius agreed. "I'd like to wash that foul wine out of my mouth too."

"Look," Harpago put in, "Aurelia must be just around the next bend. Why don't we ride on a little further and see—"

"Ride yourself if you want to be a damned fool," snapped Vettius. He didn't like to be pushed, especially when he was right.

Harpago flushed. He saluted formally. When Vettius ignored him, he wheeled and rode off.

Vettius unstrapped his shield and looked around while the Cappadocian slurped water from his cupped hand. The adjutant was out of sight now, but the swift clinking of his horse's hooves reached them clearly.

"If that young jackass doesn't learn manners, somebody's going to break his neck before he gets much older," Vettius grumbled. "Might even be me."

Dama dried his face on his sleeve and began filling the water bottles. "It's something in the air here," he explained. "We're all tight."

The soldier began scuffing at a stump fixed beside the roadway. Decayed wood flaked away under his hobnails and the wasted remnants of a bronze nail clinked on the pavement. "They crucified somebody here," he said.

"Um?"

"These posts along the road," Vettius explained. "There were several others back a ways. They're what's left of crosses when the top rots away."

Around the bend the hoofbeats faltered and a horse neighed in terror. Vettius swore and slipped his left arm through the straps of his shield. Metal crashed on stone.

Someone screamed horribly.

The big soldier vaulted into his saddle. With one swift jerk Dama loosed the cloak tied to his pommel, snapped it swiftly through the air to wrap protection around his left arm. He scrambled astride his horse.

"Wait!" Vettius said. "You aren't dressed for trouble. Ride back and get help."

"I don't think I will," the merchant remarked,

drawing the short infantry sword that was belted over his tunic. "Ready?"

"Yes," Vettius said. His spatha shimmered in his hand.

They rounded the bend at a gallop. Wind caught at their garments. The Cappadocian's tunic bulked out into a squat troll shape while Vettius's short red officers' cape flew straight back from his shoulders. When a man looked up at their approach, the soldier let out the terrible banshee howl he had learned from his first command, a squadron of Irish mercenaries, as they slaughtered pirates on the Saxon Shore.

One of the men in the road howled back.

Harpago's horse pitched wildly as two filthy, skin-clad men sawed at its reins. Startled by Vettius's howl, a dozen similar shapes in the middle of the road parted to disclose the adjutant himself. He lay on his back with his eyes wide open to the moon. One of the slayers was still lapping at the blood draining from Harpago's torn throat.

The bandits surged to meet them. A youngster with matted hair and a wool tunic too dirty to show its original color swung a club at Vettius. It boomed dully on his shield, and the bandit snarled in fury. Vettius struck back with practiced grace, felling the club wielder with an overarm chop, then stabbing another opponent over his own back as he recovered his blade. Dropping the reins, he smashed his shield down into the face of a third who was hacking at his thigh below his studded leather apron. Her rough cloak fell away from her torso as she pitched backwards.

Dama had ridden down one of the bandits. He was trading furious strokes with a second, a purple-garbed patriarch with a sword, when a third man crawled under his horse's belly and stabbed upward with a fire-hardened spear. The beast screamed in agony and threw the Cappadocian into the gully. He struggled upright barely in time to block the blow of a human thighbone used as a bludgeon, then thrust his assailant through the neck.

"Get Harpago's horse!" Vettius shouted as he cut through the melee to relieve his friend.

Dama caught at the beast's reins. A bandit, his mouth smeared with gore, clubbed him across the shoulders and he dropped them again. Stunned, he staggered into the horse. Before his opponent could raise his weapon for another blow, Vettius had slashed through his spine. Drops of blood sailed off the tip of the soldier's sword as each blow arced home.

Dama threw himself onto the saddle. As he struggled to swing a leg astride, the purple-clad swordsman who had engaged him earlier slipped behind Vettius's horse and cut at the blond merchant's face. Vettius wheeled expertly and lopped off the bandit's right arm.

The handful of surviving bandits fell back in mewling horror. Then a baby bawled from the darkness as his mother tore him from her breast and dropped him to the ground. The woodline crackled with frantic movement. Savage forms rushed from the black pines—children scarcely able to walk and feral women. In the hush their bare feet scratched on the stone. Their men, braced by their numbers, moved forward purposefully.

All looked bestially alike.

Vettius took the reeling bandit chief by the hair and thrust his blade against the bony throat. The ghoulish horde moaned in baffled rage, but hesitated.

Then one of the women snarled deep in her throat and rushed at the riders alone. Dama, reeling in his saddle, slashed at her. She ducked under his sword and raked the merchant's leg with teeth and horny nails. Dama hacked awkwardly at her back. The woman cried shrilly each time the heavy blade struck her, but only at the fourth blow did she sag to the pavement.

"Let's get out of here!" Dama cried, gesturing at the clot of savage forms. He could face their crude weapons, but the bloodlust in their eyes was terrifying.

Vettius was chopping at the bandit's neck with short strokes. At last the spine parted and the soldier howled again, flaunting his trophy as he kicked his horse into a gallop.

As they rounded the next bend, Dama glanced over his shoulder. Harpago's body was again covered by writhing men. Or things shaped like men.

A mile down the road they halted for a moment, looking to their wounds and gulping air. The merchant hung his head low to clear it. His face was still pale when he straightened.

Vettius had dropped his trophy into a saddlebag, so that he could grip the reins again with his left hand. He continued to rest the spatha on his saddlebow instead of sheathing it.

"We'd better be going," he said curtly.

The eastern sky was perceptibly brighter when their foam-spattered horses staggered into another stretch of dismantled roadway. The riders' skin crawled as they forced their way between the files of trees, but the passage was without incident. Beyond lay Aurelia, a huddle of mean houses surrounded by the tents of the merchants come for the fair.

Light bobbed as a watchman raised his lantern toward them. "You!" he called. "Where did you come from?"

"South of here," Vettius replied bleakly.

"Gods," the watchman began, "nobody's come that way in—" The riders had come within the circle of lantern light and his startled eyes took in their torn clothes and bloody weapons. "Gods!" he blurted again. "Then the story *is* true."

"What story?" Dama croaked, his gaze fixed on the watchman. Absently, he wiped his sword on his ruined tunic.

"There was a family of bandits—cannibals, really—living on that stretch—"

"You knew of that and did nothing?" Vettius roared, his face reddening with fury. "By the blood of the Bull, I'll have another head for this!"

"No!" the watchman squealed, cringing from the upraised sword. "I tell you it's been fifty years! For a long time they killed everybody they attacked, so it went on for years and years without anyone knowing what was happening. But when somebody got away, the governor brought in a squadron of cavalry. He crucified them all up and down the road and left them hanging there to rot."

Vettius shook his head in frustration. "But they're still there!" he insisted.

The watchman gulped. "That's what my grandfather said. That's why they had to close that road fifty years ago. Because they were still there—even though all of them were dead."

"Lucius," the merchant said softly. He had

opened his friend's saddlebag. A moment later the severed head thumped to the ground.

Rosy light reflected from eyes that were suddenly vacant sockets. Skin blackened, sloughed, and disappeared. The skull remained, grinning at some secret jest the dead might understand.

From The Dark Waters

The brassy sea rocked as a small shark felt the bite of hooks deep in its belly and tried to tear loose. Hlovida was crouched low over her tile oven in the shelter forward, scrunching something in her teeth. "Careful, careful," she cackled in a voice still burred with the German of her early childhood. "One'll fill his belly with you, Dercetus, I can see it."

The Libyan mate, braced ready with a boat pike for the captive his crewmates were hauling aboard, ignored the wizened cook. Sweat beads jewelled his scarred black skin but could not cool him in the breathless air.

"Shut up, old fool," Vettius muttered. With his merchant friend he lay under the awning that stretched from the deckhouse to the broken stump of the mast. The light canvas hung as limp as the jib sail, seeming to trap more heat than it turned. Dama only shrugged moodily and leaned his slight form sideways out of the shadow. The sternpost of their ship, the *Purple Ibis*, curled over the deckhouse in a gentle sweep. It had been too many years since the encaustic paint had been renewed on its bird's-head finial, but it was still a graceful piece of carving. A handsome enough ship, in fact, before the storm. Eighty feet long, it had a three-sided deckhouse aft and a low, roofed shelter in the bow for the cook and her traps. Between mast and bow, a single open hatch gave access to the hold. Forward from the deckhouse ran a low rail, polished by decades of calloused hands. The smooth line broke amidships on the starboard side where raw splinters still gaped . . .

After the first thrashing, the little shark drove straight away from the merchantman. The line and wire leader were heavy but the full shock of the fish would have snapped either. There was no need to wear the shark down, though. A brown-mottled tiger shark struck its lesser kinsman, scalloping out a huge mouthful that cut the hooked beast nearly in half. Its tail lashed briefly in the instant before a dozen other sharks ripped it apart in savage hunger. In the bloody explosion of teeth and fragments, the fishline parted and the sailor holding it stumbled backward.

Dama's face was impassive. His eyes were turned towards the sea, but in his mind it was the dark, pitching surface of the night before.

They were scudding in the bright moonlight, the breeze off the Mauretanian coast nudging them gently towards Massilia and only the helmsman awake. The first gust came as lightning from a clear sky. It heeled the vessel on to her beam-ends. Dama's right hand locked on a stanchion in a reflex developed during years of shepherding cargoes through foul weather. Vettius's massive body hit the slatted wall of the deckhouse, but his long cavalry sword was clear in his hand. The wind slackened momentarily.

The high, wet clouds that piled up over the vineyards of the shore began to flow across the moon. Catfooted crewmen scurried to reef the sail. The ship rocked back sluggishly, logy with the weight of bolted silk in her hold. Then, in the dread silence punctuated only by the captain's frantic orders, the second gust struck. The half-furled sail, a new panel of stout Egyptian linen, blasted out of the hands of the seamen. The full force of the wind snapped at the mast that was as old as the hull, dried and weathered by the sucking heat of forty years. It parted with a crash, taking the captain and three sailors over the side with it.

The merchantman wallowed in the swells like a drunken whore. There was a single chance of saving the seamen clinging to the mast and air-bulged sail. Vettius sheathed his sword as naturally as he had drawn it and wrapped his powerful legs around the deck rail. The rising wind muffled the swish of the lead rope as he spun the loaded end twice around his head. Ignoring storm and the ship's pitching, he arced the rope over the drifting mass of top hamper.

The captain dropped the sheet he held and tugged at the lead. Already the vessel had drifted fifty yards. The floating man's triumphant cry crescendoed horribly as foam and a colored shadow bloomed in the water around him. The moon glared through the clouds for one last time as the dark sea filled with fins roiling in ghastly delight. The mast trembled among them. Crippled, the Purple

Ibis *continued drifting. Rain began to slash down, but the survivors could still hear the screams from the darkness.*

"Another hook," Dercetus ordered in a husky voice. He breathed with his whole body, slowly but in deep, sudden intakes.

The seaman who held the line picked himself up from the deck. He did not look at the mate. For an instant his eyes caught those of the remaining common sailor, a Syrian like himself, before replying in the bad Greek of the sea lanes, "There's no wire for leaders. It's no use."

The mate's left hand, dark and as broad as a wine bowl, took the seaman gently behind the jaw and brought his face around. The pike Dercetus still held added no more to the threat than did the spiked plate on a war elephant's forehead. "There's wire," the mate said. "There's wire enough to string every shark in this sea—and by Moloch! I will."

Vettius chuckled deep in his throat as he watched the seaman slink towards the companionway. "Afraid," he explained conversationally to Dama. "Mithra, I know them. Like the centurion who told me an outpost had already been overrun when I ordered him to relieve it. When he learned he could lead out his section or have me flay him alive—" the big soldier grinned as his finger traced down the scabbard of the cavalry sword—"he led it out. Which was just as well for him."

Dama indicated the mate's broad back with a not-quite-casual thumb. "I know how he feels, with him and the captain as close as they were . . ."

Vettius gestured obscenely with both hands, his smile tolerant but amused.

". . . but this won't bring anybody back. And feeding the sharks around us doesn't make me feel easier, at any rate."

Hlovida shuffled towards the mate from the cooking shelter, hunched as if her bones were on the verge of shattering. Twenty years before, she had been beautiful; time had been cruel. At forty her fine blonde hair had become white and dull, so brittle that the left side of her skull was half naked like an ill-thatched roof. Grey-brown discolorations marked her wrinkled skin and both cheeks bore flat sores. Her clothes were shapeless and filthy, so old that she might have been wearing them when the slavers bought her from a garrison on the Rhastian frontier.

"No, don't do that," she said, her voice breaking in the middle of an attempt to caress. She reached a crooked hand towards the mate's bare shoulder. "I told you, you'll be in a shark's belly soon if you try to hook another. I can see things, now that I've got my beauty back; yes I can."

Dercetus turned suddenly from the pattern of fins and grey shadows streaking the sea. His look of rapt loathing twisted into nausea as he took in the clawed fingers on his arm. Grunting an oath, he jerked away and lurched down the ladder in search of the seaman.

Hlovida's glance brushed the remaining sailor regretfully, then locked on to the passengers. The Cappadocian merchant's blond hair reminded her of her youth, but his stubby body was beneath her addled fancy. Instead, she curtsied under the awning and seated herself at Vettius's side. "Yes, I can see everything," she said, stroking her own cheek. Her voice had an odd rhythm, not wholly distasteful. "The king's coming for poor Dercetus, and he'll take the rest of us too."

Vettius turned his back ostentatiously.

"Ooh!" the woman shrilled, "he's so strong and wise—what do I need with you men?"

"What indeed?" Dama agreed under his breath as the cook rose and flounced to the rail, but her voice jagged on saying, "He's wise, you know? Not like a fish, not even like a man. Down in the deep he lives, and he eats the men the wrecks send to him. Down in the deep, where the seas are as black as he is white . . . but once in a lifetime, in lifetimes, he comes up to take his food live. He's the king, the king of all the seas."

Dama scowled. "She's mad for men, Dercetus mad for sharks . . . why don't you and I try to pilot this hulk to Circe's island or the Styx, Lucius? Then we could all be mad together."

The ship trembled as something rough-scaled brushed the keel. The merchant broke off his fantasy to call, "Get away from the rail, old woman; there's fish out there that wouldn't make three gulps of you."

Hlovida tittered, irrationally gay again. "Hoo! Not yet. But wait till the king comes. He's bigger than this whole ship, and he'll eat us all, one and one and one and one and one. See how fast he's coming? He's still deep now but rising, rising . . ."

Vettius shook his head. "A shark eighty feet long?" he said with a grimace. "She *is* mad."

"Maybe she means a physeter," Dama suggested idly. "I saw a herd spouting once near Taprobane."

"She's mad," Vettius repeated.

Calloused feet scuffled on the companionway. First the Syrian appeared on deck, then the heavily-muscled mate with a dozen bronze leaders coiled over his arm. "String it," Dercetus ordered the seaman, tossing the wire at his feet; and to the cook, "Give him some pork."

"There's not much . . ." Hlovida suggested doubtfully.

"There'll be enough," Dercetus stated with a short, barking laugh. "As far north as the storm blew us, we'll fetch up on the coast of Spain any day. And maybe I'll boat one of these before he's eaten by his friends—then we'll have meat!"

The cook rummaged barehanded in the deck well where several amphoras were buried to their necks in sand. The gobbet she finally flipped to the sailor was so ripe and blackened that Dama was as glad as not to see it go over the side. Two thick-shanked hooks hid in its heart. A fifteen-foot hammerhead, misshapen and savage even among its present company, slammed the bait and took it straight down. The line hummed.

Dama shook his head and walked to the other rail, divorcing himself from the useless struggle.

"They're as bad as men," Vettius said, amused to watch other killers at work. "As soon as they see one of their own hurt, they're on him. This one doesn't feel the hooks yet. Wait till he does and tries to throw them out—Dercetus won't need the pike to finish any of this pack."

The seaman bracing against the line had fashioned mittens from a hide in the cargo. As the leather dragged on it, the hard linen cord purred and stank. Unexpectedly, the other sharks avoided the hooked hammerhead although their movements changed. Instead of slipping lazily around the becalmed vessel, each began circling its own wake. One leaped, a grisly sight with its jaws spread and a glazed yellow eye glaring at the ship. Something had gone wrong. Even Dercetus, poised at the rail as blank-eyed as the shark, felt that.

The sea was a sheet of hammered bronze. Dama could see deep down below its foamless surface. Miles, it seemed, but that was the distortion. He had never known air to be so still.

"She's rising!" someone called, and the merchant could hear the sailor's quick steps as the man tried to coil the line. It slackened faster than he could pull it in. And something was rising in the liquid depths of Dama's vision, too, a colorless dot quivering in the amber water. It grew, took an indeterminate shape. It was speeding straight up at the ship with the speed of a falling star. An outline formed and flowed with color: the dirty white of an old shroud.

"Shark!" Dama bawled. He leaped back from the port rail.

Alone of the men on deck, Vettius glanced at the puzzled Cappadocian. The hammerhead was alongside now, strangely quiescent as the Syrian jerked its head out of the water and bent over the rail for another handful of line. "Hold him!" Dercetus ordered sharply. His right arm poised to slam the heavy pike through the shark's brain case.

The sea fountained an enormous cone of pallid white. Jaws crunched together, their sound muted by the roar of falling water and a glancing impact that rocked the vessel. Ignored in the brittle chaos, the hammerhead arrowed off with the severed leader still trailing from its mouth. The Syrian had locked his calves around the rail. They remained there. Six-inch teeth had sheared off the man's body above his loincloth while his blood sprayed a semicircle of deck behind him.

The huge shark, white except where blood had spattered it, shot out of the sea like a cork bobber released on the bottom. With its dorsal fin still under water, the pointed snout already towered twenty feet above the surface. Dercetus screamed in indecision. He tripped away in fear; then, with the shark still rising, hatred carried him back in a lunge, jabbing his pike into the great side.

The iron head threw sparks as it scrunched harmlessly across the scales; it was as if the mate had speared a thrusting block of coral. Instead of sliding back into the sea, the shark twisted its body stiffly towards the ship. The rail shattered. Dama dived over the hatch coaming, head first. Dercetus was left nakedly alone amidships when Vettius leaped for his bundled gear in the deck-house. Letting his useless spear clatter over the side, the big Libyan tried to follow the merchant. His feet skidded on blood and shot him outward towards the rail.

The shark's jaws thudded harmlessly above him but the deck's pitch tipped Dercetus into something worse. Caught between the shark and the planking, he screamed. As the huge beast continued to grind back into the sea, its belly scales rasped the mate to bloody ruin. Face and chest, touched by the serrated hide, were flayed to the bones. Nothing but a carmine track remained of the right leg below the knee, and the full length of the left fibula was exposed. The sea slapped thunderously, rolling the ship again.

Vettius stripped layers of oil-rich wool from his bow case, ignoring the remaining Syrian frozen open-mouthed beside him. Dercetus made enough noise for two, the soldier thought with detachment. Or a dozen. Well, he couldn't howl for long.

Dama's head, haloed by the sunlight, poked above the deck. "Clear," the bigger man said. "It went back over the side." Dama hopped the rest of the way out of the hatch. His tunic was torn and in his right hand he clasped a hatchet snatched up in the hold.

"Ah," Hlovida crooned softly. She darted to Dercetus's side and began binding tourniquets above the blood spurting from his maimed limbs. Neither Vettius nor the little merchant considered helping her. Each had seen dying men before; also men better off dead. The cook's German-thickened voice buzzed as she worked, saying, "Oh, poor darling. How could you be so reckless when your Hlovida warned you?"

"By the Blood, do fish get that big?" Vettius marveled to his friend. His hornbow was strung in his hands now. Its fat cord stretched over a yard between ivory tips. Again the sea wove with sharks, their dark sinuosities grimly overshadowed by the pale monster now leading them.

"Isn't he strong, dear one?" Hlovida chortled as she sponged the weakly-protesting Dercetus. "And wise, too. He never comes to the surface when anyone might escape."

The dorsal fin of the white shark was a dozen feet high and all of it was out of the water. Unlike any other shark Vettius had seen, this one was from belly to fins a uniform moldy hue that made the big soldier think of grave worms. No albino, though, not with its cruel yellow eyes. More like something which had spent centuries in the depths, which was absurd. It swam stiffly, as if an obelisk with fins.

"It's not for him to be killed by men," the old Marcomann woman concluded cheerfully, "so he'll kill us all soon." Dercetus shrieked as the sponge touched a rib gnawed to the marrow by adamantine scales.

Vettius drew his bow and shot without pausing for conscious aim. The bowstring slapped the inside of his left wrist, leaving a welt because he had not taken time to strap on his bracer. He cursed, less at the pain than the ineffectiveness of his shot. The arrow struck as intended at the root of the high dorsal fin; the narrow iron point may have penetrated, but the transmitted impact shattered the shaft. Vettius nocked another arrow but did not draw the bow. "Now what?" he snarled.

"Now we wait for a breeze to bring us to land," Dama answered, wiping his palms on his tunic before regripping the hatchet.

"Oh, there won't be any wind while he's here," Hlovida said, nodding archly towards the great shark. "*He* rules the sea." She tittered as she dragged the mate towards her shelter.

At midnight the air was silent. Vettius stirred, spat. He and Dama could follow the ripples in the moonlight, spreading faintly until they shivered apart in the track of the circling sharks. The remaining seaman was huddled in the deckhouse. From forward came a faint scraping noise that Dama tried to ignore.

"We have to kill that fish," Vettius said flatly, his back to the mast and his stubbled jaw cradled between his knees.

The merchant grinned and spread his hands, palms down. "Sure, and I'd like a chance to study the carcase. Don't know how we'll get it aboard, but if you can kill something that big, you can figure that out too . . ."

"Well, we can't just wait here and watch it," the soldier growled irritably. "You saw what it did to him and the other." Vettius's spade-broad hand gestured forward.

"I didn't say we should get too near the rail," protested Dama more seriously, "but we're sure to strike land soon."

"How do we know?" Vettius demanded. He slapped his bow against his thigh for emphasis, setting the waxed cord singing. "What if that bitch is right again and we'll never see land so long as that thing dogs us?"

Dama let out a skeptical hiss.

"Anyway, I want to kill it," the bigger man admitted sheepishly. "It's out there laughing at us and . . . I want to end it."

Dama laughed out loud. "Well, there's a fine reason to risk our lives. But if neither spears nor arrows do the job, what do we do?"

"Um," the soldier grunted. "Well, I've got a notion about arrows, enough of them in the right places. Now if you're willing . . ."

The sun had merged sea and sky so that the *Purple Ibis* seemed to float within a bronze drum. The perpendicular rays exposed every dreadful line of the white shark. It cruised just as it had all the morning and the previous day. More sharks followed it than before. As far down as Dama's eyes could peer into the clear, golden water, nothing swam but sharks. He tossed the pork-baited line over the side. The fat meat floated a dozen feet from the ship, rocking slightly from the unbalanced weight of the leader. None of the smaller sharks left their grim formation.

The great white shark sank smoothly, the tip of its dorsal fin leaving a narrow track of foam before it, too, dipped below the surface. The shrinking torpedo shape continued to circle down into the lucid depths for as long as it was visible.

"He's gone," the soldier announced tensely, peering over the port rail. Dama licked his lips. He leaned over the rail, but his weight was balanced on the balls of his feet.

Vettius half-drew his bow. Three more arrows poked out of his left hand, each point gripped between a pair of fingers. He remembered how his friend had described the first appearance of the shark, a growing dot far down in the water. Now he saw it himself—

"Ready!" Vettius called. He drew the arrow to the head but still looked over his shoulder back into the sea. "Ready, ready—NOW!"

Dama porpoised, flinging himself down the companionway. He was still in the air when the white shark burst upward, a corpse-colored volcano. Its gullet was pale pink, a cathedral of flesh arched darkly on either side by five gill slits. Washed clean by the sea, its saw-edged teeth winked in the sun.

Vettius slapped his first arrow into the center of the rising belly. If the great fish noticed, its actions gave no sign. Curving its body like a fifty-ton boar tusk, the shark arced over the high stern of the *Ibis*. Deck stringers cracked under the awesome impact. Vettius dropped his weapons and thrust himself backward reflexively as the white bulk hurtled towards him. He had expected to fire three, perhaps all four of his readied arrows, but it had not occurred to him that the fish might throw itself aboard. Ferocity had guided it, that or something else not to be considered at the instant.

Two-thirds of the shark's length lay on the deck, the snout a pace short of Hlovida's shelter. The enormous tail threshed out of the water and slashed across the deckhouse from starboard to port. Light wood exploded into splinters that fanned the sea. With them pitched the screaming sailor, bloodied by the tearing impact but all too conscious of the shapes arrowing towards where he must land. Water choked his cry; then a column of bloody froth spurted high into the air.

The ship wallowed. Forward of the mast stump, where the deck sloped nearest the sea, there was almost no freeboard left. The shark's body loomed over Vettius, a scaly, deadly surge that reached the port rail just as he cleared it. The soldier's biceps knotted hugely as they took the shock of his full weight on the rail. He hung there, his hobnailed boots skittering in the water as the ship rolled. A corner of his mind doubted any of the other sharks would leave the water to strike, but the overburdened vessel was perilously near foundering.

There was a mighty splash to starboard and the ship yawed violently to port as the shark dropped back into the sea. Vettius went under to the throat. As the ship righted itself, he used his momentum to spring out of the sea and back on to the deck. Behind him, teeth clashed.

The fish had left only shambles behind it. The mast stump was gone, broken off flush with the planking. The beast's flailing body had sheared away almost everything from the stern forward: bitts, deckhouse, railings, and the steering oar. At least the jib sail had survived, though it hung limp as Tiberius's prick. Mithra, unless there came a breeze . . .

Dama climbed on deck with a questioning eyebrow cocked. "I hit him," Vettius said morosely. He glanced around for his bow. "For all the good it did. Look at him there."

The sharks were all circling again. There was nothing else on the sea or in it.

"I told you you'd never kill him," the blurred voice said. The soldier's face went gray beneath his wiry black hair and eyebrows. He turned to the cook.

Dama touched the big man's arm. "We're not sharks," he said quietly.

Blissfully ignorant of how close she had come to death, Hlovida prattled on, "You'll starve, you know. There's nothing left but a little grain and enough oil to coat the jar." She giggled. "All the meat's gone, over the side, lost—and you'll not be fishing more, will you?"

In three jumps, both men were under the shelter and jerking the stoppers from amphoras. Dercetus's left leg was stuck to the neck of one jar. The black ichor oozing through the bandage cracked as Dama eased the mate aside, and he screamed himself awake. The amphora held less than a peck of wheat. The meat containers sloshed with stinking brine, nothing else.

"Did they hurt you, dearest?" Hlovida cooed as she ran her speckled hands down Dercetus's face. She had wrapped the mate mummy-fashion in what had been one or more layers of her own garments. It would not have helped for them to start clean, Dama thought grimly, considering the way Dercetus leaked where his skin was gone.

"The bitch hid the rest of the grain on her," Vettius suggested huskily. His great hands closed on the cook's shoulders and threw her back on the deck. Insanely, the woman began to scream, "Oh! Oh! You'll rape me for my beauty!"

Dama jerked loose her sash. A paper-wrapped packet hidden somewhere within the Marcomann's clothing thumped the deck and skittered down a broken plank. The Cappadocian's hand speared it before it could slip into the hold. "Castor and Pollux, she *has* got something!" he cried.

Through a chorus of sobs, Hlovida shrieked, "No, you won't take my beauty?"

Vettius back-handed her into silence.

The blond merchant peeled away two layers of scrap papyrus while his friend watched anxiously. Inside lay a large, flat crystal. It was clear in the center, translucently white around the chipped edges. Part of one side had been scraped concave by a sharp instrument. "Rock salt?" Vettius queried. He ignored the cook groaning softly behind him.

"I don't . . ." Dama muttered. He touched a loose granule to his tongue. It tasted faintly metallic and had a gritty, insoluble texture. The merchant spat it out, spat again to clear the saliva from his mouth. "Poison!" he said. "There's enough arsenic here to wipe out a city."

His tongue touched his lips as another thought occurred to him. "What does a cook do with poison, old woman?"

Hlovida was on her knees and snuffling. "He wouldn't look at me because I wasn't pretty any more," she mumbled. "I saved some of the money each time I bought supplies—"

"Stole it, she means," Vettius interjected sardonically, but the merchant hushed him swiftly.

"My sisters, they used to use it to make men look at them. So white, such white skins they had. Oh!" she concluded with a wail, "nobody would look at me any more!"

"*Dis*," the Cappadocian whispered, "no wonder her mind's gone."

"Don't take it, will you?" Hlovida begged. A gnarled, poison-blotched hand crept towards the crystal.

Vettius's great paw caught it first, tossed it in the air. "We've got a better use for it," he stated flatly.

"Umm," Dama agreed, "but he may not take it. He's . . . that is, it isn't . . . well, it doesn't act like a shark."

"It'll take the bait we offer it," Vettius promised with a stark grin. "And that's all we have, isn't it?"

Dama followed the big soldier's eyes forward. "Yes," he admitted, "I guess it is." He checked the edge of his hatchet.

Knocking Hlovida down wasn't enough. Vettius finally tied the screaming woman to the rail before he could return to Dama in the forward shelter. For a man as near death as he was, Dercetus fought like a demon. It took all the soldier's strength to hold him down while Dama smashed through the bone at mid-thigh, just beneath the new tourniquet. The merchant drained his grisly trophy over the side, watching the blood dilute outward in semicircles.

A brown-mottled tiger shark broke momentarily from the pack, then rejoined it without noticeable interchange with any of the other sharks. The white shark rolled so that its left eye glared at the ship through the air; then it dived away more swiftly than before. The others—the sea was rotten with sharks—went wild in leaping and corkscrews but did not approach the *Purple Ibis*.

"Quick," the merchant requested. Vettius's dagger ripped a deep channel into the thigh muscle and he inserted the crystal. Two quick twists of rag and a knot closed the flesh back over the poison. Dama grunted and threw the leg overboard.

"Should have the pike ready," he said.

"What for?" the soldier queried with a chuckle. "Think he'll fool with us any more if this doesn't work?"

The great shark shot skyward with all its rigid power. The mate's leg was there and then gone, and spray fountained as the fish bellied back into the sea. The white shadow slipped beneath the ship. Wood rasped, then splintered tremulously as the keel tore away. The whole leaping, gasping pack of killers was approaching the vessel from all sides. Perhaps they sensed as both men did that the ship could break up at any moment.

Dama swore. "Even that wasn't enough poison," he said. "Look—it knows something's wrong but it's not about to roll belly up."

The white shark paused in its assault on the hull and shook itself side to side. It did not appear seriously disordered and the trembling slackened to an end. "You'll never kill him!" Hlovida shrieked from where she was bound. She lashed her head so violently that some of the brittle hair snapped and floated into the sea. "Men can't kill him!"

Vettius grimaced and started for the cook. Dama again caught his arm. "Let her rave, Lucius."

"Raving or not, she's been right too often," the

soldier growled. "I don't want her finding more of that to say. It comes true."

Before he could act, the shark slid back towards the ship through foam-muddled water. "Watch it!" Dama called, but Vettius had already seen the danger. One tail flick, a second, and the shark was on them. But instead of another graceful leap to bring its body down shatteringly on weakened timbers, the sleek movements dissolved into a spasm working forward from the tail. The shark's nose bumped the ship almost gently and the beast backed off. It vomited hugely into the sea: Dercetus's leg already bleached white by stomach acid, and a less identifiable lump that must have been the sailor.

"He'll come out of it now," Dama said bleakly. He had seen enough men poisoned to know that the survivors were the ones who turned their stomachs out quickly. A glance overboard gave him the dizzy feeling that he could step off the rail and run across the backs of the sharks. A big hammerhead, the bronze glint of a leader trailing back from its mouth, nuzzled the ejecta avidly. Seared again by the poison, the white shark lurched forward uncontrolled and snouted its T-headed relative. The lesser shark turned lazily. Its jaws opened incredibly wide, so wide they appeared to dislocate in the instant before they slammed closed on the white shark's belly.

"God of Calvary," Dama breathed, his lips forming words unspoken since his childhood. His fingers gouged bruises in Vettius's rigid arm. "Lord of the meek, be with us now!"

The huge fish arched into a flat bow, ripping loose the slaty hammerhead. A bloody gobbet of flesh had torn away. Scales proof against Man's weapons crunched apart under jaw muscles with thirty tons of rending power.

The rest of the pack went mad.

The sea blasted apart in a fury of blood and froth. The other sharks ringed the great white like doles about a wounded tiger. Twisting mightily, the white shark broke away in a dive. Already a score of platter-sized gaps in its hide streamed red into the sea. But there was time in the depths for wounds to scar; for reflection, perhaps, if a shark's mind could reflect . . .

Poison-riddled muscles spasmed again, shattering the smooth thrust for sanctuary. The rest was carnage. When the enormous tail flipped a small blue through the air broken-backed, the nearest of the pack bolted the new victim. The others continued to squirm toward the wounded white with deadly intent. The great fish did not die easily, but nothing could have survived that thrashing chaos. Logy with arsenic, ever more tattered by its maddened kin, the shark hurled itself from the carmine water in a convulsive arc. As it fell back, Dama caught its eye. It was glazed and empty.

"There's a cloud south of us," Dama said at last. "Maybe we're due for some wind."

Vettius continued to scan the bloody water about the ship. It had suddenly been drained of life. Dercetus moaned, out of sight forward.

"Rest easy, darling," Hlovida cackled grossly. "I'll never leave you."

Nemesis Place

Vettius and his half-section of troops in armor filled the innkeeper's narrow office. "The merchant Daoud of Petra," he said, pointing his finger like a knifeblade at the shocked civilian's throat. "Which room?"

"S-second floor," stuttered the innkeeper, his face gone the color of tallow when the emperor's soldiers burst in on him. "Nearest the ladder."

"Ulcius, you watch him," nodded the big legate to the nearest of his men. The other soldiers and Dama were already swinging toward the ladder that served as sole means of access to the inn's upper floors. Dama was half the bulk of any of the burly troops, an elfin man of Cappadocian stock whose blond hair was now part silver. He was not visibly armed, but neither had Vettius brought his friend on the raid to fight.

The fat teamster who had started down the ladder had sense enough to change direction as the soldiers came scrambling up. Their hobnailed sandals rasping the tiles were the only sound they made as they formed a semi-circle around the indicated doorway. Dulcitius, the Thracian centurion with a godling's face and a weasel's eyes, drew his sword silently. Vettius checked the position of his men, shifted so that his own armored body masked Dama, and kicked in the latched wooden door. All five of them were inside before the room's gray-haired occupant could sit up on his mattress.

"Your name and business, *now*!" Vettius thundered in Aramaic. He had not drawn his own long spatha, but either of his knotted fists was capable of pulping the frail man on the bed.

"Sirs, I'm Daoud, son of Hafiz, nothing more than a trader in spices," the old man whined. His hands trembled as they indicated the head-sized spice caskets arrayed beneath the room's barred window.

"You were told right," Dama said with flat assurance. He had traded in more countries than most of the empire knew existed, and the local dialects were as much a part of his memories as the products the people bartered. "That's not an Arab accent," he went on, "it's pure Persian. He may be a spice trader, but he's not from Petra or anywhere else inside the empire."

The legate's square face brightened with triumph. "Amazing," he said, irony barbing his words. "I didn't realize there was anybody in Antioch who wasn't too busy listening for treason to bother telling us about a Persian spy."

The old man cowered back against the wall, deforming the billet that served as pillow at the head of his bed. Vettius's practiced eye caught the angular hardness in the cloth. His hand shot out, jerking away the billet and spilling to the floor the dagger within it. Briefly no one moved. The Persian was hunched as though trying to crawl backwards into the plaster.

Dama toed the knife, listening critically to its ring. "Silver," he announced. "I don't think it's meant for a weapon. It's magic paraphernalia, like the robe it was wrapped in."

"Uh?" Vettius glanced at the coarse woolen blanket he had snatched. Unrolled, it displayed a garment of gauzy black silk as fine as a spider's weaving. In metal threads on the hem were worked designs that appeared notational but in no script with which the legate was familiar. Vettius kicked the silver dagger, the arthame, into the passageway and tossed the robe after it. He deliberately turned his back on the man who called himself Daoud. Bending, he grasped a handle and snaked out one of the bottom layer of spice caskets. It was of leather like the rest, its tight lid thonged to the barrel; but the workmanship was exceptionally good, and a recent polishing could not hide signs of great age. Vettius fumbled at the knot, then popped the fastening with a quick flexion of his fingers.

The old Persian gave a wordless cry and leaped for the legate's back. Dulcitius's sword darted like pale lightning, licking in at the Persian's jaw hinge and out the opposite temple in a spray of blood. Vettius spun with a bellow and slapped his centurion down with a bear-quick motion. "You idiot, who told you to kill him? Was he going to hurt *me*?"

Dulcitius clanged as he bounced against the wall, his face as white as his tunic except where Vettius's broad handprint glowed on his cheek.

His sword was still imbedded in the skull of the dead man on the floor, but a murderous rage roiled in his eyes. Unseen to the side, Dama freed the small knife concealed in his tunic.

"There was no call to do that," Dulcitius said slowly.

"There wasn't bloody call to kill the man before we even started to question him!" Vettius snarled back. "If you're too stupid to see that, you've got no business with officer rank—and I can see to that mistake very promptly, damn you. Otherwise, get downstairs with Ulcius. Find out from the innkeeper who this Daoud saw, what he did—every damn thing about him since he came to Antioch."

Vettius was by birth a Celtiberian, one of the black-haired, black-hearted race who had slammed a bloody door on the Teutoni and sent them stumbling back into the spears of Rome and Marius. Four and a half centuries had bled neither the courage of his forefathers nor their savagery from the tall legate; Dulcitius stared at him, then turned and left the room with neither a curse nor a backward glance.

"Start looking through his gear," Vettius said mildly to the remaining soldiers. "He's not going to tell us much himself."

The casket in his own hands sucked as he opened it to reveal a scroll and a glass bottle, round and nested in a leather hollow that held it firm. Vettius weighed the sphere in his hand. The silvery mercury that filled it had just enough air trapped with it beneath the seal to tremble.

Dama was already glancing at the scroll. "It's in Aramaic," he said frowning, "most of it. 'The record of the researches of Nemesius—' "

"His real name was Nemesius?" the legate interrupted.

" '—of Nemesius of Antioch,' " continued Dama unperturbed, " 'in the third year of the reign of the Emperor Valerianus.' "

The line troops had paused from opening chests filled only with spices. Vettius himself had the look of a man uncertain as to who is playing the trick on him. "Valerian," he repeated. "But he was killed. . . ."

"Almost a century ago," the Cappadocian finished for him in agreement. "What was a Persian wizard doing with a parchment written a century ago by a Greek philosopher?"

Vettius's tongue prodded his left cheek. He could command troops or seduce women in eight languages, was truly fluent in five of them; but only in Latin and Greek could he claim literacy. "I'll be pretty busy the next few days," he lied unnecessarily. "Why don't you read it yourself and tell me what you think of it?"

"Sestia'll probably be glad that I've found something to do for a few days besides pester her," Dama said with a fond smile. "Sure, it can't hurt for me to take a look at it."

The moon and three triple-wicked oil lamps lighted the pillared courtyard. Servants had cleared away the last of the platters, leaving the two friends to Chian wine and the warm Syrian night.

"I'm sorry Sestia got a headache at the last minute," Dama said. "I'd like the two of you to get better acquainted."

"She got the headache when she heard I was coming for dinner," remarked Vettius, more interested in straightening his tunic than in what he was saying.

"You don't usually have that problem with women," gibed the merchant.

"She knows the kind of guy I am, that's all."

"Nobody who really knows you, Lucius, would think you'd seduce a friend's wife."

"Yeah, that's what I mean."

Dama drew an aimless design in wine lees on the marble table top. The legate glanced up, flushed, and gulped down the contents of his own cup. "Mithra," he apologized, "I've drunk too much already." Then, "Look, have you gotten anything out of the scroll? Neither the innkeeper nor anything we found in the room gives us a notion of what this Daoud was up to."

The Cappadocian set the leather case on the table and drew the parchment out of it. "Umm, yes, I've got a notion . . . but it's no more than that and you may want to call me a fool when I tell you."

"You aren't a fool," said Vettius quietly. "Tell me about the scroll."

"Nemesius of Antioch was searching for the secret of life and a way of turning base metals into gold. He wrote an account of his attempts here—" Dama spread the scroll slightly to emphasize it—"after he succeeded in both. Or so he says."

"Even that long ago I'd have heard of him if that was true," the soldier snorted.

"Except," Dama pointed out, "that was the year the Persians sacked Antioch. And Nemesius's villa was outside the walls." He spun the parchment to a passage he had noted. " '. . . leaving in place of the lead a column of living gold, equal to me in height and in diameter some three cubits.' Now, what I suspect is that your Daoud was no spy. He was a wizard himself, not of the ability of Nemesius but able to understand the processes he describes and to believe they might work. He was a scholar, too, enough of one to read this scroll in a casket looted on whim a century ago; and a gambler besides to risk his life on its basis in a hostile empire."

"But for what?" Vettius demanded. "You said the place was sacked."

"Nemesius had an underground laboratory. He describes the secret entrance to it in this parchment," Dama replied. "It just could be that the Persian who found the chest—and probably Nemesius—above ground missed the passageway below. If so, the gold might still be there."

Vettius's intake of breath was that of a boy seeing for the first time a beautiful woman nude. "That much *gold*," he whispered. He sat up on his couch and leaned forward toward his friend, mind working like a tally board. "Hundreds of talents, maybe thousands. . . . If we could find that, we'd each be as rich as the emperor's freedmen. What would you do with wealth like that, Dama?"

"I'd leave it to rot in the ground," the merchant said without inflection. Vettius blinked at the violence of the words and the Cappadocian's hard blue eyes. "I read you what Nemesius created," Dama went on. "I didn't read you how he went about it. Neither for eternal life nor for all the gold on earth would I have done half the things he claims to have done. There's an evil to that gold. It's dangerous, the danger reeks all through this parchment, though Nemesius never puts a name to why. Maybe he was afraid to. Let the gold lie for somebody in more need of trouble than you or I are."

Vettius took the bulb of mercury from the casket to occupy his hands while he pondered. The bubble danced through the transparence, a mobile facet in the light of the oil lamps. The cap was of thin, carven gold, but the short neck of the bottle had been sealed with wax before the gold was applied.

"Why two seals, do you suppose?" Vettius asked, rather than voice what was really on his mind.

"Quicksilver combines with gold, rots it into a paste," Dama explained. "The wax is the real closure, the metal over it just for show." He paused, continued when he saw the soldier was still not ready to speak. "Nemesius used quicksilver in his searching, both for life and for gold. He says he always carried this bottle with him, why I don't know. The manuscript doesn't explain."

"You've spent your life gathering gold, trading for gold, haven't you?" the big Spaniard rumbled, slipping the mercury back into the case and then looking at his wine cup.

"Yeah, I have," Dama agreed, his posture a conscious disavowal of the tension lacing the night. "Spices from Taprobane, silks from India. Once I went all the way to the Serian lands for silk, but the extra profit wasn't worth the danger."

"All your life looking for gold and you tell *me* not to dig an emperor's ransom out of the ground when it's right here waiting. I don't understand it, Dama." Vettius raised his voice and his eyes together. "You're playing a game of some sort and I don't know what it is!"

"No game at all," said Dama, still quietly. He faced his friend as he had once faced a gut-shot bear. The merchant had seen other men suddenly besotted with an idea—a cavalryman hammered into fanaticism by the majesty of his Arian God, a shipmaster so certain that a fourth continent lay west of Ireland that he convinced a full crew to disappear with him in search of it. A jest, even a misspoken word, would send such men into murderous frenzies. "Sure, I love gold, but I know it. I'm not joking at all, Lucius, when I say there's a wrong feel to this hoard. I'll help you any way I can to see that you find it, but I'll have no portion of what Nemesius left."

Slowly Vettius reached for the wine bowl and bent a rueful smile onto his face. "That's fair," he said as he poured for both of them. "A good bit too fair, but we'll worry over that when the gold's in our hands, hey?" He paused; then, too eagerly for his pretense of calm, he blurted, "You think there's a real chance of locating Nemesius's cellars after this time?"

Dama nodded. "Let me think about it. There's a way to do most things if you think about them a while."

The soldier sipped, then gulped his unmixed wine to the lees and stood up. The light bronzed his skin and made each bristle of his nascent beard a spearpoint. "I'll be off, then," he said. "I—I really appreciate all you've done, will do, Dama. It isn't for me, not really; but if I had wealth enough to make those idiots in Constantinople listen to what I say about the army. . . ."

Dama clapped him on the arm. "As you said, we'll talk about that when the gold's in your hands."

After his friend had left behind his lamp-carrier, drunken but erect and with a vicious smile on his face that no footpad would dare to trouble, Dama returned to the courtyard. Sestia's room would be locked. From past experience Dama knew to stay out of her wing of the house and not make a fool of himself before her servants, trying to wheedle his wife out of her pique through bolted wood. Instead, he fingered the bulb of mercury, then reopened the scroll beside it. When dawn began to sear the marble facings of the court he was still at the table dictating notes to the sleepy clerk he had dragged from bed three hours before.

"You're sure that's the place?" said Vettius, a neutral figure in the dusk unless one noted the tip of the scabbard lifting the hem of his long travelling cloak. The mud-brick warren around them scampered with the sounds of furtive life, some of it human, but no one approached the friends.

"I'm not *sure* the sun will rise in the morning," retorted Dama, "but there's plenty of evidence, yes, that Nemesius's villa was here. He disappeared in the first sack, probably burned with his buildings. His heirs sold the tract to a developer to run up a cheap apartment block—land outside the walls wasn't considered a safe place for fancy houses right then. Which shows good sense, because when the Persians came back three years later they burned the apartments too."

There had been signs of that during daylight, ancient scorch marks on the rubble still heaped among the rank weeds. "Strange that no one rebuilt since," said Vettius, squinting to sharpen his twilit image of the barren acre before him.

"The site had gotten a reputation." Dama shrugged his own worn cloak loose, shifting his grip on the leathern chest he carried. "That's really what made it possible to find it." He gestured. "There's a lot of people in the city—the dregs who live here, even the ones a few levels removed who associate with them—who know what you mean when you ask about Nemesius's estate that was somewhere off the Sidon road. 'Oh, yeah,' they say, 'Nemesis Place.' Their faces tighten up and they add, 'What do you want with that, anyway? Nobody goes around there.' "

The little merchant flicked his gaze once more around the darkness. "Not quite true, of course. People cut down saplings for firewood here. Probably some of them sleep in the ruins now and again. They don't stay long, though. Nothing in particular, just uneasiness. 'Nemesis Place.' "

"Balls," said Vettius, beginning to stride into the clearing. "I don't feel uneasy."

"You didn't look very comfortable when we slipped out the gate this afternoon," commented Dama as he trotted alongside, casket thumping his thigh. "Second thoughts, or you just don't like to sneak by your own men and not be able to scream that their bronze hasn't been polished?"

Vettius slowed and glanced at his friend. Surprise audible in his voice, he said, "You know me too well. I don't like them thinking they can ignore me just because I've told them we'll be gone three days, hunting in the hills. Dulcitius was supposed to command the gate guard today, but because they think I'm gone already he seems to have traded time with Furianus without having cleared it with me."

Dama stumbled, more in anger than from the fragment of stone in the brush. "Dulcitius," he repeated. "I've seen him hanging around my gate. Tell him for me that I'll kill him if I ever catch him there again."

"Don't fool with that one," said Vettius very softly.

"I'm not afraid," Dama snapped.

"Dama, you know about a lot of things I don't," the soldier said. "But take my word about killers. Don't ever think of going up against Dulcitius alone."

"This is far enough," said Dama, changing the subject as a pile of masonry loomed up in front of them. Beside it he knelt to light a thick tallow candle with the slow match he had brought in a terra-cotta jar. "They followed the villa's groundplan when they built the apartments," he explained. "Used the old foundations. I checked yesterday and the cap slab over the hidden stairway is still in place."

"Did you open it?"

Dama ignored the suspicion leaking out in his friend's tones. "I couldn't, not without either you or a team of mules. Finally decided I'd use you."

The air was so still that the candle flame pulsed straight up at the moonless sky. By its light Vettius saw set in what had been a courtyard pavement the mosaic slab beneath which Nemesius had described his stairway as lying. The pattern laid over a counter-weighted bronze plate was of two intertwined dragons, one black and the other white. It was impossible to tell whether the beasts were battling, mating, or—just possibly—fissioning. Their tails were concealed beneath a concrete panel which had skewed across the mosaic when the building collapsed.

"I brought a sledge," said Dama, extracting the tool from the double sling beneath his right arm, "but I'll let you do the work."

"Umm," mumbled Vettius, considering the obstructing concrete. It had been part of a load-bearing wall, a hand's-breadth thick and fractured into a width of about three feet. The far end disappeared under a pile of other rubble. Vettius tossed aside his cloak and squatted over the slab, his hands turned backward to grip its irregular edge.

Dama frowned. "Dis, you'll need the hammer."

"Very likely," Vettius agreed, "but that's a lot of racket that I'd like to avoid if we can." He stiffened, his face flushing as tendons sprang out on his neck. The slab quivered. His linen tunic ripped down to his waist. Then his thighs straightened and the slab pivoted on its buried end, sliding back a foot before the off-balance soldier sat down on it.

"After—what? Twenty-six years?—you still have the ability to surprise me, Lucius," said Dama. He knelt and twisted at one of the circular tiles in the border until metal clicked. The mosaic rocked upward at an additional finger's pressure on one end.

Vettius stood, shrugged, and straightened his scabbard. "Let's go," he said, reaching for the candle.

"A moment." Dama folded his cloak, lumpy with hints of further preparations against unknown needs. From his sash he stripped everything but an additional candle and his own sword, a foot shorter than Vettius's spatha but heavy and chisel-sharp on both edges. Drawing it before he lifted the casket in his left hand he said, "All right, I'm ready."

"Are you that worried?" Vettius asked with a grin. "And if you are, why're you lugging that box along?"

"Because I *am* that worried. Nemesius says he carried it, and he knew a lot more about what he was getting into than you or I do."

The flight of brick steps was steep and narrow, dropping twenty feet to a pavement of living rock. The candle burned brightly although the air had a metallic odor, a hint that was more an aftertaste. The gallery into which the stairwell opened was a series of pilastered vaults whose peaks reached close to the surface. The candle suggested the magnitude it could not illuminate.

"Mithra," Vettius said, raising the light to the full height of his arm, "how can you have a secret vault when it's so big half of Antioch must have been down here swinging picks to excavate it?"

"Yes, I've wondered how he got it excavated too," Dama said. He did not amplify the question.

The walls were veneered with colored marble. A narrow shelf at shoulder height divided the panels, smooth below but relieved with all manner of symbols and fanciful beasts from ledge to ceiling. The technical craftsmanship was good, but execution of the designs showed a harshness akin to that of battle standards.

"He doesn't seem to have needed all this room," the soldier remarked as they entered the third vault. It held a dozen long racks of equipment and stoppered bottles, but even that was but partial use of its volume.

They circled the racks. The last of the four vaults was not empty either. "Oh dear Jesus," whispered Dama while his bigger companion muttered, "Mithra, Mithra, Mithra," under his breath. A low stone dais stood in the center of the chamber. Nemesius must have been a tall man. The column of gold he referred to as being as tall as he was would have overtopped even Vettius standing beside it. He must have measured by the long cubit as well, for the diameter of the mass was certainly over five feet. Its surface was irregular, that of waves frozen as they chopped above a rip tide, and bloody streaks shot through the bulk of yellower metal.

"Oh, yes . . ." Vettius said, drawing his spatha and stepping toward the gold.

"Careful, Lucius," Dama warned. "I don't think we'd better hack off a piece yet. Nemesius gives a formula for 'unbinding' the column. I think I ought to read that first."

Vettius made a moue of irritation but said only, "We haven't found any tricks, but yeah, that doesn't mean that he didn't play some." He held the candle close as Dama opened the casket and unrolled the parchment to the place he needed.

The merchant had sheathed his own sword. Kneeling and drawing a deep breath, he read aloud in Aramaic, "In the names by which you were bound, Saloë, Pharippa, Phalertos, I unbind you."

Voice gathering strength from the husky whisper with which he had begun, Dama read the next line in Persian, using the old pronunciation: "By the metals in which you were locked in death, lead, sulphur, quicksilver, I free you to life."

There were five more sentences in the spell, each of them in a different tongue; Vettius understood none of them. One reminded him of phrases mumbled by a horseman who rode with a squadron of Sakai irregulars but who came from much farther east. At the climax, Dama's voice was an inhuman thunder explicable only as a trick of the room's acoustics. "Acca!" he shouted, "Acca! Acca!"

The words struck the gold like hammer-blows

and it slumped away from them. The column sagged, mushroomed, and began to flow across the dais before resolidifying. A single bright streak zigged from the main mass like a stream across mudflats. "What in the name of Dis did you do?" Vettius cried. The candle in his hand trembled as he held it up.

The metal seemed rigid. It had fallen into an irregular dome over most of the dais and some of the rock beneath it. "As if we'd heated it," Dama said. "But. . . ." He reached up, ignited his other taper from the flame of the first, and set it on the floor beside the leather case. Then he stepped toward the dais while Vettius waited, torn by anger and indecision.

Two rivulets streamed outward to meet the Cappadocian's approach. He paused. Vettius shifted the spatha in his hand and said, "Dama, I—"

Dama sprang back as the golden streamlets froze, then scissored through the air. Hair-fine and rigid as sword edges, they slit the flapping hem of his tunic but missed the flesh. The dome itself lurched toward the men, moving from the dais with the deceptive speed of a millipede crawling across a board set in its path.

Dama scooped at the handle of the leather box. He caught it, missed his footing, and skidded it a dozen feet across the stone. Vettius had turned and run back toward the chamber's entrance. His candle went out at his first loping stride but the one still lighted on the floor caught a glittering movement ahead of him. "Lucius!" Dama shouted, but the big soldier had seen the same tremor and his sword was slashing up and outward to block the golden thread extruded when the column first collapsed. Steel met gold and the softer metal sang as it parted. The severed tip spun to the floor and pooled while the remainder of the thin tentacle wavered, still blocking the only exit. Ruddy streaks rippled through the main bulk as it closed on its victims.

Vettius cut again at the gold before him but it had thickened after its initial injury, forming a bar that only notched on impact. With a python's speed it looped on the blade and snatched it from the Spaniard's grip. Dama had taken two steps and jumped, using his left hand to help boost his whole lithe body up onto the shoulder-high ledge. Vettius saw the leap, spun like a tiger to follow. Nemesius's casket was open on the floor. Dama stared, understood, and cried, "The quicksilver! Break it on—"

Vettius bent and snatched up the glittering bulb of liquid. He raised it high as the fluid mass threw out a sheet which lapped across his ankles. Able but unwilling to act he moaned, "Oh dear Gods, the gold!" and the sheet bulged into a quilt as the whole weight of metal began to flow over him.

Dama leaned forward, judging distance with the cool precision with which he would have weighed a bolt of silk in his warehouse. The swift arc of his sword overbalanced him as he knew it would. He was falling onto the swelling monster below at the instant his point shattered the glass ball in his friend's hand. Droplets of mercury spewed across the mass of gold and fused with it.

The chamber exploded in a flash of red. Momentarily the walls blazed with the staring, shadowless eyes of the beasts limned on the frieze. Slowly, dazzled but not blinded, the two men pulled themselves free of gritty muck while their retinas readapted to the light of the single candle.

Where they had been exposed to the flash, their skins had the crinkly, prickly feel of sunburn.

"You took a chance there," Vettius said matter-of-factly. Most of the gold seemed to have disintegrated into a powder of grayish metal, lead to judge by its weight. Where the mercury had actually splashed were clinging pools with an evil, silvery luster. "When I locked up like I did, you could have gotten out along the ledge."

"I've got enough on my conscience without leaving a friend to that," Dama said.

"I knew what had to be done, but I just couldn't . . . destroy it," the soldier explained. He was on his knees, furrowing the edge of the lead dust deeply with his hands. "That gold . . . and I'm damned if I can understand why, now, but that gold was worth more to me than my life was. Guess that's what you need friends for, to do for you what you won't do for yourself."

Dama had retrieved the candle and held it high. "Some other time we'll talk that over with a philosopher. Now let's get out of here before we find some other goody our friend Nemesius left."

"Give me a moment. I want to find my sword."

The merchant snorted. "If you cared as much about some woman— *one* woman—as you do about that sword, Lucius, you'd be a happier man. You know, right now I feel like I had been gone the three days I told Sestia I would."

"Found it," said Vettius, carefully wiping hilt and blade on his tunic before sheathing the weapon. "Let's go back and greet your wife."

Later that night Dama understood a number of things. As stunned as a hanged man, he gurgled "Sestia!" through the shattered door to his wife's chamber. The centurion's sword and dagger were on a table near the bed, and Dulcitius was very quick; but Vettius had drawn before he kicked in the panel. Nothing would stop the overarm cut of his spatha, certainly not the bedding nor the two squirming bodies upon it.

Dragons' Teeth

The sound of squealing axles drifted closer on the freezing wind. The watching Roman raised his eyes an inch above the rim of his brush-screened trench. A dozen Sarmatian wagons were hulking toward him into the twilight. Their wheels of uncured oak, gapped and irregular at the fellies, rumbled complainingly as they smashed stiff grass and bushes into the unyielding soil.

A smile of grim satisfaction brushed Vettius's lips as the Sarmatians approached. He did not touch the bow that lay beside him; it was still too soon.

The enormous weight of the wagons turned every finger's breadth of rise into a steep escarpment up which the oxen had to plod. They grunted out great plumes of breath as they threw their weight into the traces. Sexless, almost lifeless in their poses of stolid acceptance, the drivers hunched on the high wagon seats. Like the oxen, they had been at their killing work since dawn. The wind slashed and eddied about the canopies of aurochs hide which covered the boxes. Tendrils of smoke from heating fires within squirmed through the peaks. They hung for a moment in the sunset before scudding off invisibly.

The last of the wagons was almost within the defile, Vettius noted. It would be very soon now.

Among the Sarmatians the whole family travelled together, even to war. The children and nursing mothers huddled inside the wagons. So did the warriors; their work, like that of the horses tethered behind each wain, was yet to come. Soon the wagons would halt and laager up in the darkness. Using night as a shroud, the reivers would mount and thunder across the frozen Danube. Laughingly they would return before dawn with booty and fresh Roman ears.

The only picket Vettius could see from where he lay was a single rider slightly ahead and to the left of the wagons. Earlier in the day he might have been guide or outrider. Hours had passed. Wagons had bunched or straggled according to the strength of their teams and the temper of their drivers. Now, while the sun bled like an open wound in the western sky, the rider was almost a part of the jumbled line and no protection for it. Vettius smiled again, and his hand was on the bow.

The wind that moaned around the wagons scuffed up crystals from the snow crusts lying in undulant rills among the brush. The shaggy pony's rump and belly sparkled. The beast's torso, like its rider's, was hidden under armor of broad horn scales, each one painstakingly sewn onto a leather backing by the women of the family. Across his pommel rested a slender lance more than eighteen feet long. The Sarmatian fondled its grip as he nodded over his mount's neck, neglecting to watch the bushes that clawed spiked shadows from the sun.

A sound that trickled through the wind made him straighten; unexpected movement caught his eye. Then the Roman archer rose up from behind a bush far too small to conceal a man the way it had. The Sarmatian, spurring his horse in incredulous panic, heard the slap of the bowstring, heard the loud pop as one scale of his cuirass shattered. After the bodkin-pointed arrow ripped through his chest he heard nothing at all.

"Let's get 'em!" Vettius shouted, nocking another arrow as his first target pitched out of the saddle. The trumpeter crouching behind him set the silver-mounted warhorn to his lips and blasted out the attack. Already the shallow hillsides were spilling soldiers down on the unprepared Sarmatians.

The driver of the lead wagon stood up, screaming a warning. The nearest Roman thrust her through the body with his spear. With two slashes of his short-sword, the legionary cut open the canopy behind her and plunged inside with a howl of triumph.

Sarmatians leaped out of the second wagon, trying to reach their horses. Three legionaries met them instead. Vettius had set fifty men in ambush, all picked veterans in full armor. None of the others had bows—the legate had feared a crossfire in the dusk—but sword and spear did the butcher's work on the startled nomads. The Sarmatians were dressed for war in armor of boiled leather or aurochs horn, but they had no shields and their light swords were no match for the heavy Roman cut and thrust blades. One at a time the nomads jumped down to be stretched on the ground by a stab, a quick chop, or even the heavy smash of a shield rim. Death trebled, the legionaries stood waiting for each victim. The fading sunlight gleamed from their polished helmets and greaves and touched with fire the wheels of bronze and vermilioned leather that marked the shields.

The legate's practiced eye scanned the fighting. The wrack showed the Sarmatians had battled with futile desperation. A baby lay beside the fourth wagon. Its skull had been dashed in on the wagon box, but its nails were stained with Roman blood. The oxen bellowed, hamstrung in the yoke. One was spurting black jets through a heart-deep channel. This day was Rome's vengeance; retribution for a thousand sudden raids, a thousand comrades crumpled from a chance arrow or a dagger thrust in the night.

Only toward the rear where three wagons had bunched together was there real fighting. Vettius ran down the line of wagons though his quiver was almost emptied when he saw one of his men hurtle through the air in a lifeless somersault. The legionary crashed to the ground like a load of scrap metal. His whole chest and body armor had been caved in by an enormous blow. Measurably later the man's sword completed its own parabola and clanked thirty feet away.

"Get back!" Vettius shouted when he saw the windrow of ruined bodies strewn in front of him. "Stand clear!" Before he could say more, the killer was lumbering toward him around the back of the wagon.

The horsehair crest wobbling in the waning sunlight increased the figure's titanic height, but even bareheaded the giant would have been half again as tall as the six-foot soldier. Worse, he was much heavier built than a man, a squat dwarf taller than the wagon. He carried no shield but his whole body shone with a covering of smooth bronze plates. Both gauntleted hands gripped the haft of an iron-headed mace. The six-foot helve was as thick as a man's calf and the head could have served as an anvil.

The giant strode toward Vettius with terrifying agility.

Vettius arched his bow. The shaft of his arrow splintered on the monster's breastplate. It left only a bright scar on the metal. Vettius stepped back, nocking another missile and shifting his aim to the oddly sloped helmet. The face was completely covered except for a T-shaped slot over the eyes and nose. The light was very dim but the narrow gap stood out dead black against the helmet's luster. As the giant started to swing his mace parallel to the ground, Vettius shot again.

The arrow glanced off the bronze and howled away into the darkness.

Vettius leaped upward and fell across the wagon seat as the giant's mace hurtled toward him. The spiked head smashed into a wheel with awesome force, scattering fragments of wood and making the whole wagon shudder. As it rocked, the driver's hacked corpse tumbled to the ground, leaving the Roman alone on the seat as he sighted along his last arrow.

The giant had reversed his grip on the mace. Now he swung his weapon upward with no more apparent effort than a man with a flywhisk. As the head came level with the giant's hips, the mace slipped from his fingers to fly forward and burst through the side of the wagon. The titan reeled backwards. A small tuft of feathers was barely visible where the helmet slot crossed the bridge of his nose.

The earth trembled when he fell.

Shaking with reaction himself, Vettius dropped his now-useless bow and craned his neck to peer over the wagon's canopy at the remaining fighting. Some of the wains were already burning. Confusion or the victors had spilled the heating flames from their earthenware pots and scattered coals into the cloth and straw of the bedding.

"Save me a prisoner!" Vettius bellowed against the wind. "For Mithra's sake, save me a prisoner!"

He jumped to the ground and cautiously approached the fallen giant. The helmet came off easily when he grasped it by the crest and yanked. Beneath the bronze the face was almost human. The jaw was square and massive; death's rictus had drawn thin lips back from leonine tushes, yellowed and stark. The nose squatted centrally like a smashed toad, and from it the face rose past high flat eyesockets to enormous ridges of bone. There was virtually no forehead so that the brows sloped shallowly to a point on the back of the skull. Only their short tight coils distinguished the eyebrows from the black strands that covered the rest of the head.

No wonder the helmet looked odd, Vettius thought bleakly. He would believe in the face, in a man so large, because they were there for him to touch; but he would have called another man a liar for claiming the existence of something so impossible. Perhaps believing in the impossible was the secret of the success of the Christians whose god, dead three hundred years, was now beginning to rule the empire.

The trumpeter approached from behind with his horn slung and a bloody sword in his right hand. The torque he now wore was of gold so pure and soft that he had spread it by hand to get if off a dead nomad and rebent it around his own neck.

"Sir!" he called, "are you all right?"

"Give me a hand here," Vettius grunted unresponsively as he tugged at the mace. Together the men pulled the weapon from the fabric of the wagon. Vettius gave a curt order and hefted it alone as his subordinate stepped back. "Ha!" he snorted in disbelief. The mace weighed at least two talents, the weight of a small man or a fair-sized woman.

He let it thud to the ground and walked away from it. "May the Bull bugger me if I don't learn more about this," he swore.

The doorkeeper had difficulty slamming the door against the gust of wind that followed Vettius into the anteroom. Moist air from the baths within condensed to bead the decorated tiles and rime the soldier's cape of black bearskin. He wore the bear's head as a cowl. The beast's glass eyes usually glared out above Vettius' own; now they too were frosted and the doorkeeper, turning, shuddered at the look of blank agony they gave him.

Vettius shrugged off the cape and stamped his muddy boots on the floor. The doorkeeper sighed inwardly and picked up his twig broom. The damned man had been stomping through the muck like a common soldier instead of riding decently in a litter as befit his rank. The slave said nothing aloud as he swept, though; the legate had a reputation for violence and he already wore a dark glower this afternoon.

Walking through the door of the changing room, Vettius tossed his cape to one of the obsequious attendants and began to unlace his boots. While he sat on a bench and stripped off his thick woolen leggings, the other attendant looked delicately at the miry leather and asked with faint disdain, "Will you have these cleaned while you bathe, sir?"

"Dis, why should I?" the soldier snarled. "I've got to wear them out of here, don't I?"

The attendant started at his tone. Vettius chuckled at the man's fear and threw the filthy leggings in his face. Laying both his tunics on the bench, he surveyed the now apprehensive slaves and asked, "Either of you know where Dama is?"

"The Legate Vettius?" called a voice from the inner hallway. A third attendant stuck his head into the changing room. "Sir? If you will follow me. . . ."

The attendant's sandals slapped nervously down the hallway past steam rooms on the right and the wall of the great pool on the left. Tiles of glaucous gray covered floors and most of the walls, set off by horizontal bands of mosaic. A craftsman of Naisso who had never been to the coast had inset octopuses and dolphins cavorting on a bright green sea. The civilization I protect, Vettius thought disgustedly. The reason I bow to fat fools.

At the corner of the hall the attendant stopped and opened one of the right-hand doors. Steam puffed out. Vettius peered in with his hand on the jamb to keep from slipping on the slick tile. He could make out two figures through the hot fog, a small man lying on a bench with a masseur beside him. The slap of hands on flesh had paused when the door opened.

"Dama?" the solder called uncertainly.

The man on the bench raised up on his elbow. "Come on in, Lucius," he invited with genuine pleasure. "Urso, we'll have no further need of you today."

Coins jingled. The masseur bowed low to the merchant, nodded respectfully to Vettius, and thudded the door shut behind him.

"Have a bench," Dama offered. "How did it go?"

Vettius grunted. "Anyone with big ears likely to bust in here?"

"I doubt it," the merchant replied. "I think Dazos misunderstood when I told him we'd not want to be disturbed, but he knows I pay well for privacy."

The soldier stepped gingerly through the gloom. Even so his foot brushed one of the perforated tiles through which boilers in the basement forced steam into the room. He swore fiercely. The only light seeped through the skylight, a tracery of mica plaquets now virtually opaqued by the layers of ice and soot above. Even the minatory red glaze of the ducts blurred to gray in the dark.

Vettius stretched his solid form on the bench. "Why don't they light this place?" he growled.

"There's a lamp on the wall, but I think it's out of oil," his friend said. "Just lie down and relax; your eyes will adjust. Did you talk to the Count?"

The soldier swore again. He flexed his thigh and shoulder muscles, letting the anger work out through opening pores. At last he loosened and sighed, "Yeah, I talked to Celsus. Did you ever have anything to do with him, Dama?"

"Not directly. It's worth his while to let me sell silk in his region."

"The gods waste me if he's not an idiot!" Vettius snapped angrily. He sat up, swinging his legs over the side of his bench. "Look, I'm just a soldier—but I damned well know how to soldier. I keep my sector of border safe and a thousand of the toughest whoresons in the Eastern Army happy. Anybody can see I know my business!"

He paused, breathing hard. Dama too sat up, trying to scan the big man's face in the darkness. "You told him what you told me this morning?" he asked. "I mean, you told him about the giant?"

"I told him, sure," Vettius answered. He rubbed his forehead with his knuckles while he remembered. "More. We got this prisoner to talk after I left you. It's as bad as I thought it might be, maybe worse. That wasn't the only giant, and he wasn't a freak Sarmatian. Mithra, you could see from the face that he wasn't any sort of Sarmatian."

"If he wasn't a Sarmatian," Dama considered, "where could he have come from?"

"Oh, he came from Torgu," explained Vettius. "It's one of those tent villages, maybe a hundred miles across the river. In summer there's only a handful of permanent buildings and most of them wattle and daub. In the winter a thousand or so Sarmatians gather with their wagons and all their livestock, trading and drinking and going off to raid in little groups. Only there's a shaman there now who seems to have taken the place over—"

"I didn't think the Sarmatians ever let a shaman become chief," the merchant interrupted.

"I didn't either," Vettius agreed, "but that's not

the last odd thing we heard about Hydaspes." The soldier chuckled evilly and added, "And I don't think the prisoner was lying by the time we were through with him.

"Hydaspes—that's the shaman—is something beyond the usual hedge wizard. His magic looks so real that the prisoner was more afraid of what the chief a hundred miles away could do to him than what we could, until he scarcely had mind left to answer questions."

Vettius fell silent. Torture was a part of his job. Sometimes following a Sarmatian raid it became more personal than that, but the successful ambush had left him feeling almost kindly toward the defeated. There had been no savor in what he and his interrogators were doing to the broken, drooling prisoner. Normally Vettius would have forgotten the incident as soon as possible.

Normally: had he not spoken to Celsus. Stupid, short-sighted Celsus with his dark suspicions of a subordinate who showed initiative. Vettius had wanted to smash his simpering commander off the delicately carven ivory stool he affected, wanted at least to clench his great fists and watch the Count pale. Self interest had held him rigid instead. In his mind though, he once again inserted the glowing rod while the Sarmatian screamed in helpless agony on the rack.

Dama said nothing. He knew why his friend's hands clamped tight on the bench. A handball game was in progress on the other side of the steam room's back wall. Words came through the masonry as little more than high-pitched squeals, but the unfaltering slap-slap-slap of the ball wove a fabric for contemplation. Either one man was practicing alone or two perfectly matched experts were having a bout as precise as a dance of oreads.

Vettius rumbled, clearing his throat in embarrassment. "I must have drifted off," he apologized, lying back down on the bench. He felt ashamed of the red savagery that had bubbled through his brain, ashamed because it was misdirected. Perhaps he would do something for the human wreckage in the detention cell, buy the fellow and send him to the steward of his British estates with a chit for a soft job. A comfortable enough life. Fear of a wizard across the Danube couldn't reach that far.

"Where did Hydaspes get a giant?" Dama prompted to divert the soldier's revery.

"Giants," Vettius corrected. "The prisoner says there were ten more at Torgu when his family was sent out with this one. Thing is, he couldn't say where they came from. He thought it was a part of the shaman's magic, that Hydaspes was building the men out of clay and breathing life into them. That's crap, by the way, we didn't have time or transport to bring the body back, but I don't need a philosopher's word to know that he was a normal man, no statue."

"Then why did the Sarmatian think otherwise?" Dama queried.

"Well, the giants just seemed to appear," his friend replied. The question had been bothering him. "They weren't at Torgu when the family we ambushed got there in the late fall. Hydaspes was there, though, nervous as the emperor's taster and fussing around the village to look over each new arrival. He wasn't claiming much authority, either.

"About two months ago a horseman rode in

from eastward alone. Our prisoner didn't talk with the fellow but he saw him give a package to Hydaspes. Nothing big—the size of a fist, he says. That was what Hydaspes had been waiting for. He laughed and capered all the way to his tent and didn't come out again for a week. When he did, he started giving orders like a king. With a nine-foot giant behind him, everyone obeyed. In back of Hydaspes's tent there was a long trench in the frozen ground and a lot of dirt was missing."

The merchant began rapping one fingertip on his bench as he pondered, beating out an unconscious counterpoint to the handball game outside the room. "So . . ." he articulated slowly. "It looks as though Hydaspes was able to dig up a giant, literally. If only one, then maybe he just knew where to dig . . . but you say there were more of them?"

"Ten more, one at a time," Vettius agreed with a nod of his head. "And there was another hole in the ground the morning each one appeared. Nobody the prisoner knew hung about at night to see what was happening behind the shaman's tent, though. They were all scared to death by then."

"So scared that they found enough bronze to build a colossus and used it to armor Hydaspes's creations," Dama mused.

The soldier grunted assent. "Some they gave to him. A lot of it he bought from other tribes or from traders at Tyras, paying for it with raw gold."

"Gold and a giant bodyguard," Dama continued softly, "and a one-time hedge wizard had united a tribe under him. If he can do that, he might as easily become king of the whole nation. A real leader, not a figurehead like most Sarmatian kings.

What would happen, Lucius, if the Sarmatians stopped squabbling among themselves and crossed the river together, obeying one man?"

The white fear that had been shimmering around the edges of Vettius's mind broke through and again all his muscles tensed. Consciously forcing himself to relax, the soldier said, "A century ago the Persians unified Mesopotamia against us. Constant fighting. Some victories, more losses. But we could accept that on one frontier—it's a big empire. On two sides at the same time. . . . I can't really say what would happen."

"We'd better deal with Hydaspes soon," Dama summarized flatly, or Hydaspes will deal with us."

"That's what I tried to tell Celsus," Vettius muttered. His fury had burned out and frustration had given way to bleak despair. "The prisoner told us each of the giants was sent with a single family to raid our border posts. Messengers had gone out to call the other tribes to a meeting and he thought that if the raids were successful the others would come. I begged Celsus for a quick expedition against Torgu before Hydaspes could settle with the other chiefs."

"And?" the merchant demanded.

"The Count was more interested in criticizing the ambush I'd set.

"Yeah, that's what I said," Vettius continued over Dama's grunt of surprise. His voice rose high, taking on a mocking simper. " 'Don't you know how hard it is to find and train men, legate? You took fifty men out into the heart of Sarmatia and despite incredible luck in getting back at all, you took heavy casualties.' Damn that man!"

The echoes of his voice shouted back at Vettius. The incongruity struck him. He began to chuckle and, while the merchant blinked, filled the rooms with peals of laughter.

"Oh, Dama," the soldier gasped, clasping his friend's hands, "the sky is falling down on our heads and I'm mad. A simpleton doesn't appreciate my tactical genius, so I'm mad. Oh!

"We killed at least eighty Sarmatians, and only six of my boys didn't make it back. It could have been better but Mithra! I didn't figure on a giant. At the very best they would have done more damage if they'd have gotten to this side of the river. But Celsus didn't like the ambush and he didn't think I should have gone along anyway. Undignified for a legate, he said."

At that Dama laughed, trying to imagine Vettius too dignified for a fight.

"That's the sort he is," the soldier agreed with a rueful smile. "He expects me to keep my cutthroats in line without dirtying my boots. A popular attitude this side of the river, it seems. But Mithra, I know my men. They're so stubborn they'd not follow Venus to bed—but they'd follow me to Hell because they know I'd be leading them when the war horns blew. Leading, damn it, not in the rear sitting on a white horse."

The handball game across the partition ended with a crash of flesh on wood. The door had suddenly opened behind the players and one of them, leaping back, had struck it. A voice shrilled through the wall, "You crowbait fool, you might have killed me! I don't care who you are, you've no right to come bursting in here like that. And I never heard of your fool soldier!"

Both men in the steam room looked up sharply. Knuckles rapped on their door.

"Sirs, quickly!" Dazos hissed from outside.

Dama threw the door open for the frightened attendant. "Sirs," the slave explained, "the Count has come for the legate Vettius. I misdirected him, thinking you might want to prepare, but he'll be here any moment."

"I'll put on a tunic and meet him in the changing room," the soldier decided. "I've no desire to be arrested in the nude."

The frightened changing room attendants had disappeared into the far reaches of the building, leaving the friends to pull on their linen tunics undisturbed. Celsus burst in on them without ceremony, followed by two of his runners. He's not here to charge me after all, Vettius thought, not without at least a squad of troops. Though Mithra knew, his wishes would have supported a treason indictment.

"Where have you been?" the official stormed. His round face was almost the color of his toga's broad maroon hem.

"Right here in the bath, your excellency," Vettius replied without deference.

"Word just came by heliograph," the count sputtered. "There were ten attacks last night, ten! Impregnable monsters leading them—Punicum, Novae, Frasuli, Anarti—posts wiped out!"

"I told you there were other attacks planned," the soldier replied calmly. "None of them were in my sector. I told you why that was too."

"But you lied when you said you killed a monster, didn't you?" accused Celsus stamping his foot. "At Novae they hit one with a catapult and the bolt only bounced off!"

"Then they didn't hit him squarely," Vettius retorted. "The armor isn't that heavy. And I told you, I shot mine through the viewslit in his helmet."

The Count motioned his runners away. Noticing Dama for the first time he screamed, "Get out! Get out!"

The merchant bowed and exited behind the runners. He stood near the door.

"Listen," Celsus whispered, plucking at the soldier's sleeve to bring his ear lower, "you've got to do something about the giants. It'll look bad if these raids continue."

"Fine," Vettius said in surprise. "Give me my regiment and the Fifth Macedonian, and some cavalry—say the Old Germans. I'll level Torgu and everyone in it."

"Oh no," his pudgy superior gasped. "Not so much. The emperor will hear about it and the gods know what he'll think. Oh no—fifty men, that was enough before."

"Are you—" Vettius began, then rephrased his thought. "This isn't an ambush for one family, your excellency. This is disposing of a powerful chief and maybe a thousand of his followers, a hundred miles into Sarmatia. I might as well go alone as with fifty men."

"Fifty men," Celsus repeated. Then, beaming as if he was making a promise, he added, "You'll manage, I'm sure."

The two riders were within a few miles of Torgu before they were noticed.

"I shouldn't have let you come," Vettius grumbled to his companion. "Either I should have gone myself or else marched my regiment in and told Celsus to bugger himself."

Dama smiled. "You don't have any curiosity, Lucius. You only see the job to be done. Myself, I want to know where a nine-foot giant comes from."

They eyed the sprawling herd of black cattle which were finding some unimaginable pasturage beneath the snow crust. Perhaps they were stripping bark from the brush that scarred the landscape with its black rigidity. A cow scented the unfamiliar horses approaching it. The animal blatted and scrambled to its feet, splashing dung behind it. When it had bustled twenty feet away, the cow regained enough composure to turn and stare at the riders, focusing the ripple of disturbance that moved sluggishly through other bovine minds. Face after drooling, vacant face rotated toward them; after long moments, even the distant herdsman looked up from where he huddled over his fire in the lee of a hill.

Dama's chest grew tight. There was still another moment's silence while the Sarmatian made up his mind that there really were Romans riding toward Torgu through his herd. When at last he grasped the fact, he leaped to his feet yipping his amazement. For an instant he crouched bowlegged, waiting for a hostile move. When the intruders ignored him, the Sarmatian scampered to his horse and lashed it into a startled gallop for home.

The merchant chewed at his cheeks, trying to work saliva into a mouth that had gone dry when he realized they would be noticed. He'd known they were going to meet Sarmatians: that was the whole purpose of what they were doing. But now it was too late to back out. "About time we got an escort," he said with false bravado. "I'm surprised the Sarmatians don't patrol more carefully."

"Why should they?" Vettius snorted. "They know they're safe over here so long as a brainless scut like Celsus is in charge of the border."

They jogged beyond the last of the cattle. Without the Sarmatian's presence the beasts were slowly drifting away from the trampled area where they had been herded. If they wandered far they would be loose at night when the wolves hunted.

"Cows," Vettius muttered. "It's getting hard to find men, my friend."

Half a mile away on the top of the next rolling hill an armored horseman reined up in a spatter of snow. He turned his head and gave a series of short yelps that carried over the plain like bugle calls. Moments later a full score of lancers topped the brow of the hill and pounded down toward the interlopers.

"I think we'll wait here," the soldier remarked.

"Sure, give them a sitting target," Dama agreed with a tense smile.

Seconds short of slaughter the leading Sarmatian raised his lance. The rest of the troop followed his signal. The whole group swept around Vettius and Dama to halt in neighing, skidding chaos. One horse lost its footing and spilled its rider on the snow with a clatter of weapons. Cursing, the disgruntled Sarmatian lurched toward the Romans with his short, crooked sword out. From behind Dama, the leader barked a denial and laid his lance in front of the man. The merchant breathed deeply but did not relax his grip on the queerly shaped crossbow resting on his saddle until the glowering Sarmatian had remounted.

The leader rode alongside Vettius and looked up at the soldier on his taller horse. "You come with us to Torgu," he ordered in passable Greek.

"That's right," Vettius agreed in Sarmatian. "We're going to Torgu to see Hydaspes."

There was a murmur from the Sarmatians. One of them leaned forward to shake an amulet bag in the soldier's face, gabbling something too swiftly to be understood.

The leader had frowned when Vettius spoke. He snapped another order and kicked his horse forward. Romans and Sarmatians together jogged up the hill, toward the offal and frozen muck of Torgu.

On the bank of a nameless, icebound stream stood the village's central hall and only real building. Dama glanced at it as they rode past. Its roughly squared logs were gray and streaked with odd splits along the twisted grain. Any caulking there might have been in the seams had fallen out over the years. The sides rose to a flaring roof of scummed thatch, open under the eaves to emit smoke and the stink of packed bodies. The hall would have seemed crude in the most stagnant backwaters of the Empire; the merchant could scarcely believe that a people to whom it was the height of civilization could be a threat.

Around the timber structure sprawled the nomad wagons in filthy confusion. Their sloping canopies were shingled with cow droppings set out to dry in the wan sunlight before being burned for fuel. The light soot that had settled out of thousands of cooking fires permeated the camp with an unclean, sweetish odor. Nothing in the village but the untethered horses watching the patrol return looked cared for.

Long lances had been butted into the ground beside each wagon. As he stared back at the flat glares directed at him by idle Sarmatians, Dama realized what was wrong with the scene. Normally, only a handful of each family group would have been armored lancers. The rest would be horse archers, able to afford only a bow and padded linen protection. Most of their escort hung cased bows from their saddles, but all bore the lance and most wore scale mail.

"Lucius," the merchant whispered in Latin, "are all of these nobles?"

"You noticed that," Vettius replied approvingly. "No, you can see from their looks that almost all of them were just herdsmen recently. Somebody made them his retainers, paid for their equipment and their keep."

"Hydaspes?" the merchant queried.

"I guess. He must have more personal retainers than the king then."

"You will be silent!" ordered the Sarmatian leader.

They had ridden almost completely through the camp and were approaching a tent of gaily pennoned furs on the edge of the plains. At each corner squatted an octagonal stump of basalt a few feet high. The stones were unmarked and of uncertain significance, altars or boundary markers or both. No wains had been parked within fifty paces of the tent. A pair of guards stood before its entrance. Dama glanced at the streamers and said, "You know, there really is a market for silk in this forsaken country. A shame that—"

"Silence!" the Sarmatian repeated as he drew up in front of the tent. He threw a rapid greeting to the guards, one of whom bowed and ducked inside. He returned quickly, followed by a tall man in a robe of fine black Spanish wool. The newcomer's face was thin for a Sarmatian and bore a smile that mixed triumph and something else. On his shoulder, covered by the dark hood, clung a tiny monkey with great brown eyes. From time to time it put its mouth to its master's ear and murmured secretly.

"Hydaspes," Vettius whispered. "He always wears black."

"Have they been disarmed?" the wizard questioned. The escort's leader flushed in embarrassment at his oversight and angrily demanded the Romans' weapons. Vettius said nothing as he handed over his bow and the long cavalry bow he carried even now that he commanded an infantry unit. The merchant added his crossbow and a handful of bolts to the collection.

"What is that?" Hydaspes asked, motioning his man to hand him the crossbow.

"It comes from the east where I get my silk," Dama explained, speaking directly to the wizard. "You just drop a bolt into the tall slot on top. That holds it while you pull back on the handle, cocking it and firing it all in one motion."

"From the east? I get weapons from the east," the Sarmatian said with a nasty quirk of his lip. "But this, this is only a toy surely? The arrow is so light and scarcely a handspan long. What could a man do with such a thing?"

Dama shrugged. "I'm not a warrior. For my own part, I wouldn't care to be shot with this or anything else."

The wizard gestured an end to the conversation, setting the weapon inside his tent for later perusal. "Dismount, gentlemen, dismount," he continued in excellent Greek. "Perhaps you have heard of me?"

"Hydaspes the wizard. Yes," Vettius lied, "even within the Empire we think of you when we think of a powerful sorceror. That's why we've come for help."

"In whose name?" the Sarmatian demanded shrewdly. "Constantius the emperor?"

"Celsus, Count of Dacia," Vettius snapped back. "The Empire has suffered the absurdities of Constantius and his brothers long enough. Eunuchs run the army, priests rule the state, and the people pray to the tax gatherers. We'll have support when we get started, but first we need some standard to rally to, something to convince everyone that we have more than mere hopes behind us. We want your giants, and we'll pay you a part of the Empire to get them."

"And you, little man?" Hydaspes asked the merchant unexpectedly. Dama had been imagining the Count's face if he learned his name was being linked with raw treason, but he recovered swiftly and fumbled at his sash while replying, "We merchants have little cause to love Constantius. The roads are ruinous, the coinage base; and the rapacity of local officials leaves little profit for even the most daring adventurer."

"So you came to add your promise of future gain?"

"Future? Who knows the future?" Dama grunted. Gold gleamed in his hand. A shower of coins arced unerringly from his right palm to his left and back again. "If you can supply what we need, you'll not lament your present payment."

"Ho! Such confidence," the wizard said, laughing cheerfully. The monkey chittered, stroking its master's hair with bulbous fingertips. "You really believe that I can raise giants from the past?

"I can!"

Hydaspes's face became a mask of unreason. Dama shifted nervously from one foot to the other, realizing that the wizard was far from the clever illusionist they had assumed back at Naisso he must be. This man wasn't sane enough to successfully impose on so many people, even ignorant barbarians. Or was the madness a recent thing?

"Subradas, gather the village behind my tent," Hydaspes ordered abruptly, "but leave space in the middle as wide and long as the tent itself."

The leader of the escort dipped his lance in acknowledgement. "The women, Lord?"

"All—women, slaves, everyone. I'm going to show you how I raise the giants."

"Ho!" gasped the listening Sarmatians. The leader saluted again and rode off shouting. Hydaspes turned to re-enter his tent, then paused. "Take the Romans, too," he directed the guards. "Put them by the flap and watch them well.

"Yes," he continued, glancing back at Vettius, "it is a very easy thing to raise giants, if you have the equipment and the knowledge. Like drawing a bowstring for a man like you."

The Hell-lit afterimage of the wizard's eyes continued to blaze in the soldier's mind when the furs had closed behind the black figure.

As the rest of the Sarmatians dismounted and began to jostle them around the tent, Dama whispered, "This isn't working. If it gets too tight, break for the tent. You know about my bow?"

Vettius nodded, but his mind was chilled by a foretaste of death.

As the prisoner had said, eleven long trenches bristled outward from the wall of Hydaspes's tent.

Each was shallow but too extensive for the wizard to have dug it in the frozen ground in one night. Dama disliked the way the surface slumped over the ditches as if enormous corpses had clawed their way out of their graves.

Which was what the wizard seemed to claim had happened.

The guards positioned the two Romans at the center of the back wall of the tent where laces indicated another entrance. Later comers crowded about anxiously, held back in a rough circle by officers with drawn swords. Twenty feet to either side of the Romans stretched the straight wall of the tent paralleled by a single row of warriors. From the basalt posts at either corner curved the rest of the tribe in milling excitement, warriors in front and women and children squirming as close as they could get before being elbowed back.

The Sarmatians were still pushing for position when Hydaspes entered the cleared space, grinning ironically at Vettius and Dama as he stepped between them. A guard laced the tent back up. In the wizard's left hand was a stoppered copper flask; his right gripped a small packet of supple cowhide.

"The life!" Hydaspes shouted to the goggle-eyed throng, waving the flask above his head from the center of the circle. He set the vessel down on the dirt and carefully unrolled the leather wrappings from the other objects.

"And the seed!" the wizard cried at last. In his palm lay a pair of teeth. They were a dull, stony gray without any of the sheen of ivory. One was a molar, human but inhumanly large. The other tooth, even less credible, seemed to be a canine fully four inches long. With one tooth in either hand, Hydaspes goat-footed about the flask in an impromptu dance of triumph.

His monkey rider clacked its teeth in glee.

The wizard stopped abruptly and faced the Romans. "Oh yes. The seed. I got them, all thirteen teeth, from the Serians—the people who sell you your silk, merchant. Dragons' teeth they call them—hee hee! And I plant them just like Cadmus did when he built Thebes. But I'm the greater prince, oh yes, for I'll build an empire where he built a city."

Dama licked his lips. "We'll help you build your empire," he began, but the wizard ignored him and spoke only to Vettius.

"You want my giants, Roman, my darlings? Watch!"

Hydaspes plucked a small dagger from his sash and poked a hole in the ground. Like a farmer planting a nut, the wizard popped the molar into the hole and patted the earth back down. When he straightened he shouted a few words at the sky. The villagers gasped, but Dama doubted whether they understood any more of the invocation than he did. Perhaps less—the merchant thought he recognized the language, at least, one he had heard chanted on the shores of the Persian Gulf on a dead, starless night. He shuddered.

Now the wizard was unstoppering his flask and crooning under his breath. His cowl had fallen back to display the monkey clinging fiercely to his long oily hair. When the wizard turned, Dama could see the beast's lips miming its master obscenely.

Droplets splattered from the flask, bloody red and glowing. The merchant guessed wine or blood, changed his mind when the fluid popped and sizzled on the ground. The frozen dirt trembled like a stricken gong.

The monkey leaped from Hydaspes's shoulder, strangely unaffected by the cold. It faced the wizard across the patch of fluid-scarred ground. It was chanting terrible squeaky words that thundered back from Hydaspes.

The ground split.

The monkey collapsed. Hydaspes leaped over the earth's sudden gape and scooped up the little creature, wrapping it in his cloak.

Through the crack in the soil thrust an enormous hand. Earth heaved upward again. The giant's whole torso appeared, dribbling dirt back into the trench. Vettius recognized the same thrusting jaw, the same high flat eyesockets, as those of the giant he had killed.

The eyes were Hydaspes's own.

"Oh, yes, Roman," the wizard cackled. "The life and the seed—but the mind too, hey? There must be the mind."

The giant rose carefully in a cascade of earth. Even standing in the trench left by his body, he raised his pointed skull eight feet into the air.

"My mind!" Hydaspes shrieked, oblivious to everyone but the soldier. "Part of me in each of my darlings, you see? Flowing from me through my pet here to them."

One of the wizard's hands caressed the monkey until it murmured lasciviously. The beast's huge eyes were seas of steaming brown mud, barely flecked by pinpoint pupils.

"You said you knew me," continued the wizard. "Well, I know you too, Lucius Vettius. I saw you bend your bow, I saw you kill my darling—

"I saw you kill me, Roman!"

Vettius unclasped his cape, let it slip to the ground. Hydaspes wiped a streak of spittle from his lips and stepped back to lay a hand on the giant's forearm. "Kill me again, Roman," the wizard said softly. "Go ahead; no one will interfere. But this time you don't have a bow.

"Watch the little one!" he snapped to the guard on Dama's right. The Sarmatian gripped the merchant's shoulder.

Then the giant charged.

Vettius dived forward at an angle, rolling beyond the torn up section of the clearing. The giant spun, stumbled in a ditch that had cradled one of his brothers. The soldier had gained the room he wanted in the center of the open space and waited in a loose-armed crouch. The giant sidled toward him splay footed.

"Hey!" the Roman shouted and lunged for his opponent's dangling genitalia. The giant struck with shocking speed, swatting Vettius in midair like a man playing handball. Before the Roman's thrusting fingers could make contact, the giant's open-handed blow had crashed into his ribs and hurled him a dozen feet away. Only the giant's clumsy rush saved Vettius from being pulped before he could jump to his feet again. The soldier was panting heavily but his eyes were fixed on the giant's. A thread of blood dribbled off the point of his jaw. Only a lip split on the hard ground—thus far. The giant charged.

Two faces in the crowd were not fixed on the one-sided battle. Dama fingered the hem of his cloak unobtrusively, following the fight only from the corners of his eyes. It would be pointless to watch his friend die. Instead the merchant watched Hydaspes, who had dug another hole across the clearing and inserted the last and largest tooth into it. The wizard seemed to ignore the fighting. If he watched at all, it was through the giant's eyes as he claimed; and surely, mad as he was, Hydaspes would not have otherwise turned his back on his revenge. For the first time Dama thought he recognized an unease about the monkey which rode again on the wizard's shoulder. It might have been only fatigue. Certainly Hydaspes seemed to notice nothing unusual as he tamped down the soil and began his thirteenth invocation.

Dama's guard was wholly caught up in the fight. He began to pound the merchant on the back in excitement, yelling bloodthirsty curses at Vettius. Dama freed the slender stiletto from his cloak and palmed it. He did not turn his head lest the movement catch the guard's attention. Instead he raised his hand to the Sarmatian's neck, delicately fingering his spine. Before the moth-light touch could register on the enthusiastic Sarmatian, Dama slammed the thin blade into the base of his brain and gave it a twist. The guard died instantly. The merchant supported the slumping body, guiding it back against the tent.

Hydaspes continued chanting a litany with the monkey, though the noise of the crowd drowned out his words. The wizard formed the inaudible syllables without noticing either Dama or the stumbling way his beast answered him. There was a look of puzzlement, almost fear, in the monkey's eyes. The crowd continued to cheer as the merchant opened the flap with a quick slash and backed inside Hydaspes's tent.

Within, a pair of chalcedony oil lamps burned with tawny light. The floor was covered with lush furs, some of which draped wooden benches. On a table at one end rested a pair of human skulls, unusually small but adult in proportions. More surprising were the cedar book chests holding parchments and papyri and even the strange pleated leaf-books of India.

Dama's crossbow stood beside the front entrance. He ran to it and loosed the bundle of stubby, unfletched darts beside it. From his wallet came a vial of pungent tarry matter into which he jabbed the head of each dart. The uncovered portions of the bronze points began to turn green. Careful not to touch the smears of venom, the merchant slipped all ten missiles into the crossbow's awkward vertical magazine.

Only then did he peer through the tent flap.

Vettius leaped sideways, kicking at the giant's knee. The ragged hobnails scored his opponent's calf, but the giant's deceptively swift hand closed on the Roman's outer tunic. For a heartsick instant the fabric held; then it ripped and Vettius tumbled free. The giant lunged after him.

Vettius backpedaled and, as his enemy straightened, launched himself across the intervening space. The heel of his outstretched boot slammed into the pit of the giant's stomach. Again the iron nails made a bloody ruin of the skin. The titan's breath whooshed out, but its half-ton bulk did not falter at the blow.

Vettius, thrown back by the futile impact, twisted away from the giant's unchecked rush. The creature's heels grazed past, thudded with mastodontic force. The soldier took a shuddering breath and lurched to his feet. A long arm clawed for his face. The Roman staggered back, barely clear of the spade-like talons. The monster pressed after him relentlessly, and Vettius was forced at last to recognize what should have been hopelessly obvious from the first: he could not possibly kill the giant with his bare hands.

With desperate purpose Vettius began to circle and retreat before his adversary. He should have planned it, measured it, but now he could only trust to luck and the giant's incredible weight. Backed almost against a corner post, he crouched and waited.

Arms wide, the giant hesitated—then rushed in for the kill. Vettius met him low, diving straight at his opponent instead of making a vain effort to get clear again. The Roman's arms locked about his opponents ankles as the taloned fingers clamped crushingly on Vettius' ribs.

The unyielding basalt altar met the giant's skull with shattering force. Bone slammed dense rock with the sound of a maul on a wedge. Warm fluids spattered the snow while the Sarmatians moaned in disbelief.

Hydaspes knelt screaming on the ground, his fists pummeling terror from a mind that had forgotten even the invocation it had just completed.

The earth began pitching like an unmastered horse. It split in front of the wizard where the tooth had been planted. The crack raced jaggedly through the crowd and beyond.

"Lucius!" Dama cried, lifting the corner of the tent.

The soldier pulled his leg free from the giant's pinioning body and rolled toward the voice, spilling endwise the only Sarmatian alert enough to try to stop him. Dama dropped the tent wall and nodded toward the front, his hands full of crossbow. "There's horses waiting out there. I'll slow them up."

Vettius stamped on a hand that thrust into the tent.

"Get out, damn you!" the merchant screamed. "There aren't any more weapons in here."

A Sarmatian rolled under the furs with a feral grimace and a dagger in his hand. The soldier hefted a full case of books and hurled it at his chest. Wood and bone splintered loudly. Vettius turned and ran toward the horses.

The back flap ripped apart in the haste of the Sarmatians who had remembered its existence. The first died with a dart through his eye as Dama jerked the cocking handle of his weapon. The next missile fell into position. The merchant levered back the bow again. At full cock the sear released and snapped the dart out into the throat of the next man. The Sarmatian's life dissolved in a rush of red flame as the bolt pricked his carotid to speed its load of poison straight to the brain.

The third man stumbled over his body, screamed. Two darts pinged off his mail before one caught the armpit he bared when he threw his hands over his face.

Relentless as a falling obelisk, Dama stroked out the full magazine of lethal missiles, shredding the lives of six screaming victims in the space of a short breath. The entrance was plugged by a clot of men dying in puling agony. Tossing his empty bow at the writhing chaos behind him, Dama ran through the front flap and vaulted onto his horse.

"We'll never get clear!" Vettius shouted as he whipped his mount. "They'll run us down in relays before we reach the Danube."

Wailing Sarmatians boiled around both ends of the tent, shedding helmets, weapons—any encumbrances. Their voices honed a narrow blade of terror.

"The control," Dama shouted back as the pair dodged among the crazy pattern of wagon tongues.

"He used his own mind and a monkey's to control something not quite a man."

"So what?"

"That last tooth didn't come from a man. It didn't come from anything like a man."

Something scaly, savage and huge towered over the wreckage of the tent. It cocked its head to glare at the disappearing riders while scrabbling with one stubby foreleg to stuff a black-robed figure farther into its maw. Vettius twisted in his saddle to stare in amazement at the coffin-long jaws gaping twenty feet into the air and the spined backfin like that of no reptile of the past seventy million years.

The dragon hissed, leaving a scarlet mist of blood to hang in the air as it ducked for another victim.

The Barrow Troll

Playfully, Ulf Womanslayer twitched the cord bound to his saddlehorn. "Awake, priest? Soon you can get to work."

"My work is saving souls, not being dragged into the wilderness by madmen," Johann muttered under his breath. The other end of the cord was around his neck, not that of his horse. A trickle of blood oozed into his cassock from the reopened scab, but he was afraid to loosen the knot. Ulf might look back.

Johann had already seen his captor go into a berserk rage. Over the Northerner's right shoulder rode his axe, a heavy hooked blade on a four foot shaft. Ulf had swung it like a willow-wand when three Christian traders in Schleswig had seen the priest and tried to free him. The memory of the last man in three pieces as head and sword arm sprang from his spouting torso was still enough to roil Johann's stomach.

"We'll have a clear night with a moon, priest; a good night for our business." Ulf stretched and laughed aloud, setting a raven on a fir knot to squawking back at him. The berserker was following a ridge line that divided wooded slopes with a spine too thin-soiled to bear trees. The flanking forests still loomed above the riders. In three days, now, Johann had seen no man but his captor, nor even a tendril of smoke from a lone cabin. Even the route they were taking to Parmavale was no mantrack but an accident of nature.

"So lonely," the priest said aloud.

Ulf hunched hugely in his bearskin and replied, "You soft folk in the south, you live too close anyway. Is it your Christ-god, do you think?"

"Hedeby's a city," the German priest protested, his fingers toying with his torn robe, "and my brother trades to Uppsala. . . . But why bring me to this manless waste?"

"Oh, there were men once, so the tale goes," Ulf said. Here in the empty forest he was more willing for conversation than he had been the first few days of their ride north. "Few enough, and long enough ago. But there were farms in Parmavale, and a lordling of sorts who went a-viking against the Irish. But then the troll came and the men went, and there was nothing left to draw others. So they thought."

"You Northerners believe in trolls, so my brother tells me," said the priest.

"Aye, long before the gold I'd heard of the Parma troll," the berserker agreed. "Ox broad and stronger than ten men, shaggy as a denned bear."

"Like you," Johann said, in a voice more normal than caution would have dictated.

Blood fury glared in Ulf's eyes and he gave a savage jerk on the cord. "You'll think me a troll, priestling, if you don't do just as I say. I'll drink your blood hot if you cross me."

Johann, gagging, could not speak nor wished to.

With the miles the sky became a darker blue, the trees a blacker green. Ulf again broke the hoof-pummeled silence, saying, "No, I knew nothing of the gold until Thora told me."

The priest coughed to clear his throat. "Thora is your wife?" he asked.

"Wife? Ho!" Ulf brayed, his raucous laughter ringing like a demon's. "Wife? She was Hallstein's wife, and I killed her with all her house about her! But before that, she told me of the troll's horde, indeed she did. Would you hear that story?"

Johann nodded, his smile fixed. He was learning to recognize death as it bantered under the axehead.

"So," the huge Northerner began. "There was a bonder, Hallstein Kari's son, who followed the king to war but left his wife, that was Thora, behind to manage the stead. The first day I came by and took a sheep from the herdsman. I told him if he misliked it to send his master to me."

"Why did you do that?" the fat priest asked in surprise.

"Why? Because I'm Ulf, because I wanted the sheep. A woman acting a man's part, it's unnatural anyway.

"The next day I went back to Hallstein's stead, and the flocks had already been driven in. I went into the garth around the buildings and called for the master to come out and fetch me a sheep." The berserker's teeth ground audibly as he remembered. Johann saw his knuckles whiten on the axe helve and stiffened in terror.

"Ho!" Ulf shouted, bringing his left hand down

on the shield slung at his horse's flank. The copper boss rang like thunder in the clouds. "She came out," Ulf grated, "and her hair was red. 'All our sheep are penned,' says she, 'but you're in good time for the butchering.' And from out the hall came her three brothers and the men of the stead, ten in all. They were in full armor and their swords were in their hands. And they would have slain me, Ulf Otgeir's son, *me*, at a woman's word. Forced me to run from a woman!"

The berserker was snarling his words to the forest. Johann knew he watched a scene that had been played a score of times with only the trees to witness. The rage of disgrace burned in Ulf like pitch in a pine faggot, and his mind was lost to everything except the past.

"But I came back," he continued, "in the darkness, when all feasted within the hall and drank their ale to victory. Behind the hall burned a log fire to roast a sheep. I killed the two there, and I thrust one of the logs half-burnt up under the eaves. Then at the door I waited until those within noticed the heat and Thora looked outside.

" 'Greetings, Thora,' I said. 'You would not give me mutton, so I must roast men tonight.' She asked me for speech. I knew she was fey, so I listened to her. And she told me of the Parma lord and the treasure he brought back from Ireland, gold and gems. And she said it was cursed that a troll should guard it, and that I must needs have a mass priest, for the troll could not cross a Christian's fire and I should slay him then."

"Didn't you spare her for that?" Johann quavered, more fearful of silence than he was of misspeaking.

"Spare her? No, nor any of her house," Ulf

thundered back. "She might better have asked the flames for mercy, as she knew. The fire was at her hair. I struck her, and never was a woman better made for an axe to bite—she cleft like a waxen doll, and I threw the pieces back. Her brothers came then, but one and one and one through the doorway, and I killed each in his turn. No more came. When the roof fell, I left them with the ash for a headstone and went my way to find a mass priest—to find you, priestling." Ulf, restored to good humor by the climax of his own tale, tweaked the lead cord again.

Johann choked onto his horse's neck, nauseated as much by the story as by the noose. At last he said, thick-voiced, "Why do you trust her tale if she knew you would kill her with it or not?"

"She was fey," Ulf chuckled, as if that explained everything. "Who knows what a man will do when his death is upon him? Or a woman," he added more thoughtfully.

They rode on in growing darkness. With no breath of wind to stir them, the trees stood as dead as the rocks underfoot.

"Will you know the place?" the German asked suddenly. "Shouldn't we camp now and go on in the morning?"

"I'll know it," Ulf grunted. "We're not far now—we're going down hill, can't you feel?" He tossed his bare haystack of hair, silvered into a false sheen of age by the moon. He continued, "The Parma lord sacked a dozen churches, so they say, and then one more with more of gold than the twelve besides, but also the curse. And he brought it back with him to Parma, and there it rests in his barrow, the troll guarding it. That I have on Thora's word."

"But she hated you!"

"She was fey."

They were into the trees, and looking to either side Johann could see hill slopes rising away from them. They were in a valley, Parma or another. Scraps of wattle and daub, the remains of a house or a garth fence, thrust up to the right. The firs that had grown through it were generations old. Johann's stubbled tonsure crawled in the night air.

"She said there was a clearing," the berserker muttered, more to himself than his companion. Johann's horse stumbled. The priest clutched the cord reflexively as it tightened. When he looked up at his captor, he saw the huge Northerner fumbling at his shield's fastenings. For the first time that evening, a breeze stirred. It stank of death.

"Others have been here before us," said Ulf needlessly.

A row of skulls, at least a score of them, stared blank-eyed from atop stakes rammed through their spinal openings. To one, dried sinew still held the lower jaw in a ghastly rictus; the others had fallen away into the general scatter of bones whitening the ground. All of them were human or could have been. They were mixed with occasional glimmers of buttons and rust smears. The freshest of the grisly trophies was very old, perhaps decades old. Too old to explain the reek of decay.

Ulf wrapped his left fist around the twin handles of his shield. It was a heavy circle of linden wood, faced with leather. Its rim and central boss were of copper, and rivets of bronze and copper decorated the face in a serpent pattern.

"Good that the moon is full," Ulf said, glancing

at the bright orb still tangled in the fir branches. "I fight best in the moonlight. We'll let her rise the rest of the way, I think."

Johann was trembling. He joined his hands about his saddle horn to keep from falling off the horse. He knew Ulf might let him jerk and strangle there, even after dragging him across half the northlands. The humor of the idea might strike him.

Johann's crucifix, his knucklebone of St. Martin in a silver-gilt reliquary—everything he had brought from Germany or purchased in Schleswig save his robe—had been left behind in Hedeby when the berserker awakened him in his bed. Ulf had jerked a noose to near-lethal tautness and whispered that he needed a priest, that this one would do, but that there were others should this one prefer to feed crows. The disinterested bloodlust in Ulf's tone had been more terrifying than the threat itself. Johann had followed in silence to the waiting horses.

In despair, he wondered again if a quick death would not have been better than this lingering one that had ridden for weeks a mood away from him.

"It looks like a palisade for a house," the priest said aloud in what he pretended was a normal voice.

""That's right," Ulf replied, giving his axe an exploratory heft that sent shivers of moonlight across the blade. "There was a hall here, a big one. Did it burn, do you think?" His knees sent his roan gelding forward in a shambling walk past the line of skulls. Johann followed of necessity.

"No, rotted away," the berserker said, bending over to study the post holes.

"You said it was deserted a long time," the priest commented. His eyes were fixed straight forward. One of the skulls was level with his waist and close enough to bite him, could it turn on its stake.

"There was time for the house to fall in, the ground is damp," Ulf agreed. "But the stakes, then, have been replaced. Our troll keeps his front fence new, priestling."

Johann swallowed, said nothing.

Ulf gestured briefly. "Come on, you have to get your fire ready. I want it really holy."

"But we don't sacrifice with fires. I don't know how—"

"Then learn!" the berserker snarled with a vicious yank that drew blood and a gasp from the German. "I've seen how you Christ-shouters love to bless things. You'll bless me a fire, that's all. And if anything goes wrong and the troll spares you—I won't, priestling. I'll rive you apart if I have to come off a stake to do it!"

The horses walked slowly forward through brush and soggy rubble that had been a hall. The odor of decay grew stronger. The priest himself tried to ignore it, but his horse began to balk. The second time he was too slow with a heel to its ribs, and the cord nearly decapitated him. "Wait!" he wheezed. "Let me get down."

Ulf looked back at him, flat-eyed. At last he gave a brief crow-peck nod and swung himself out of the saddle. He looped both sets of reins on a small fir. Then, while Johann dismounted clumsily, he loosed the cord from his saddle and took it in his axe hand. The men walked forward without speaking.

"There . . ." Ulf breathed.

The barrow was only a black-mouthed swell in the ground, its size denied by its lack of features.

Such trees as had tried to grow on it had been broken off short over a period of years. Some of the stumps had wasted into crumbling depressions, while from others the wood fibers still twisted raggedly. Only when Johann matched the trees on the other side of the tomb to those beside him did he realize the scale on which the barrow was built: its entrance tunnel would pass a man walking upright, even a man Ulf's height.

"Lay your fire at the tunnel mouth," the berserker said, his voice subdued. "He'll be inside."

"You'll have to let me go—"

"I'll have to nothing!" Ulf was breathing hard. "We'll go closer, you and I, and you'll make a fire of the dead trees from the ground. Yes. . . ."

The Northerner slid forward in a pace that was cat soft and never left the ground a finger's breadth. Strewn about them as if flung idly from the barrow mouth were scraps and gobbets of animals, the source of the fetid reek that filled the clearing. As his captor paused for a moment, Johann toed one of the bits over with his sandal. It was the hide and paws of something chisel-toothed, whether rabbit or other was impossible to say in the moonlight and state of decay. The skin was in tendrils, and the skull had been opened to empty the brains. Most of the other bits seemed of the same sort, little beasts, although a rank blotch on the mound's slope could have been a wolf hide. Whatever killed and feasted here was not fastidious.

"He stays close to hunt," Ulf rumbled. Then he added, "The long bones by the fence; they were cracked."

"Umm?"

"For marrow."

Quivering, the priest began gathering broken-off trees, none of them over a few feet high. They had been twisted off near the ground, save for a few whose roots lay bare in wizened fists. The crisp scales cut Johann's hands. He did not mind the pain. Under his breath he was praying that God would punish him, would torture him, but at least would save him free of this horrid demon that had snatched him away.

"Pile it there," Ulf directed, his axe head nodding toward the stone lip of the barrow. The entrance was corbelled out of heavy stones, then covered over with dirt and sods. Like the beast fragments around it, the opening was dead and stinking. Biting his tongue, Johann dumped his pile of brush and scurried back.

"There's light back down there," he whispered.

"Fire?"

"No, look—it's pale, it's moonlight. There's a hole in the roof of the tomb."

"Light for me to kill by," Ulf said with a stark grin. He looked over the low fireset, then knelt. His steel sparked into a nest of dry moss. When the tinder was properly alight, he touched a pitchy faggot to it. He dropped his end of the cord. The torchlight glinted from his face, white and coarse-pored where the tangles of hair and beard did not cover it. "Bless the fire, mass-priest," the berserker ordered in a quiet, terrible voice.

Stiff-featured and unblinking, Johann crossed the brushwood and said, "In nomine Patris, et Filii, et Spiritus Sancti, Amen."

"Don't light it yet," Ulf said. He handed Johann the torch. "It may be," the berserker added, "that you think to run if you get the chance. There is no Hell so deep that I will not come for you from it."

The priest nodded, white-lipped.

Ulf shrugged his shoulders to loosen his muscles and the bear hide that clothed them. Axe and shield rose and dipped like ships in a high sea.

"Ho! Troll! Barrow fouler! Corpse licker! Come and fight me, troll!"

There was no sound from the tomb.

Ulf's eyes began to glaze. He slashed his axe twice across the empty air and shouted again, "Troll! I'll spit on your corpse, I'll lay with your dog mother. Come and fight me, troll, or I'll wall you up like a rat with your filth!"

Johann stood frozen, oblivious even to the drop of pitch that sizzled on the web of his hand. The berserker bellowed again, wordlessly, gnashing at the rim of his shield so that the sound bubbled and boomed in the night.

And the tomb roared back to the challenge, a thunderous *Bar Bar Bar* even deeper than Ulf's.

Berserk, the Northerner leaped the brush pile and ran down the tunnel, his axe thrust out in front of him to clear the stone arches.

The tunnel sloped for a dozen paces into a timber-vaulted chamber too broad to leap across. Moonlight spilled through a circular opening onto flags slimy with damp and liquescence. Ulf, maddened, chopped high at the light. The axe burred inanely beneath the timbers.

Swinging a pair of swords, the troll leapt at Ulf. It was the size of a bear, grizzled in the moonlight. Its eyes burned red.

"Hi!" shouted Ulf and blocked the first sword in a shower of sparks on his axe-head. The second blade bit into the shield rim, shaving a hand's length of copper and a curl of yellow linden from beneath it. Ulf thrust straight-armed, a blow that would have smashed like a battering ram had the troll not darted back. Both the combatants were shouting; their voices were dreadful in the circular chamber.

The troll jumped backward again. Ulf sprang toward him and only the song of the blades scissoring himself from either side warned him. The berserker threw himself down. The troll had leaped onto a rotting chest along the wall of the tomb and cut unexpectedly from above Ulf's shield. The big man's boots flew out from under him and he struck the floor on his back. His shield still covered his body.

The troll hurtled down splay-legged with a cry of triumph. Both bare feet slammed on Ulf's shield. The troll was even heavier than Ulf. Shrieking, the berserker pistoned his shield arm upward. The monster flew off, smashing against the timbered ceiling and caroming down into another of the chests. The rotted wood exploded under the weight in a flash of shimmering gold. The berserker rolled to his feet and struck overarm in the same motion. His lunge carried the axehead too far, into the rock wall in a flower of blue sparks.

The troll was up. The two killers eyed each other, edging sideways in the dimness. Ulf's right arm was numb to the shoulder. He did not realize it. The shaggy monster leaped with another double flashing and the axe moved too slowly to counter. Both edges spat chunks of linden as they withdrew. Ulf frowned, backed a step. His boot trod on a ewer that spun away from him. As he cried out, the troll grinned and hacked again like Death the Reaper. The shield-orb flattened as the top third of it split away. Ulf snarled and chopped at the troll's knees. It leaped above the steel and cut left-handed, its blade nocking the shaft an inch from Ulf's hand.

The berserker flung the useless remainder of his shield in the troll's face and ran. Johann's torch was an orange pulse in the triangular opening. Behind Ulf, a swordedge went *sring*! as it danced on the corbels. Ulf jumped the brush and whirled. "Now!" he cried to the priest, and Johann hurled his torch into the resin-jeweled wood.

The needles crackled up in the troll's face like a net of orange silk. The flames bellied out at the creature's rush but licked back caressingly over its mats of hair. The troll's swords cut at the fire. A shower of coals spit and crackled and made the beast howl.

"Burn, dog-spew!" Ulf shouted. "Burn, fish-guts!"

The troll's blades rang together, once and again. For a moment it stood, a hillock of stained gray, as broad as the tunnel arches. Then it strode forward into the white heart of the blaze. The fire bloomed up, its roar leaping over the troll's shriek of agony. Ulf stepped forward. He held his axe with both hands. The flames sucked down from the motionless troll, and as they did the shimmering arc of the axe-head chopped into the beast's collarbone. One sword dropped and the left arm slumped loose.

The berserker's axe was buried to the helve in the troll's shoulder. The faggots were scattered, but the troll's hair was burning all over its body. Ulf pulled at his axe. The troll staggered, moaning. Its remaining sword pointed down at the ground. Ulf yanked again at his weapon and it slurped free. A thick velvet curtain of blood followed it. Ulf raised his dripping axe for another blow, but the troll tilted toward the withdrawn weapon, leaning forward, a smoldering rock. The body hit the ground, then flopped so that it lay on its back. The right arm was flung out at an angle.

"It was a man," Johann was whispering. He caught up a brand and held it close to the troll's face. "Look, look!" he demanded excitedly, "it's just an old man in bearskin. Just a man."

Ulf sagged over his axe as if it were a stake impaling him. His frame shuddered as he dragged air into it. Neither of the troll's swords had touched him, but reaction had left him weak as one death-wounded. "Go in," he wheezed. "Get a torch and lead me in."

"But . . . why—" the priest said in sudden fear. His eyes met the berserker's and he swallowed back the rest of his protest. The torch threw high-lights on the walls and flags as he trotted down the tunnel. Ulf's boots were ominous behind him.

The central chamber was austerely simple and furnished only with the six chests lining the back of it. There was no corpse, nor even a slab for one. The floor was gelatinous with decades' accu-mulation of foulness. The skidding tracks left by the recent combat marked paving long undisturbed. Only from the entrance to the chests was a path, black against the slime of decay, worn. It was toward the broken container and the objects which had spilled from it that the priest's eyes arrowed.

"Gold," he murmured. Then, "Gold! There must—the others—in God's name, there are five more and perhaps all of them—"

"Gold," Ulf grated terribly.

Johann ran to the nearest chest and opened it one-handed. The lid sagged wetly, but frequent use had kept it from swelling tight to the side panels. "Look at this crucifix!" the priest marveled. "And the torque, it must weigh pounds. And Lord in heaven, this—"

"Gold," the berserker repeated.

Johann saw the axe as it started to swing. He was turning with a chalice ornamented in enamel and pink gold. It hung in the air as he darted for safety. His scream and the dull belling of the cup as the axe divided it were simultaneous, but the priest was clear and Ulf was off balance. The berserker backhanded with force enough to drive the peen of his axehead through a sapling. His strength was too great for his footing. His feet skidded, and this time his head rang on the wall of the tomb.

Groggy, the huge berserker staggered upright. The priest was a scurrying blur against the tunnel entrance. "Priest!" Ulf shouted at the suddenly empty moonlight. He thudded up the flags of the tunnel. "Priest!" he shouted again.

The clearing was empty except for the corpse. Nearby, Ulf heard his roan whicker. He started for it, then paused. The priest—he could still be hiding in the darkness. While Ulf searched for him, he could be rifling the barrow, carrying off the gold behind his back. "Gold," Ulf said again. No one must take his gold. No one ever must find it unguarded.

"I'll kill you!" he screamed into the night. "I'll kill you all!"

He turned back to his barrow. At the entrance, still smoking, waited the body of what had been the troll.

KILLER*

Rain was again trickling from the grayness overhead, and the damp reek of the animals hung on the misty droplets. A hyena wailed miserably, longing for the dry plains it would never see again. Lycon listened without pity. Let it bark its lungs out here in Brundisium, or die later in the amphitheater at Rome. He remembered the Ethiopian girl who had lived three days after a hyena had dragged her down. It would have been far better had the beast not been driven off before it had finished disembowelling her.

"Wish the rain would stop," complained Vonones. The Armenian dealer's plump face was gloomy. "A lot of these are going to die otherwise, and I'll be caught in the middle. In Rome they only pay me for live delivery, but I have to pay you regardless."

Which is why I'm a hunter and you're a dealer, mused Lycon without overmuch sympathy. "Well,

**with Karl Edward Wagner*

it won't ruin you," he reassured the dealer. "Not at the prices you pay. You can replace the entire lot for a fifth of what they'll bring in Rome."

The tiger whose angry cough had been cutting through the general racket thundered forth a full-throated roar. Lycon and the Armenian heard his heavy body crash against the bars of his cage. Vonones nodded toward the sound. "There's one I can't replace."

"What? The tiger?" Lycon's tone was surprised. "I'll grant you he's the biggest I've ever captured, but I brought you back two others with him that are near as fine."

"No, not the tiger," Vonones grunted. "I meant the thing he's snarling at. Come on, I'll show you. Maybe you'll know what it is"

The Armenian put on his broad felt hat and snugged up his cloak against the drizzle. Lycon followed, not really noticing the rain that beaded his close-cut black hair. He had been a mercenary scout in his youth, before he had sickened of butchering Rome's barbarian enemies and turned instead to hunting animals for her arenas. A score of years in the field left him calloused to the weather as to all else.

For the beasts themselves he felt only professional concern, no more. As they passed a wooden cage with a dozen maned baboons, he scowled and halted the dealer. "I'd get them into a metal cage, if I were you. They'll chew through the lashings of that one, and you'll have hell catching them again."

"Overflow," the Armenian told him vexedly. "Had to put them there. It's all I've got with your load and this mixed shipment from the Danube getting here at the same time. Don't worry, they move tomorrow when we sort things out for the haul to Rome."

Beasts snarled and lunged as the men threaded through the maze of cages. Most of the animals were smeared with filth, their coats worn and dull where they showed through the muck. A leopard pining in a corner of its cage reminded Lycon of a cat he once had force fed—a magnificent mottled brown beast that he had purchased half-starved from a village of gap-toothed savages in the uplands of India. He needed four of his men to pin it down while he rammed chunks of raw flesh down its throat with a stake. That lithe killer was now the empress' plaything, and her slavegirls fed it tid-bits from silver plates.

"There it is," Vonones announced, pointing to a squat cage of iron.

The creature stared back, ignoring the furious efforts of the tiger alongside to slash his paw through the space that separated their cages.

"You've got some sort of wild man!" Lycon blurted with first glance.

"Nonsense!" Vonones snorted. "Look at the tiny scales, those talons! There may be a race somewhere with blue skin, but this thing's no more human than a mandrill."

After that first startled impression, Lycon had to agree. The thing seemed far less human than any mandrill, which it somewhat resembled. Probably those hairless limbs made him think it was a man—that and the aura of evil intelligence its stare conveyed. But the collector had never seen anything like it, not in twenty years of professional hunting along the fringes of the known world. Lycon could not even decide whether it was mammal or reptile. It was scaled and exuded an acrid reptilian scent, but its movements and poise were feline. Apelike, it could walk erect and would be about man height if it straightened. Its face was cat-like, low browed and without much jaw. A flat, earless skull thrust forward on a snaky neck. Its eyes looked straight forward with human intensity, but were slit-pupiled with a swift nictitating membrane.

"This came from the Danube?" Lycon questioned wonderingly.

"It did. There was a big lot of bears and aurochs that one of my agents jobbed from the Sarmatians. This thing came with them, and all I know about it is what Dama wrote me with the shipment—that a band of Sarmatians saw a hilltop explode and found this when they went to see what had happened."

"A hilltop exploded!"

The dealer shrugged. "That's all he wrote."

Lycon studied the cage in silence.

"Why did you weld the cage shut instead of putting a chain and lock on it?"

"That's the way it came," Vonones explained. "I'll have to knock the door loose and put a proper lock on it before sending it off tomorrow, or those idiots at Rome will wreck a good cage trying to smash it open, and never a denarius for the damage. I guess the Sarmatians just didn't have a lock—I'm a little surprised they even had an iron cage."

Lycon frowned, uncomfortable at the way the beast stared back at him. "It's its eyes," he reflected. "I wish all my crew looked that bright."

"Or mine," Vonones agreed readily. "Oh, I make no doubt it's more cunning than any brute should be, but it's scarcely human. Can you see those claws? They're curled back in its palms now, but—there!"

The creature made a stretching motion, opening its paws—or were they hands? Bones stood out, slim but like the limbs themselves hinting at adamantine hardness. The crystalline claws extended maybe a couple of inches, so sharp that their points seemed to fade into the air. No wild creature should have claws so delicately kept. The beast's lips twitched a needle-toothed grin.

"Hermes!" Lycon muttered, looking away. There was a glint of bloodlust in those eyes, something beyond natural savagery. Lycon remembered a centurion whose eyes held that look, an unassuming little man who once had killed over a hundred women and children during a raid on a German village.

"What are they going to pit this thing against?" he asked suddenly.

Vonones shrugged. "Can't be sure. The buyer didn't say much except that he didn't like the thing's looks."

"Can you blame him?"

"So? He's supposed to be running a beast show, not a beauty contest. If he wants pretty things, I should bring him gazelles. For the arena, I told him, this thing is perfect—a real novelty. But the ass says he doesn't like the idea of keeping it around until the show, and I have to cut my price to nothing to get him to take it. Think of it!"

"What's the matter?" Lycon gibed sardonically. "Do you also like its looks so little you'll unload it at a sacrifice?"

"Hardly!" the dealer scoffed. "Animals are animals, and business is business. But I've got a hundred other animals here right now, and *they* don't like the thing. Look at this tiger. All day, all night he's trying to get at it—even broke a tooth on the bars! Must be its scent, because all the animals hate it. No, I have to get this thing out of my compound."

Lycon considered the enraged tiger. The huge cat had killed one of his men and maimed another for life before they had him safely caged. But even the tiger's rage at capture paled at the determined fury he showed toward Vonones's strange find.

"Well, I'll leave you to him, then," the hunter said, giving up on the mystery. "Tomorrow I'll be by to pick up my money, so try to stay out of reach of that thing's claws until then."

"You could have gone on with it," Vulpes told him. "You could have made a fortune in the arena."

Lycon tore off a hunk of bread and sopped it with greasy gravy. "I could have gotten killed—or crippled for life."

He immediately regretted his choice of words, but his host only laughed. The tavern owner's left arm was a stump, and that he walked at all was a testament to the man's fortitude. Lycon had seen him after they dragged him from the wreckage of his chariot. The surgeons doubted Vulpes would last the night, but that was twenty-five years ago.

"No, it was stupidity that brought me down," Vulpes said. "Or greed. I knew my chances of forcing through on that turn, but it was that or the race. Well, I was lucky. I lived through it and had enough of my winnings saved to open a wine shop. I get by.

"But you," and he stabbed a thick finger in Lycon's grey-stubbled face. "You were too good, too smart. You could have been rich. A few years was all you needed. You were as good with a sword as any man who's ever set foot in the arena—fast, and you knew how to handle yourself. All those years you spent against the barbarians seasoned you. Not like these swaggering bullies the crowds dote on these days—gutless slaves and flashy thugs who learned their trade in dark alleys! Pit a combat-hardened veteran against this sort of trash and see whose lauded favorite gets dragged off by his heels!"

Vulpes downed a cup of his wares and glared about the tavern truculently. None of his few customers was paying attention.

Lycon ruefully watched his host refill their cups with wine and water. He wished his friend would let old memories lie. Vulpes, he noted, was getting as red-faced and paunchy as the wineskins he sold here. Nor, Lycon mused, running a hand over his close cropped skull, was he himself as young as back then. At least he stayed fit, he told himself—but then, Vulpes could hardly be faulted for inaction.

Tall for a Greek, Lycon had only grown leaner and harder with the years. His face still scowled in hawk-like intensity; his features resembled seasoned leather stretched tightly over sharp angles. Spirit and sinew had lost nothing in toughness as Lycon drew closer to fifty, and his men still talked of the voyage of a few years past when he nursed an injured polar bear on deck while waves broke over the bow and left a film of ice as they slipped back.

Vulpes rumbled on. "But you, my philosophic Greek, found the arena a bore. Just walked away and left it all. Been skulking around the most forsaken corners of the world for—what is it, more than twenty years now? Risking your life to haul back savage beasts that barely make your expenses when you sell them. And you could be living easy in a villa near Rome!"

"Maybe this is what I wanted," Lycon protested. He tried to push away memories of sand and sweat and the smell of blood and the sound of death and an ocean's roar of voices howling to watch men die for their amusement.

Vulpes was scarcely troubling to add water to their wine. "What you wanted!" he scoffed. "Well, what *do* you want, my moody Greek?"

"I'm my own master. Maybe I'm not rich, but I've journeyed to lands Odysseus never dreamed of, and I've captured stranger beasts than the Huntress ever loosed arrow after."

"Oh, here's to adventure!" mocked Vulpes good-humoredly, thumping his wine cup loudly.

Lycon, reminded of the blue-scaled creature in Vonones's cage, smiled absently.

"I, too, am a philosopher," Vulpes announced loftily. "Wine and sitting on your butt all day makes a good Roman as philosophic as any wander-witted Greek beast collector." He raised his cup to Lycon.

"And you, my friend, you have a fascination with the deadly, for the killer trait. Deny it as you will, but it's there. You could have farmed olives, or studied sculpture. But no, it's the army for you, then the arena, and what next? Are you sick of killing? No, just bored with easy prey. So now you spend your days outwitting and ensnaring the most savage beasts of all lands!

"You can't get away from your fascination for the killer, friend Lycon. And shall I tell you why?

It's because, no matter how earnestly you deny it, you've got the killer streak in your own soul too."

"Here's to philosophy," toasted Lycon sardonically.

Lycon had done business with Vonones for many years, and the fat Armenian was one of the handful that the hunter more or less considered as friends. Reasonably honest albeit shrewd, Vonones paid with coins of full weight and had been known to add a bonus to the tally when a collector brought him something exceptional. Still, after a long night of drinking with Vulpes, Lycon was not pleased when the dealer burst in upon him well before noon in the room he shared with five other transients.

"What in the name of the buggering Twins do you mean getting me up at this hour!" Lycon snarled, surprised to see daylight. "I said I'd come by later for my money."

"No—it's not that!" Vonones moaned, shaking his arm. "Come on, Lycon! You've got to help me!"

Lycon freed his arm and rolled to his feet. Someone cursed and threw a sandal in their direction. "All right, all right," the hunter yawned. "Let's get out of here and let other people sleep."

The stairs of the apartment block reeked of garbage and refuse. It reminded Lycon of the stench at Vonones's animal compound—the sour foulness of too many people living within cramped walls. Beggars clogged the stairs, living there for want of other shelter. Now and again the manager of the block would pay a squad of the watch to pummel them out into the street. Those who could pay for a portion of a room were little cleaner themselves.

"Damn it, Vonones! What is it!" Lycon protested, as the frantic Armenian took hold of his arm again.

"Outside—I can't. . . . That animal escaped. The blue one."

"Well," Lycon said reasonably, "you said you didn't get much for the thing, so it can't be all that great a loss. Anyway, what has it to do with me?"

But Vonones set his lips and tugged the hunter down the stairs and out onto the cobbled street where eight bearers waited with his litter. He pushed Lycon inside and closed the curtains before speaking in a low, agitated voice. "I don't dare let this get out! Lycon, the beast escaped only a few miles out of town. It's loose in an estate now—hundreds of little peasant grainplots, each worked by a tenant family."

"So?"

"The estate is owned by the emperor, and that blue beast killed one of his tenants within minutes of escaping! You've got to help me recapture it before worse happens!"

"Hermes!" swore Lycon softly, understanding why the loss of the animal had made a trembling wreck of the dealer. "How did it get loose?"

"That's the worst of it," Vonones whimpered. "It must have unlocked the cage somehow—I checked the fastenings myself before the caravan left. But nobody will believe that—they'll think I was careless and didn't have the cage locked properly in the first place. And if the emperor learns that one of his estates is being ravaged . . ."

"Domitian shows his displeasure in interesting ways," Lycon finished somberly. "Are you sure it isn't already too late to hush the business up?"

Vonones struggled for composure. "For now it's

all right. The steward is no more interested in letting this get out than I am, knowing the emperor's temper. But there's a limit to what he can cover up, and . . . it won't take very much of what happened to that farmer to exceed that limit. You've got to catch the thing for me, Lycon!"

"All right," Lycon decided. He knew he was plunging into a mess that might call down Domitian's wrath on all concerned, but his voice was edged with excitement. "Let's get out to where the thing escaped."

The caravan was still strung out along the road when they arrived in Vonones's mud-spattered carriage. There were thirty cars, most loaded with only a single cage to avoid fights between the bars. Despite wind, rain and jostling, the beasts seemed less restive than in the compound. Perhaps there was a reason. The third cage from the end stood open.

Lycon stepped between a pair of carts—then ducked quickly as a taloned paw ripped through the bars at him. Disappointed, the huge tiger snarled as he hunched back in his cage.

The hunter glanced to be certain his arm was still in place. "There's one to watch out for," he cautioned Vonones. "That one was a man-killer when we captured him—and out of preference, not just because he was lame or too old to take other prey. When they turn him loose in the arena, he'll take on anything in sight."

"Maybe," muttered the Armenian. "But he'd like to start with that blue thing. I never saw anything drive every animal around it to a killing rage the way it does. Maybe it's its scent, but at times I could swear it was somehow taunting them."

Lycon grunted noncommittally.

"Suppose I should let the rest of the caravan go on?" Vonones suggested. "They're just causing comment stopped here like this."

Lycon considered. "Why not get them off the road as much as you can and spread out. Don't let them get too far away though, because I'll need some men for this. Say, there aren't any hunting dogs here, are there?"

Vonones shook his balding head. "No, I don't often handle dogs. There is a small pack in Brundisium for the local arena though. I know the trainer, and I think I can have them here by noon."

"Better do it, then," Lycon advised. "It's going to be easiest just to run the thing down and let the dogs have it. If we can pull them off in time, maybe there'll be enough left for your buyer in Rome."

"Forget the sale," Vonones urged him. "Just *get* that damned thing!"

But Lycon was studying the lock of the cage. It clearly had not been forced. There were only a few fine scratches on the wards.

"Any of your men mess with this?"

"Are you serious? They don't like it any better than the animals do."

"Vonones, I think it had to have opened the lock with its claws."

The Armenian looked sick.

Twenty feet from the cart were the first footprints of the beast, sunk deeply into the mud of the wheat field beside the road. In the black earth their stamp was as undefinable as the beast itself. More lizard than birdlike, Lycon decided. Long toes leading a narrow, arched foot, with a thick spurred heel.

"First I knew anything was wrong," explained the arm-waving driver of the next cart back, "was when this thing all of a sudden swings out of its cage and jumps into the field. Why, it could just as easy have jumped back on me—and then where would I have been, I ask you?"

Lycon did not bother to tell him. "Vonones, you've got a couple archers in your caravan, haven't you?"

"Yes, but they weren't any use—it was too sudden. The one in the rear of the column shot where he could see the wheat waving, but he didn't really have a target. If only the thing *had* turned back on the rest of the caravan instead of diving through the hedges! My archers would have skewered it for sure then, and I wouldn't be in this fix. Lycon, this creature is a killer! If it gets away . . ."

"All right, steady," the hunter growled. "Going to pieces isn't going to help." He rose from where he knelt in the wheat.

"You won't be so self-assured once you see the farmer," Vonones warned.

The tenant's hut was a windowless beehive of wattle and daub, stuck up on the edge of his holdings. Huddled in the doorway, three of his children watched the strangers apathetically, numbed by the cold drizzle and their father's death.

The farmer lay about thirty yards into the field. A scythe, its rough iron blade unstained, had fallen near the body. Blank amazement still showed in his glazed eyes. A sudden, tearing thrust of the creature's taloned hands had eviscerated the man—totally, violently. He lay on his back in a welter of gore and entrails, naked ribs jagged through his ripped open chest cavity.

Lycon studied the fragments of flesh strewn over the furrows. "What did you feed it in the compound?"

"The same as the other carnivores," Vonones replied shakily. "Scrap beef and parts of any animals that happened to die. It wasn't fussy."

"Well, if you manage to get it back alive, you'll know what it really likes," Lycon said grimly. "Do you see any sign of his liver?"

Vonones swallowed and stared at the corpse in dread. The archers held arrows to their bows and looked about nervously.

Lycon, who had been following the tracks with his eye as they crossed the gullied field, suddenly frowned. "How is your bow strung?" he asked sharply of the nearest archer.

"With gut," he answered, blinking.

Lycon swore in disgust. "In this rain a gut string is going to stretch like a judge's honor! Vonones, we've got to have spears and bows strung with waxed horsehair before we do anything. I don't want to be found turned inside out with a silly expression like this poor bastard!"

Lycon chose a dozen of Vonones's men to follow the dogs with him. After that nothing happened for hours, while Vonones fumed and paced beside the wagons. At the prospect of extricating himself from his dilemma, the Armenian's sick fear gave way to impatience.

About mid-afternoon a battered farm cart creaked into view behind a pair of spavined mules. The driver was a stocky North Italian, whose short whip and leather armlets proclaimed him the trainer of the six huge dogs that almost filled the wagon bed. Following was a much sharper carriage packed with hunting equipment, nets as well as bows and spears.

"What took you so long, Galerius!" Vonones demanded. "I sent for you hours ago—told you to spare no expense in hiring a wagon! Damn it, man—the whole business could have been taken care of by now if you hadn't come in this wreck!"

"Thought you'd be glad I saved you the money," Galerius scowled with dull puzzlement. "My father-in-law lets me use this rig at a special rate."

"It doesn't matter," Lycon headed off the quarrel. "We had to wait for the weapons anyway. How about the dogs? Can they track in this drizzle?"

"Sure, they're real hunting dogs—genuine Molossians," the trainer asserted proudly. "They weren't bred for the arena. I bought them from an old boy who used to run deer on his estate before he offended Domitian."

Vonones began to chew his ragged nails.

At least the pack looked fully capable of holding up its end of things, Lycon thought approvingly. The huge, brindle-coated dogs milled about the wagon bed, stiff-legged and hackles lifted at the babel of sounds and scents from Vonones's caravan. Their flanks were lean and scarred, and their massive shoulders bespoke driving strength. Their trainer might be a slovenly yokel himself, but his hounds were excellent hunting stock and well cared for. With professional interest, Lycon wondered whether he could talk Galerius into selling the pack.

"Don't you have horses?" the trainer asked. "Going to be tough keeping up with these on foot."

"We'll have to do it," Lycon snorted. The trainer's idea of hunting was probably limited to the arena. Well, this wasn't some confused animal at bay in the center of an open arena. "Look at the terrain. Horses would be worse than useless!"

Beneath gray clouds, the land about them was broken with rocky gullies, shadowy ravines, and stunted groves of trees. Gateless hedgerows divided the tenant plots at short intervals, forming dark, thorny barriers in a maze-like pattern throughout the estate. There were a few low sections where a good horse might hurdle the hedge, but the rain had turned plowed fields into quagmires, and the furrows were treacherous footing.

Lycon frowned at the sky. The rain was now only a dismal mist, but the overcast was thick and the sun well down on the horizon. Objects at a hundred yards blurred indistinctly into the haze.

"We've got one, maybe two hours left if we're going to catch the thing today," he judged. "Well, let's see what they can do."

Galerius threw open the back gate of the wagon, and the pack bounded onto the road. They milled and snarled uncertainly while their trainer whipped them into line and led them past the remaining wagons. As soon as they neared the open cage, the hounds began to show intense excitement. One of the bitches gave a throaty bay and swung off into the wheat field. The other five poured after her, and no more need be done.

They hate it too, mused Lycon, as the excited pack bounded across the field in full cry. "Come on!" he shouted. "And keep your eyes open!"

Taking a boar spear, the hunter plunged after the baying pack. Vonones's men strung out behind him, while the dogs raced far ahead in the wheat. Too heavy for a long run, Vonones held back with the others on the road. Fingering a bow nervously, he stood atop a wagon and watched the hunt disappear into the mist. He looked jumpy enough to loose an arrow at the first thing to come out of the woods, and Lycon reminded himself to shout when they returned to the road.

Already the dogs had vanished in the wheat, so that the men heard only their distant cries. Trailing them was no problem—the huge hounds had torn through the grainfield like a chariot's rush—but keeping up with them was impossible. The soft earth pulled at their legs, and sandals were constantly mired with clay and straw.

"Can't you slow them up?" Lycon demanded of the trainer who panted at his side.

"Not on a scent like this!" Galerius gasped back. "They're wild, plain wild! No way we can keep up without horses!"

Lycon grunted and lengthened his stride. The trainer quickly fell back, and when Lycon glanced over his shoulder he saw the other had paused to clean his sandals. Of the others he saw only vague forms farther behind still. Lycon wasted a breath to curse them and ran on.

The dogs had plunged through a narrow gap in the first hedge. Lycon followed, pushing his boar spear ahead of him. Had the gap been there, or had their quarry broken it through in passing? Clearly the thing was powerful beyond proportion to its slight bulk.

The new field was already harvested, and stubble spiked up out of the cold mud to jab Lycon's toes. His side began to ache. Hermes, he thought, the beast could be clear to Tarantum by now if it wanted to be. If it did get away, there was no help for Vonones. Lycon himself might find it expedient to spend a few years beyond the limits of the empire. That's what happens when you get involved in things that really aren't your business . . .

Another farmhouse squatted near the next hedgerow. "Hoi!" the hunter shouted. "Did a pack of dogs cross your hedge?"

There was no sound within. Lycon stopped in sudden concern and peered through the open doorway.

A half-kneaded cake of bread was turning black on the fire in the center of the hut. The rest of the hut was mottled throughout with russet splashes of blood that dried in the westering sun. There were at least six bodies scattered about the tiny room. The beast had taken its time here.

Lycon turned away, shaken for the first time in long years. He looked back the way he had come. None of the others had crawled through the last hedgerow yet. This time he felt thankful for their flabby uselessness.

He used a stick of kindling to scatter coals into the straw bedding, and tossed the flaming brand after. With luck no one would ever know what had happened here. As Vonones had said, there was a limit. They had better finish the beast fast.

The pack began to bay fiercely not far away. From the savage eagerness of their voices, Lycon knew they had overtaken the creature. Whatever the thing was, its string had run out, Lycon thought with relief.

Recklessly he ducked into the hedge and wormed through, not pausing to look for an opening. Thorns shredded his tunic and gouged his limbs as he pulled himself clear and began running toward the sounds.

No chance of recapturing the beast alive now. Any one of the six Molossians was nearly the size of the blue creature, and the arena would have taught the pack to kill rather than to hold. By the time Vonones's men arrived with the nets, it would be finished. Lycon half regretted that—the beast fascinated him. But quite obviously the thing was too murderously powerful to be loose and far too clever to be safely caged. It was luck the beast had kept close to its kill instead of running farther. The pack was just beyond the next hedgerow now.

With an enormous bawl of pain, one of the hounds suddenly arched into view, flailing in the air above the hedge. A terrified clamor abruptly broke through the ferocious baying of the pack. Beyond the hedge a fight was raging—and by the sound of it, the pack was in trouble.

Lycon swore and made for the far hedge, ignoring the cramp in his side. His knuckles clamped white on the boar spear.

He could see three of the dogs ahead of him, snarling and milling uncertainly on the near side of the hedge. The other three were not to be seen. They were beyond the hedge, Lycon surmised—and from their silence, dead. The beast was cunning; it had lain in wait for the pack as it squirmed through the hedge. But surely it was no match for three huge Molossians!

Lycon was less than a hundred yards from the hedge, when the blue-scaled killer vaulted over the thorny barrier with an acrobat's grace. It writhed through the air, and one needle-clawed hand slashed out—tearing the throat from the nearest Molossian before the dog was fully aware of its presence. The creature bounced to the earth like a cat, as the last two snarling hounds sprang for it together. Spinning and slashing as it ducked under and away, the thing was literally a blur of motion. Deadly motion. Neither hound completed its leap, as lethal talons tore and gutted—slew with nightmarish precision.

Lycon skidded to a stop on the muddy field. He did not need to glance behind him to know he was alone with the beast. Its eyes glowed in the sunset as it turned from the butchered dogs and stared at its pursuer.

The hunter advanced his spear, making no attempt to throw. As fast as it moved, the thing would easily dodge his cast. And Lycon knew that if the beast leaped, he was dead, dead as Pentheus. His only chance was that he might drive his spear home, might take his slayer with him—and he thought the beast recognized that.

It crouched, its lips drawn in a savage grin—then vaulted back over the hedge again.

Lycon tried to make his dry mouth shape a prayer of thanks. Eyes intent on the hedge, he held his spear at ready. Then he heard feet splatting at a clumsy run behind him.

Galerius puffed toward him, accompanied by several of the others in a straggling clot. "That hut back there caught fire!" he blurted. "Didn't you see it? Just a ball of flame by the time we could get to it. Don't know if anyone was there, or if they got out, or . . ."

He caught sight of the torn bodies and trailed off. His voice drawled in wonder. "What happened here!"

Lycon finally let his breath out. "Well, I found the animal we were supposed to be hunting—while you fools were back there gawking at your fire!

Now I think Vonones owes you for a pack of dogs."

Lycon waited long enough to make certain the beast no longer lay in wait beyond the hedge. After seeing the hounds, no one had wanted to be first to wriggle through to the other side. Thinking of those murderous claws, the hunter had no intention of doing so either. There was a gap in the hedge some distance away, and he sent half the men to circle around. There was no sign of the beast other than three more mutilated hounds. In disgust Lycon hiked back to the caravan, letting the others follow as they would.

As he reached the road a shrill voice demanded, "Who's there!"

Lycon swore and yelled before nervous fingers released an arrow. "Don't shoot, damn you! Hermes, that's all it would take!"

Vonones thumped heavily on to the roadbed from his perch on the wagon. His face was anxious. "How did it go? Did you get the thing? Where are the others?"

"Drag-assing back," Lycon grunted wearily. "Vonones, there isn't one of your men I'd trust to walk a dog."

"They're wagon drivers, not hunters," the dealer protested. "But what about the beast?"

"We didn't get it."

And while the others slowly drifted back, Lycon told the dealer what had happened. The damp stillness of the dusk settled around the wagons as he finished. Vonones slumped in stunned silence.

Lycon's weathered face was thoughtful. "You got a hold of something from an arena, Vonones. I don't know where or whose—maybe the Sarmatians raided it from the Chinese. But the way it moves, the way its claws are groomed—the way it kills for pleasure. . . . Somebody lost a fighting cock, and you bought it!"

The Armenian stared at him without comprehension. Licking his lips, Lycon continued. "I can't say who could have owned it, or what the beast is—but I know the arena, and I tell you that thing is a superbly trained killer. The way it ambushed the dogs, slaughtered them without a wasted motion! And that thing moves fast! I'm fast enough that I've jumped back from a pit trap I didn't know was there until my feet started to go through. I knew a gladiator in Rome who moved faster than any man I've seen. He'd let archers shoot at him from sixty yards, then dodge the arrow, and I never could believe I saw it happen. But that thing out there in the fields is so much faster there's no comparison."

How did the Sarmatians capture it then!" Vonones demanded.

"Capture? They took its surrender!" Lycon exploded. "A band of mounted archers on a thousand miles of empty plains—they could have run it down and killed it easily, and that damned thing knew it! Then they welded it into an iron cage, and strong as it is, the beast can't snap iron bars."

"But it can pick locks."

"Yeah."

The dealer took a deep breath, shrugging all over and seeming to fill his garments even more fully. "How do we recapture it, then?"

"I don't know."

Lycon chewed his lips, looking at the ground rather than the Armenian. "If the beast sleeps, maybe we could sneak up and get a shot. Maybe with a thousand men we could spread out through the hedgerows and gullies, encircle it somehow."

"We don't have a thousand men," Vonones stated implacably.

"I know."

Smoky clouds were sliding past the full moon. With dusk the drizzle at last had lifted; the overcast was clearing. A few stars began to spike through the cobwebby sky. Across the twilit fields, shadows crept out from hedgerows and trees, flowed over the rocky gullies.

"I can lay my hands on a certain amount of money at short notice," Vonones thought aloud. "There will be ships leaving Brundisium in the morning . . ."

But Lycon was staring at the nearest cage.

"Vonones," the hunter asked pensively. "Have you ever seen a tiger track a man down?"

"What? No, but I've heard plenty of grisly reports about man-killers who will . . ."

"No, I don't mean hunt down as prey. I mean track down for, well, revenge."

"No, it doesn't happen," the dealer replied. "A wolf maybe, but not one of the big cats. They don't go out of their way for anything, not even revenge."

"I saw it happen once," Lycon said. "It was a female, and one of my men had cleaned out her litter while she was off hunting. We figured later she must have followed him fifty miles before she caught up to him."

"She followed her cubs, not the man."

The hunter shook his head. "He'd given me the cubs. The man was three villages away when she got him. Her left forepaw had an extra toe; there was no mistake."

"So what?"

"Vonones, I'm going to let that tiger out."

The Armenian choked in disbelief. "Lycon, are you mad? This isn't the same at all! You can't . . ."

"Have you got a better idea? You know how all the animals hate this thing . . . that tiger even broke a tooth trying to chew his way to the beast. Well, I'm going to give him his chance."

"I can't let you turn yet another savage killer loose here!"

"Look, we can't get that blue-scaled thing any other way. Once it runs wild through a few more tenant holdings, Domitian isn't going to care if you turn the whole damn caravan loose!"

"So the tiger kills the beast. Then I'm responsible for turning a tiger loose on his estate! Lycon . . ."

"I caught this tiger once. I know about tigers. This thing, Vonones . . ."

The dealer's hand shook as he turned over the key.

Muttering, the drivers made an armed cluster in the middle of the road, watching Lycon as he unlocked the cage and vaulted to the roof as the door swung down. The tiger bounded onto the road almost before the door touched gravel. Tail lashing, he paused in a half-crouch to growl at the nervous onlookers. Several bows arched tautly.

Lady Artemis, breathed Lycon, let him scent that beast and follow it.

Turning from the men, the cat moved toward the other cage. He rumbled a challenge into the empty interior, then swung toward where the tracks stabbed into the damp earth. Without a backward glance, the tiger headed off across the field.

Lycon jumped down, boar spear in hand, and stepped across the ditch.

"Where are you going?" Vonones called after him.

"I want to see this," he shouted back, and loped off along the track he earlier had followed with the hounds.

"Lycon, you're crazy!" Vonones shouted into the night.

Even after the earlier run, Lycon had no trouble keeping up with the tiger. Cats have speed but are not pacers like dogs, like men. The tiger was moving at a graceless quick-step, midway between his normal arrogant saunter and the awesome rush that launched him to his kill. Loose skin behind his neck wobbled awkwardly as his shoulder blades pumped up and down. Moonlight washed all the orange from between the black stripes, and it seemed to be a ghost cat that jolted through the swaying wheat. He ignored Lycon, ignored even the blood-soaked earth where the first victim's corpse had lain—intent only on the strange, hated scent of its blue-scaled enemy.

Following at a cautious distance, Lycon marvelled that his desperate stratagem had worked. It seemed impossible that the great cat was actually stalking the other killer. It was pure hatred, the same unnatural fury that had maddened the dogs, that had turned the compound into a raging chaos as long as the creature had been among them.

And the men? None of the men had liked the blue-scaled devil either. Uncertain fear had made Vonones's crew useless in the hunt. And Vonones had unloaded the thing for a trivial sum, because neither he nor the buyer from Rome had wanted the beast around. Why then did he feel such fascination for the creature?

The tiger changed stride to clear the first hedgerow. Lycon warily climbed through after him, trotting toward the pall of reeking smoke that still hovered over the ruined hut. Vonones would see to things here, the hunter thought, praying that there would not be more such charnel scenes across the maze-like estate.

A dozen men passing and repassing had hacked a fair gap through the second hedge, and Lycon was glad he did not have to worm blindly through again. The tiger leaped it effortlessly and was speeding across the empty field at a swifter pace by the time he stepped through. Lycon lengthened his stride to stay within fifty yards.

More stars broke coldly through the clearing sky. The cat looked as deadly as Nemesis rippling through the moonlight. Lycon grimly recalled that he had thought much the same about the pack. The tiger was every bit as deadly as the blue killer, and probably was five times its weight. Speed and cunning could only count for so much.

The third hedge had not been trampled, and Lycon's belly tightened painfully as he dived through the gore-splashed gap where the killer had awaited the dogs. But the tiger had already leapt over the brushy wall, and Lycon disdained to lose time by detouring to the opening farther down. He pushed his way free and stood warily in the field beyond.

Here the soil was too sparse and rocky for regular sowing. Left fallow, small trees and weedy scrub grew disconsolately between bare rocks and shadowed gullies. The wasteland was a sharp study of hard blacks and whites etched by the pale moon.

The tiger had halted just ahead, his belly flattened to the rocky soil. He sniffed the air, coughing a low rumble like distant thunder. Then his challenging roar burst from his throat, moonlight glowing on awesome fangs. Far away an ox bawled in fear, and Lycon felt the hair on his neck tingle.

A bit of gravel rattled from the brush-filled gully just beyond. Lycon watched the cat's haunches rise, quivering with restrained tension. A man-sized shadow stood erect from the shadows of the gully, and the tiger leaped.

Thirty yards separated the cat from his prey. He took two short hops toward the blue devil, then lunged for the kill. The scaled creature was moving the instant the tiger left the ground for his final leap. A blur of energy, it darted beneath the lunge, needle-clawed fingers thrusting toward the cat's belly. The tiger squalled and hunched in mid-leap, slashing at its enemy in a deadly riposte that nearly succeeded.

Gravel and mud sprayed as the cat struck the ground and whirled. The blue killer was already upon him, its claws ripping at the tiger's neck. With speed almost as blinding, the cat twisted about, left forepaw flashing a bone-snapping blow against the creature's ribs—hurling it against a knot of brush.

The cat paused, trying to lick the stream of blood that spurted from its neck. The blue-scaled thing gave a high pitched cry—the first sound Lycon had heard from it—and leaped onto the cat's back.

By misjudgment or sudden weakness, it landed too far back, straddling the tiger's belly instead of withers. The cat writhed backward and rolled, taloned forepaws slashing, hind legs pumping. Stripped from its hold, the creature burrowed into the razor-edge fury of thrashing limbs.

It was too fast to follow. Both animals flung

themselves half erect, spinning, snarling in a crimson spray. A dozen savage blows ripped back and forth in the space of a heartbeat, as they tore against each other in suicidal frenzy.

With no apparent transition, the tiger slumped into the mud. His huge head hung loose, and bare bone gleamed for an instant. Blood spouted in a great torrent, then ebbed abruptly to a dark smear. The tiger arched his back convulsively in death as his slayer staggered away.

Lycon stared in disbelief as the blue-scaled killer took a careful step toward him. Blood bathed its bright scales like a glistening imperial cloak. Murder gleamed joyously in its eyes. Lycon readied his spear.

Another step and it stumbled, bracing itself on the ground with one deadly hand. The other arm hung broken, useless—all but torn away by the tiger's claws. It jerked erect and grinned at the hunter, its feral face a reflection of death. It lunged for him.

There was no strength to its legs. Its leap fell short a yard from the hunter. The beast skidded across the rocky soil. The claws of its good hand scored the dirt at his feet, then relaxed.

The moon glared down, drowning the stars with chilled splendor. Lycon shivered, and after a while he walked back to the road.

He felt old that night.

Ranks Of Bronze

The rising sun is a dagger point casting long shadows toward Vibulenus and his cohort from the native breastworks. The legion had formed ranks an hour before; the enemy is not yet stirring. A playful breeze with a bitter edge skitters out of the south, and the Tribune swings his shield to his right side against it.

"When do we advance, sir?" his First Centurion asks. Gnaeus Clodius Calvus, promoted to his present position after a boulder had pulped his predecessor during the assault on a granite fortress far away. Vibulenus only vaguely recalls his first days with the cohort, a boy of eighteen in titular command of four hundred and eighty men whose names he had despaired of learning. Well, he knows them now. Of course, there are only two hundred and ninety-odd left to remember.

Calvus's bearded, silent patience snaps Vibulenus back to the present. "When the cavalry comes up, they told me. Some kinglet or other is supposed to bring up a couple of thousand men to close our flanks. Otherwise, we're hanging. . . ."

The Tribune's voice trails off. He stares across the flat expanse of gravel toward the other camp, remembering another battle plain of long ago.

"Damn Parthians," Calvus mutters, his thought the same.

Vibulenus nods. "Damn Crassus, you mean. He put us *there*, and that put us *here*. The stupid bastard. But he got his, too."

The legionaries squat in their ranks, talking and chewing bits of bread or dried fruit. They display no bravado, very little concern. They have been here too often before. Sunlight turns their shield-facings green: not the crumbly fungus of verdigris but the shimmering sea-color of the harbor of Brundisium on a foggy morning.

Oh, Mother Vesta, Vibulenus breathes to himself. He is five foot two, about average for the legion. His hair is black where it curls under the rim of his helmet and he has no trace of a beard. Only his eyes make him appear more than a teenager; they would suit a tired man of fifty.

A trumpet from the command group in the rear sings three quick bars. "Fall in!" the Tribune orders, but his centurions are already barking their own commands. These too are lost in the clash of hobnails on gravel. The Tenth Cohort could form ranks in its sleep.

Halfway down the front, a legionary's cloak hooks on a notch in his shield rim. He tugs at it, curses in Oscan as Calvus snarls down the line at him. Vibulenus makes a mental note to check with the centurion after the battle. That fellow should have been issued a replacement shield before disembarking. He glances at his own. How many shields has he carried? Not that it matters. Armor is replaceable. He is wearing his fourth cuirass, now, though none of them have fit like the one his father had bought him the day Crassus granted him a tribune's slot. Vesta. . . .

A galloper from the command group skids his beast to a halt with a needlessly brutal jerk on its reins. Vibulenus recognizes him—Pompilius Falco. A little swine when he joined the legion, an accomplished swine now. Not bad with animals, though. "We'll be advancing without the cavalry," he shouts, leaning over in his saddle. "Get your line dressed."

"Osiris's bloody dick we will!" the Tribune snaps. "Where's our support?"

"Have to support yourself, I guess," shrugs Falco. He wheels his mount. Vibulenus steps forward and catches the reins.

"Falco," he says with no attempt to lower his voice, "you tell our deified Commander to get somebody on our left flank if he expects the Tenth to advance. There's too many natives—they'll hit us from three sides at once."

"You afraid to die?" the galloper sneers. He tugs at the reins.

Vibulenus holds them. A gust of wind whips at his cloak. "Afraid to get my skull split?" he asks. "I don't know. Are you, Falco?" Falco glances at where the Tribune's right hand rests. He says nothing. "Tell him we'll fight for him," Vibulenus goes on. "We won't let him throw us away. We've gone that route once." He looses the reins and watches the galloper scatter gravel on his way back.

The replacement gear is solid enough, shields that do not split when dropped and helmets forged without thin spots. But there is no craftsmanship in them. They are heavy, lifeless. Vibulenus still carries a bone-hilted sword from Toledo that required frequent sharpening but was tempered and balanced—poised to slash a life out, as it has a hundred times already. His hand continues to caress the palm-smoothed bone, and it calms him somewhat.

"Thanks, sir."

The thin-featured tribune glances back at his men. Several of the nearer ranks give him a spontaneous salute. Calvus is the one who spoke. He is blank-faced now, a statue of mahogany and strap-bronze. His stocky form radiates pride in his leader. Leader—no one in the group around the standards can lead a line soldier, though they may give commands that will be obeyed. Vibulenus grins and slaps Calvus's burly shoulder. "Maybe this is the last one and we'll be going home," he says.

Movement throws a haze over the enemy camp. At this distance it is impossible to distinguish forms, but metal flashes in the virid sunlight. The shadow of bodies spreads slowly to right and left of the breastworks as the natives order themselves. There are thousands of them, many thousands.

"Hey-*yip!*" Twenty riders of the general's bodyguard pass behind the cohort at an earthshaking trot. They rein up on the left flank, shrouding the exposed depth of the infantry. Pennons hang from the lances socketed behind their right thighs, gay yellows and greens to keep the lance heads from being driven too deep to be jerked out. The riders' faces are sullen under their mesh face guards. Vibulenus knows how angry they must be at being shifted under pressure—under his pressure—and he grins again. The bodyguards are insulted at being required to fight instead of remaining nobly aloof from the battle. The experience may do them some good.

At least it may get a few of the snotty bastards killed.

"Not exactly a regiment of cavalry," Calvus grumbles.

"He gave us half of what was available," Vibulenus replies with a shrug. "They'll do to keep the natives off our back. Likely nobody'll come near, they look so mean."

The centurion taps his thigh with his knobby swagger stick. "Mean? We'll give 'em mean."

All the horns in the command group sound together, a cacophonous bray. The jokes and scufflings freeze, and only the south wind whispers. Vibulenus takes a last look down his ranks—each of them fifty men abreast and no more sway to it than a tight-stretched cord would leave. Five feet from shield boss to shield boss, room to swing a sword. Five feet from nose guard to the nose guards of the next rank, men ready to step forward individually to replace the fallen or by ranks to lock shields with the front line in an impenetrable wall of bronze. The legion is a restive dragon, and its teeth glitter in its spears; one vertical behind each legionary's shield, one slanted from each right hand to stab or throw.

The horns blare again, the eagle standard slants forward, and Vibulenus's throat joins three thousand others in a death-rich bellow as the legion steps off on its left foot. The centurions are counting cadence and the ranks blast it back to them in the crash-jingle of boots and gear.

Striding quickly between the legionaries, Vibulenus checks the dress of his cohort. He should have a horse, but there are no horses in the legion now. The command group rides rough equivalents which are . . . very rough. Vibulenus is not sure he could accept one if his parsimonious employers offered it.

His men are a smooth bronze chain that advances in lock step. Very nice. The nine cohorts to the right are in equally good order, but Hercules! there are so few of them compared to the horde swarming from the native camp. Somebody has gotten overconfident. The enemy raises its own cheer, scattered and thin at first. But it goes on and on, building, ordering itself to a blood-pulse rhythm that moans across the intervening distance, the gap the legion is closing at two steps a second. Hercules! there is a crush of them.

The natives are close enough to be individuals now: lanky, long-armed in relation to a height that averages greater than that of the legionaires. Ill-equipped, though. Their heads are covered either by leather helmets or beehives of their own hair. Their shields appear to be hide and wicker affairs. What could live on this gravel waste and provide that much leather? But of course Vibulenus has been told none of the background, not even the immediate geography. There is some place around that raises swarms of warriors, that much is certain.

And they have iron. The black glitter of their spearheads tightens the Tribune's wounded chest as he remembers.

"Smile, boys," one of the centurions calls cheerfully, "here's company." With his words a javelin hums down at a steep angle to spark on the ground. From a spear-thrower, must have been. The distance is too long for any arm Vibulenus has seen, and he has seen his share.

"Ware!" he calls as another score of missiles arc from the native ranks. Legionaries judge them, raise their shields or ignore the plunging weapons as they choose. One strikes in front of Vibulenus and shatters into a dozen iron splinters and a knobby shaft that looks like rattan. One or two of the men have spears clinging to their shield faces. Their clatter syncopates the thud of boot heels. No one is down.

Vibulenus runs two paces ahead of his cohort, his sword raised at an angle. It makes him an obvious target: a dozen javelins spit toward him. The skin over his ribs crawls, the lumpy breadth of scar tissue scratching like a rope over the bones. But he can be seen by every man in his cohort, and somebody has to give the signal. . . .

"Now!" he shouts vainly in the mingling cries. His arm and sword cut down abruptly. Three hundred throats give a collective grunt as the cohort heaves its own massive spears with the full weight of its rush behind them. Another light javelin glances from the shoulder of Vibulenus's cuirass, staggering him. Calvus's broad right palm catches the Tribune, holds him upright for the instant he needs to get his balance.

The front of the native line explodes as the Roman spears crash into it.

Fifty feet ahead there are orange warriors shrieking as they stumble over the bodies of comrades whose armor has shredded under the impact of the heavy spears. "At 'em!" a front-rank file-closer cries, ignoring his remaining spear as he drags out his short sword. The trumpets are calling something but it no longer matters what: tactics go hang, the Tenth is cutting its way into another native army.

In a brief spate of fury, Vibulenus holds his forward position between a pair of legionaries. A native, orange-skinned with bright carmine eyes, tries to drag himself out of the Tribune's path. A Roman spear has gouged through his shield and arm, locking all three together. Vibulenus's sword takes the warrior alongside the jaw. The blood is paler than a man's.

The backward shock of meeting has bunched the natives. The press of undisciplined reserves from behind adds to their confusion. Vibulenus jumps a still-writhing body and throws himself into the wall of shields and terrified orange faces. An iron-headed spear thrusts at him, misses as another warrior jostles the wielder. Vibulenus slashes downward at his assailant. The warrior throws his shield up to catch the sword, then collapses when a second-rank legionary darts his spear through the orange abdomen.

Breathing hard with his sword still dripping in his hand, Vibulenus lets the pressing ranks flow around him. Slaughter is not a tribune's work, but increasingly Vibulenus finds that he needs the swift violence of the battle line to release the fury building within him. The cohort is advancing with the jerky sureness of an ox-drawn plow in dry soil.

A windrow of native bodies lies among the line of first contact, now well within the Roman formation. Vibulenus wipes his blade on a fallen warrior, leaving two sluggish runnels filling on the flesh. He sheathes the sword. Three bodies are sprawled together to form a hillock. Without hesitation the Tribune steps onto it to survey the battle.

The legion is a broad awl punching through a belt of orange leather. The cavalry on the left stand free in a scatter of bodies, neither threatened by the natives nor making any active attempt to drive them back. One of the mounts, a hairless brute combining the shape of a wolfhound with the bulk of an ox, is feeding on a corpse his rider has lanced. Vibulenus was correct in expecting the natives to give them a wide berth; thousands of flanking warriors tremble in indecision rather than sweep forward to surround the legion. It would take more discipline than this orange rabble has shown to attack the toad-like riders on their terrible beasts.

Behind the lines, a hundred paces distant from the legionaries whose armor stands in hammering contrast to the naked autochthones, is the Commander and his remaining score of guards. He alone of the three thousand who have landed from the starship knows why the battle is being fought, but he seems to stand above it. And if the silly bastard still has half his body guard with him—Mars and all the gods, what must be happening on the right flank?

The inhuman shout of triumph that rises half a mile away gives Vibulenus an immediate answer.

"Prepare to disengage!" he orders the nearest centurion. The swarthy non-com, son of a North African colonist, speaks briefly into the ears of two legionaries before sending them to the ranks forward and back of his. The legion is tight for men, always has been. Tribunes have no runners, but the cohort makes do.

Trumpets blat in terror. The native warriors boil whooping around the Roman right flank. Legionaries in the rear are facing about with ragged suddenness, obeying instinct rather than the orders bawled by their startled officers. The command group suddenly realizes the situation. Three of the bodyguard charge toward the oncoming orange mob. The rest of the guards and staff scatter into the infantry.

The iron-bronze clatter has ceased on the left flank. When the cohort halts its advance, the natives gain enough room to break and flee for their encampment. Even the warriors who have not engaged are cowed by the panic of those who have; by the panic, and the sprawls of bodies left behind them.

"About face!" Vibulenus calls through the indecisive hush, "and pivot on your left flank. There's some more barbs want to fight the Tenth!"

The murderous cheer from his legionaries overlies the noise of the cohort executing his order.

As it swings Vibulenus runs across the new front of his troops, what had been the rear rank. The cavalry, squat-bodied and grim in their full armor, shows sense enough to guide their mounts toward the flank of the Ninth Cohort as Vibulenus rotates his men away from it. Only a random javelin from the native lines appears to hinder them. Their comrades who remained with the Commander have been less fortunate.

A storm of javelins has disintegrated the half-hearted charge. Two of the mounts have gone down despite their heavy armor. Behind them, the Commander lies flat on the hard soil while his beast screams horribly above him. The shaft of a stray missile projects from its withers. Stabbing up from below, the orange warriors fell the remaining lancer and gut his companions as they try to rise. Half a dozen of the bodyguards canter nervously back from their safe bolthole among the infantry to try to rescue their employer. The wounded mount leaps at one of the lancers. The two beasts tangle with the guard between them. A clawed hind leg flicks his head. Helmet and head rip skyward in a spout of green ichor.

"Charge!" Vibulenus roars. The legionaries who can not hear him follow his running form. The knot of cavalry and natives is a quarter mile away. The cohorts of the right flank are too heavily engaged to do more than defend themselves against the new thrust. Half the legion has become a bronze worm, bristling front and back with spear-points against the surging orange flood. Without immediate support, the whole right flank will be squeezed until it collapses into a tangle of blood and scrap metal. The Tenth Cohort is their support, all the support there is.

"Rome!" the fresh veterans leading the charge shout as their shields rise against the new flight of javelins. There are gaps in the back ranks, those just disengaged. Behind the charge, men hold palms clamped over torn calves or lie crumpled around a shaft of alien wood. There will be time enough for them if the recovery teams land—which they will not do in event of a total disaster on the ground.

The warriors snap and howl at the sudden threat. Their own success has fragmented them. What had been a flail slashing into massed bronze kernels is now a thousand leaderless handfuls in sparkling contact with the Roman line. Only the leaders bunched around the command group have held their unity.

One mount is still on its feet and snarling. Four massively-equipped guards try to ring the Commander with their maces. The Commander, his suit a splash of blue against the gravel, tries to rise. There is a flurry of mace strokes and quickly-riposting spears, ending in a clash of falling armor and an agile orange body with a knife leaping the crumpled guard. Vibulenus's sword, flung over-arm, takes the native in the throat. The inertia of its spin cracks the hilt against the warrior's forehead.

The Tenth Cohort is on the startled natives. A moment before the warriors were bounding forward in the flush of victory. Now they face the cohort's meat-axe suddenness—and turn. At sword-point and shield edge, as inexorable as the rising sun, the Tenth grinds the native retreat into panic while the cohorts of the right flank open order and advance. The ground behind them is slimy with blood.

Vibulenus rests on one knee, panting. He has retrieved his sword. Its stickiness bonds it to his hand. Already the air keens with landing motors. In minutes the recovery teams will be at work on the fallen legionaries, building life back into all but the brain-hacked or spine-severed. Vibulenus rubs his own scarred ribs in aching memory.

A hand falls on the Tribune's shoulder. It is gloved in a skin-tight blue material; not armor, at least not armor against weapons. The Commander's voice comes from the small plate beneath his clear, round helmet. Speaking in Latin, his accents precisely flawed, he says, "You are splendid, you warriors."

Vibulenus sneers though he does not correct the alien. Warriors are capering heroes, good only for dying when they meet trained troops, when they meet the Tenth Cohort.

"I thought the Federation Council had gone

mad," the flat voice continues, "when it ruled that we must not land weapons beyond the native level in exploiting inhabited worlds. All very well to talk of the dangers of introducing barbarians to modern weaponry, but how else could my business crush local armies and not be bled white by transportation costs?"

The Commander shakes his head in wonder at the carnage about him. Vibulenus silently wipes his blade. In front of him, Falco gapes toward the green sun. A javelin points from his right eyesocket. "When we purchased you from your Parthian captors it was only an experiment. Some of us even doubted it was worth the cost of the longevity treatments. In a way you are more effective than a Guard Regiment with lasers; out-numbered, you beat them with their own weapons. They can't even claim 'magic' as a salve to their pride. And at a score of other job sites you have done as well. And so cheaply!"

"Since we have been satisfactory," the Tribune says, trying to keep the hope out of his face, "will we be returned home now?"

"Oh, goodness, no," the alien laughs, "you're far too valuable for that. But I have a surprise for you, one just as pleasant I'm sure—females."

"You found us real women?" Vibulenus whispers.

"You really won't be able to tell the difference," the Commander says with paternal confidence.

A million suns away on a farm in the Sabine hills, a poet takes the stylus from the fingers of a nude slave girl and writes, very quickly, *And Crassus's wretched soldier takes a barbarian wife from his captors and grows old waging war for them.*

The poet looks at the line with a pleased expression. "It needs polish, of course," he mutters. Then, more directly to the slave, he says, "You know, Leuconoe, there's more than inspiration to poetry, a thousand times more; but this came to me out of the air."

Horace gestures with his stylus toward the glittering night sky. The girl smiles back at him.

Dreams In Amber

The man in the tavern doorway was the one whom Saturnus saw in the dreams which ended in nightmare. The bead on Saturnus's chest tingled, and the fragmented dream-voice whispered in the agent's mind, *Yes. . . . Allectus.*

Allectus paused to view the interior, smoky with the cheap oil of the tavern lamps. He was a soft-looking man whose curly beard and sideburns were much darker than his flowing ginger moustache. Allectus wore boots, breeches, and a hooded cape buttoned up the front. All his clothing was farm garb, and all of it was unsuited to the position Saturnus knew Allectus held—Finance Minister of Carausius. The Emperor Marcus Aurelius Mausaeus Carausius, as he was styled on this side of the British Ocean which his fleet controlled. The one-time Admiral of the Saxon Shore now struck coins to show himself as co-emperor with his "brothers," Diocletian and Maximian. In the five years since disaster engulfed Maximian's fleet off Anderida, there had been no attempt from the mainland to gainsay the usurper's claim.

No attempt until now, until Gaius Saturnus was sent to Britain with instructions from an emperor and a mission from his dreams.

Allectus stepped aside as the agent approached him. He took Saturnus for another sailor leaving the tavern on the Thames dockside, the sort of man he had come to hire perhaps . . . but the finance officer was not ready to commit himself quite yet.

Saturnus touched his arm. "I'm the man you want," the agent said in a low voice.

"Pollux! Get away from me!" the finance officer demanded angrily. Allectus twitched loose as he glared at Saturnus, expecting to see either a pimp or a catamite. Saturnus was neither of those things. In Allectus's eyes, the agent was a tall, powerful man whose skin looked weathered enough to fit the shoddy clothes he also wore.

The finance officer stepped back in surprise. He had been tense before he entered the dive. Now, in his confusion, he was repenting the plan that had brought him here.

"I know what you want done," Saturnus said. He did not move closer to Allectus again, but he spoke louder to compensate for the other's retreat. "I'm the man you need." And Saturnus's arm tucked the cloak momentarily closer to his torso so that it molded the hilt of his dagger. The voice in Saturnus's mind whispered . . . *need* . . . to him again.

A customer had just left one of the blanket-screened cribs along the wall. It was a slow night, no lines, and the Moorish prostitute peered out at the men by the door as she settled her smock.

Allectus grimaced in frustration. He looked at Saturnus again. With a curse and a prayer in Greek—Allectus was a Massiliot, no more a native Briton than the Batavian Carausius—he said, "Outside, then."

Three sailors blocked the door as they tried to enter in drunken clumsiness. Normally the finance officer would have given way, even if he had his office to support him. Now he bulled through them. Anger had driven Allectus beyond good judgment; though the sailors, thank Fortune, were too loose to take umbrage.

Taut himself as a drawn bow, the Imperial agent followed the official. Maximian had sent him to procure the usurper's death. The dreams . . .

The air outside was clammy with a breeze off the river. All the way from the docks to the fort there were taverns similar to the one in which Saturnus had been told to wait: one-story buildings with thatched roofs and plaster in varying states of repair covering the post and wattle walls. The shills were somnolent tonight. Only a single guard ship remained while the Thames Squadron joined the rest of the fleet at some alert station on the Channel. Saturnus knew that the mainland emperors planned no immediate assault. He could not tell, however, whether the concentration were merely an exercise, or if it were a response to some garbled news of a threat. The threat, perhaps, that he himself posed.

There was some fog, but the moon in a clear sky gave better light than the tavern lamps in the haze of their own making. Allectus had composed himself by the time he turned to face Saturnus again. In a voice as flat and implacable as the sound of waves slapping the quay, the finance officer demanded, "Now, who are you and what do you think you're playing at?" The metal of an armored vest showed beneath Allectus's cloak as he tossed his head. His right hand was on the hilt of a hidden sword.

Saturnus laughed. The sound made Allectus jump. He was aware suddenly of his helplessness against the bigger, harder man who had accosted him. "My name doesn't matter," the agent said. "We both want a man killed. I need your help to get close to him, and you need . . ." the men looked at one another. "You were looking for a man tonight, weren't you?" Saturnus added. "A tough from the docks for a bit of rough work? Well, you found him."

The finance officer took his hand from his weapon and reached out slowly. His fingers traced the broad dimple on Saturnus's forehead. It had been left by the rubbing weight of a bronze helmet over years of service. "You're a deserter, aren't you?" Allectus said.

"Think what you like," Saturnus replied.

Allectus's hand touched the other man's cape. He raised the garment up over the agent's shoulder. Saturnus wore breeches and a tunic as coarse as the cape itself. The dagger sheathed on his broad leather belt was of uncommon quality, however. It had a silver-chased hilt and a blade which examination would have shown to be of steel watermarked by the process of its forging. The knife had been a calculated risk for the agent; but the meanest of men could have chanced on a fine weapon in these harsh times.

On the chain around Saturnus's neck was a lump of amber in a basket of gold wire. The nature of the flaw in the amber could not be determined in the light available.

Allectus let the garment flop closed. "Why?" he asked very softly. "*Why* do you want to kill Carausius?"

Saturnus touched the amber bead with his left hand. "I was at Anderida," he said.

The truth of the statement was misleading. It did not answer the question as it appeared to do. It was true, though, that in the agent's mind shimmered both his own memories and those of another mind. *Transports burned in scarlet fury on the horizon, driven back toward the mainland by the southwest wind against which they had been beating. With the sight came the crackle of the flames and, faintly—scattered by the same breeze that bore it—the smell of burning flesh. Maximian had clutched the stern rail of his flagship in his strong, calloused hands. His red cloak and those of his staff officers, Saturnus then among them, had snapped like so many pools of quivering blood. The emperor cursed monotonously. Still closer to their position in the rear guard a sail was engulfed in a bubble of white, then scarlet. Maximian had ordered withdrawal. A trumpet had keened from the flagship's bow, and horns answered it like dying seabirds.*

No one in the flagship had seen a sign of the hostile squadron. In shattered but clear images in Saturnus's mind, however, a trireme painted dark gray-green like the sea struggled with waves that were a threat to its low freeboard. The decks of the warship were empty, save for the steersmen and a great chest lashed to the bow . . . and beside the chest, the stocky figure of Carausius himself. The usurper pointed and spoke, and a distant mast shuddered upward in a gout of flame. . . .

The finance officer sagged as if he had been stabbed. "I was at Mona," he whispered. "Eight years ago. He took a chest aboard, bullion I thought, like he was going to run. But he caught the Scoti pirates and they burned. . . . He's a hero, you know? Ever since that." Allectus gave a sweep of his arm that could have indicated anything from the fort to the whole island. "To all of them. But he scares me, scares me more every day."

Saturnus felt a thrill of ironic amusement not his own. He shrugged his cape back over him. Aloud he said, "All right, we can take care of it now. They'll let me into the fort with you, won't they?"

"Now? But . . ." Allectus objected. He looked around sharply, at the empty street and the river blurred in cottony advection fog. "He's gone, isn't he? With the squadron?"

Sure with a faceted certainty where even the high official had been misled, Saturnus said, "No, Carausius is here. He sends the ships out sometimes when he doesn't want too many people around. I've been told where he is, but you'll have to get me into the fort."

The finance officer stared at Saturnus for seconds that were timeless to the agent. "If Carausius knows enough to send you to trap me," mused Allectus, "then it doesn't really matter, does it? Let's go, then." He turned with a sharp, military movement and led Saturnus up the metalled road to the fort.

The Fleet Station at London had been rebuilt by Carausius from the time he usurped the rule of

Britain. There had always been military docking facilities. Carausius had expanded them and had raised the timber fort which enclosed also the administrative center from which he ruled the island. Now only a skeleton detachment manned the gates and the artillery in the corner towers. The East Gate, opening onto the central street of the fort, was itself defended by a pair of flanking towers with light catapults. The catapults were not cocked. Their arms were upright, and the slings drooped in silhouette against the sky above the tower battlements. The bridge over the ditch had not been raised either, but the massive, iron-clad gate-leaves were closed and barred against the night.

Someone should have challenged the men as soon as they set foot on the drawbridge. Instead, Allectus had first to shout, then to bang on a gate panel with his knife hilt to arouse the watch. A pair of Frankish mercenaries finally swung open a sally port within the gateway. The Franks were surly and reeked of wine. Saturnus wondered briefly whether the finance officer's help had been necessary to get him within the fort. But the agent was inside safely, now, and a feeling of satisfaction fluttered over his skin.

Allectus looked angrily away from the guards. "All right," he said in a low voice to the agent. "What next?"

Saturnus nodded up the street, past the flanking barracks blocks to the Headquarters complex in the center of the fort. "In there," he said. He began walking up the street, leading Allectus but led himself by whispers and remembered dreams. "In the Headquarters building, not the palace."

The two central buildings were on a scale larger

than the size of the fort would normally have implied. Though the fort's troop complement was no more than a thousand men, it enclosed what amounted to an Imperial administrative center. The Headquarters building closing the street ahead of them was two-storied and almost three hundred feet to a side. Saturnus knew that beyond it the palace, which he had never seen with his own eyes, was of similar size.

The fort's interior had the waiting emptiness of a street of tombs: long, silent buildings with no sign of inhabitants. Occasionally the sound of laughter or an argument would drift into the roadway from partying members of the watch detachment. Others of the troops left behind when the squadron sailed were certainly among the few customers on the strip below the fort. Men who chanced near to Saturnus and the finance officer ducked away again without speaking. Both the men had the gait and presence of officers, and the foggy moonlight hid their rough clothes.

"How do you know this?" Allectus asked suddenly. "How do you know about—about me?"

"It doesn't matter," the agent said. He tramped stolidly along the flagstone street with his left hand clutching the bead against his chest. "Say I dreamed it. Say I have nightmares and I dreamed it all."

"It could be a nightmare," the finance officer muttered. "He must consult sorcerors to bring storms down on his enemies. He must *be* a sorceror—I've never seen any others of that sort around him."

"He's not a sorceror," Saturnus remarked grimly. "And he's not alone." "*Alone* . . ." echoed his mind.

"I can rule without sorcery," Allectus said, aloud but to himself. The agent heard. He did not respond.

The guard at the front door of the Headquarters Building was a legionary, not a barbarian from the Rhine Estuary as those in the gate-tower had been. The soldier braced to attention when he heard the pairs of boots approaching. "Who goes there?" he challenged in Latin.

"The Respectable Allectus, Chief of Imperial Accounts," the finance officer replied. "We have business inside."

The guard waited two further steps until he could visually identify the speaker. Allectus threw back his cowl to expose his face. The guard's spear clashed as he swung it to port against his body armor. "Sir!" he acknowledged with a stiff-armed salute. Then he unlatched the tall double doors before returning to attention. Saturnus watched with a sardonic smile. There were few enough units back on the mainland which could be expected to mount so sharp an interior guard. Whatever else the source of Carausius's strength, he had some first-class troops loyal to him.

"Who's the officer of the watch?" Saturnus asked.

The guard looked at him, surprised that Allectus's companion had spoken. The agent did not look to be the sort of man who entered headquarters at night. That raised the question of the way Allectus himself was dressed, but . . . "Standard-bearer Minucius, sir," the guard replied. Discipline held. It was not his business to question the authority of one of Carausius's highest officials. "You'll find him in his office."

When the big door closed behind them, it was obvious how much ambient light there had been

outside. The clerestory windows were pale bars without enough authority to illuminate the huge hall beneath them. The nave could hold an assemblage larger than the normal complement of the fort. On the south end, the tribunal was a hulking darkness with no hint of the majesty it would assume when lighted and draped with bunting.
"We'll need the officer of the watch," Saturnus remarked. He gestured.

Lamplight was showing through the columns from one of the offices across the width of the hall. "We need to get into the strongroom beneath the Shrine of the Standards."

The finance officer looked sharply at his companion. It was absurd to think that all this was a charade dreamed up by a common thief . . . absurd. "There's nothing in the strongroom but the men's private accounts," he said aloud.

Saturnus appeared to ignore the comment.

The gleam from the office was a goal, not an illumination. That did not matter to the agent. He could have walked across the building blind-folded, so often had he dreamed of it bathed in amber light. Now Saturnus strode in a revery of sorts, through the arches of the aisle and finally into the office section beyond the assembly hall. Allectus and present reality had almost disappeared from Saturnus's mind until the Standard-bearer, alerted by the sound of boots, stepped from his office behind an upraised lamp. "Who the hell are you?" the soldier demanded, groping behind him for the swordbelt he had hung over the top of the door.

Allectus stepped into the light as Saturnus paused. "Oh, *you*, sir," said the startled duty officer. "I didn't recognize your, ah, bodyguard."

"We need to check the strongroom," Allectus

said unceremoniously. He gestured with his head. "Get your keys and accompany us."

The Standard-bearer reacted first to the tone of command. He patted the ring of keys he wore on a leather shoulder-belt. Then he frowned, still touching the keys. He said, "Sir, none of that's public money, you know."

"Of course we know!" snapped Allectus. "We need to check it anyway." He did not understand the stranger's purpose, but he was not willing to be balked in any request by an underling.

"Sir, I think . . ." the Standard-bearer said in a troubled voice. "Look, the squadron should be back tomorrow or the next day at the latest. Why don't you—"

He delays us, Saturnus dreamed. His right hand swung from beneath his cape to bury the dagger to its crossguards in the pit of the soldier's stomach.

The Standard-bearer whooped and staggered backward with a look of surprise. Saturnus released the dagger-hilt in time to take the lamp before the soldier collapsed. Minucius was dead before he hit the stone floor.

Saturnus rolled the body over before he withdrew the knife. Blood followed the steel like water from a spring. None of the blood escaped the dead man's tunic and breeches to mark the stones.

"Gods," whispered the finance officer. His hand hovered short of his sword. "You just killed him!"

"We came here to kill, didn't we?" the agent reminded him bleakly. "Help me drag him back behind a pillar where he won't be noticed till morning." As Saturnus spoke, he wiped the dagger on his victim's tunic, then cut the keys loose from the belt that supported them. "Come on, for pity's sake. We haven't much time." *Time* . . . the mind in his mind repeated.

Allectus obeyed with a quickness close to panic. Vague fears and a longing for personal power had brought the finance officer to the point of murder and usurpation. Now the ordinary concerns of failure and execution to which he had steeled himself were giving way to a morass more doubtful than the original causes.

They tugged the murdered man into the empty office next to his own. Allectus then carried the lamp as he nervously followed the agent's striding figure.

The Shrine of the Standards was a small room in the center of the line of offices. It faced the main entrance across the nave, so that anyone entering the building during daylight would first see the sacred standards of the unit in their stone-screened enclosure. They were gone, now, with the squadron. The lamp threw curlique shadows across the shrine to the equally-twisted stonework on the other side. Saturnus fitted one key, then the next on the ring, until he found the one that turned the lock. His dreams were trying to speak to him, but trial and error was a better technique now than viewing the ring of keys through eyes which were knowledgeable but not his own.

Allectus sighed when the iron door swung open. Saturnus released the keys. They jangled against the lockplate. For safety's sake, the agent should have closed the door behind them. That would have disguised the fact that they were inside. He was too nervous to do so, however. The nightmare was closing on him, riding him like a raft through white water. "Come on," Saturnus said to the finance officer. He had to remember that the other man could not hear the clamor in his own mind. Saturnus bent to lift the ring-handled trap door in the center of the shrine's empty floor. "We'll need the light when we're inside."

The hinges of the door down to the strongroom were well-oiled and soundless. Saturnus did not let the panel bang open. Rather, he eased it back against the flooring. The room beneath was poorly lighted by the lamp which trembled in Allectus's hand. In any case, the strongroom was no more than a six-foot cube. It was just big enough to hold the large iron-bound chest and to give the standard-bearers room to work in their capacity as bankers for the troops of the unit. The walls of the dug-out were anchored by posts and paneled with walers of white oak to keep the soil from collapsing inward.

Saturnus used the ladder on one wall instead of jumping down as Allectus half expected. "Quietly," the agent said with exaggerated lip movements to compensate for the near silence of his command. He took the lamp from Allectus's hands.

As the finance officer climbed down into the cramped space, Saturnus put the lamp on the strongbox and drew his dagger. "Get ready," he said with a grin as sharp and cold as the point of his knife. "You're about to get your chance to be emperor, remember?"

Allectus drew his sword. The hem of his cape snagged on a reinforcing band of the strongbox. The finance officer tore the garment off with a curse. He had seen battle as a line infantryman, but that had been fifteen years before. "Ready," he said.

An ant stared at Saturnus from the wall opposite the strongbox. The creature was poised on what seemed to be a dowel rod set flush with the oak paneling. The agent's right hand held his dagger advanced. Saturnus set his left thumb over the ant and crushed the creature against the dowel that sank beneath the pressure. The whole wall pivoted inward onto a short tunnel.

With his left thumb and forefinger, Saturnus snuffed the lamp.

Allectus opened his mouth to protest. Before the whispered words came out, however, the finance officer realized that he was not in total darkness after all. The door at the tunnel's further end, twenty feet away, was edged and crossed with magenta light that slipped through the interstices of the paneling. Allectus chewed at one point of his bushy moustache. He could not see his companion until the other man stepped forward in silhouette against the hot pink lines.

For his own part, Saturnus walked in the monochrome tunnel of his mind. Light suffused the myriad facets through which he saw. He was walking toward the climax of his nightmare, the nightmare which had owned his soul ever since his parents had hung the lucky amulet of gold and amber around his neck as an infant. Unlike other well-born children, Gaius Saturnus had not dedicated the amulet with his shorn hair at age twelve when he formally became a man. The blade that would exorcize his childhood was not in the hand of a barber but rather now in Saturnus's own.

There, whispered the mind beyond Saturnus's mind as the agent's hand touched the ordinary bronze latch-lever on the further door. Saturnus had enough intellectual control over what he was about to do to check his companion's position. Allectus stood to the side and a step back. The finance officer's face would have been white had it not been lighted by the rich glow. Allectus was clear of the door's arc, however. In a single swift motion, Saturnus turned the latch and pulled the door open.

The door gave onto a room covered in swaths of ceramic-smooth substance that was itself the source of the magenta light. Carausius stood in the center of the room. Three maggots as large as men hung in the air around him with no evident support. They were vertical, save for tapered lower portions which curled under them like the tails of seahorses. To one side of the room was a large wooden box with its lid raised. The box had been built around a cocoon of the same glowing material that covered the walls. A part of the agent's mind recognized the box as the "treasure chest" which Carausius had strapped to the foredeck of the ship in which he sailed at Mona and at Anderida, where his opponents burned. The cocoon was open also, hollow and large enough to hold the maggot which began to drift soundlessly toward it.

Saturnus's amulet tingled and its commands were white fire in his brain. There were a score, a hundred ants hidden against the whorls of the magenta room. The cocoon pulsed in the myriad facets of their eyes. *The weapon* demanded the gestalt mind behind them all. *It must not turn toward you.*

The burly emperor in the center of the room gurgled like a half-drowned man recovering consciousness. He fumbled for his sword as Saturnus ignored him and leaped past.

The agent brushed the drifting maggot as it and he both made for the cocoon. The creature's skin was dry and yielding. Had Saturnus thought, he could not even have sworn that he touched a natural integument and not some sort of artificial one. He did not think. He reacted with a panicked loathing uncontrollable even by the group intelligence riding him. Saturnus cut at the maggot with the motion of a man chopping away the spider that leaped on his shoulder. There was a momentary resistance to the point. Then the steel was through in a gush and spatter of ochre fluids.

The maggot fell in on itself like a pricked bladder collapsing. It shrank to half its original size before the remainder slopped liquidly to the floor. By that time, the agent had grabbed the side of the cocoon. The object, crate and all, began to twist as if to point one of its ends toward Saturnus.

Neither of the other floating creatures was moving. Besides the way the cocoon shifted, a great lens blacker than matter started to form in place of the wall behind Carausius.

The emperor had cleared his sword as much by reflex as by conscious volition. Allectus, almost mad with fears and the impossible present, struck Carausius before the latter could parry. The blade rang on Carausius's forehead. The finance officer was no swordsman, but panic made his blow a shocking one even when the edge turned on bone and glanced away. The Emperor staggered. His sword clanged as the hilt slipped from his fingers.

Saturnus gripped the cocoon with his left hand. He could not prevent the object from turning. Like a man wrestling a crocodile, however, he kept the end from pointing toward him the way it or what controlled it desired. Then, as the dream-voices demanded, Saturnus stabbed into the spongy wall of the cocoon. His steel hissed in a dazzling iridescence. The cocoon's material boiled away from the metal, disappearing at a rate that increased geometrically as the gap expanded toward itself around its circumference.

There was a crashing sound like lightning. The box that camouflaged the cocoon from human eyes burst into flames.

Saturnus rolled back from the destruction he had caused. The blade of his dagger had warped, though its hilt was not even warm in his hand. One of the floating maggots made a sound like that of water on hot iron.

Allectus ignored the maggots as if he could thus deny their existence. The finance officer stepped between them to thrust with the full weight of his body at the reeling Carausius. His point skidded on the breastplate hidden by the Emperor's tunic. Carausius flung himself back, away from the blade. He fell into the lens and merged with the dim shape already forming there.

Carausius's whole body burned. His iron armor blazed like the heart of the sun. In its illumination, the wall began to powder and the maggots shriveled like slugs on a stove. The mind in Saturnus's mind sparkled in triumph.

Saturnus dragged Allectus back down the tunnel toward the strongroom. The agent acted by instinct rather than from any conscious desire to save the other man. The finance officer had been stunned by events and reaction to his own part in them. His skin prickled where it had been bare to coruscance a moment before, and his eyes were watering.

"What was it?" Allectus whispered. He felt his lips crack as he moved them. "What were they?"

Saturnus had been familiar since infancy with

the scene he had just lived and with a thousand variations upon that scene. "Things from far away," he said. It was the first time he had spoken to a human being about the nightmare that had ruled him for so long. "They've been helping Carausius for now, getting his support in turn for their own mission, things they need. When they were ready, more of them would come. Many more. They would smooth this world like a ball of ivory and squirm across its surface with no fellow but themselves."

"What?" mumbled Allectus. They had reached the strongroom. With Carausius gone and no one else aware of that fact, the finance minister could seize the throne himself—if he could organize his mind enough to act. The agent's words rolled off Allectus's consciousness, part of the inexplicable madness of moments before. He did not wait for Saturnus to amplify his remarks, did not *want* to hear more about things whose possible reality could be worse than human imaginings.

Saturnus paused as his human companion began to scramble up the ladder. The agent's left hand closed for the last time over the amulet on his chest. The further door of the tunnel had swung shut on the blazing carnage within. The hinges and latch glowed. As Saturnus watched, the center of the wood charred through and illuminated the tunnel harshly.

Saturnus jerked his hand down and broke the thin gold chain. The amulet was as clear in his mind as if he could see it through his clenched fist. At the heart of the amber bead was the creature trapped in pine resin sixty million years before Man walked the Earth. Trapped and preserved in sap that hardened to transparent stone. . . .

Trapped and preserved, an ant like so many billions of others in that age and in future ages. . . .

Saturnus hurled his amulet back toward the flame-shot door. A last memory remained as the amber bead left his hand. It was not the world of his nightmare, the maggot-drifting globe Saturnus had described to Allectus.

Saturnus's Roman world-view had as little concept of duration as did that of the timeless group mind to which he had so long been an appendage. *Thirty million years in the future* would have been no more than nonsense syllables to Saturnus if someone had spoken them. But he could understand the new vision that he saw. The dream-Earth crawled with the one life form remaining to it. To salute Saturnus as they left him, all the billions of six-legged units raised their antennae, under the direction of the single gestalt intelligence which had just saved the world for itself.

Then the amber bead and the vision blazed up together.

King Crocodile

The freshest of the twelve crocodile heads had been staked up only a few hours before. All twelve grinned back at Khati and the brown majesty of the Nile beyond him. In his pleasure the scarred, blocky man flexed the great shoulder muscles which had stood him in good stead when he was only a member of Nar-mer's Bodyguard. For his proven loyalty to the Great House, Khati had been picked as one of the hundreds of new stewards chosen from the army. Nar-mer had ground petty kingdoms like millet in a grain mill in his drive to the reed-choked mouths of the Nile. Now he needed trustworthy managers for the estates he had confiscated from princes and a few priesthoods—and the villages in which the new estates were located could use a loyal presence.

Many men had refused the honor and advancement, however. It meant permanent exile from the villages in the South that had been all their world before Nar-mer had made them soldiers.

Khati had his own reasons to accept and become Steward of the lands Nar-mer took from the Temple of Sebek in Usuit. The Great House hated the crocodile god and his scaly avatars; but he did not hate them as fiercely as Khati did.

"Psemthek caught this one?" Khati asked, pointing to the freshest crocodile head, that of a nine-footer. Its eyes were glazed, but they had not yet sunken into the skull.

"Psemthek and Ro," Hetep agreed. Khati's slim secretary was, like every freeman in the village but the Steward himself, a native of Usuit. His willingness to discuss his neighbors would have made the young servant invaluable to Khati even without his ability to read and write. "They were born together, they farm together—they stood their turn catching crocs together, of course. Ro's married and Psemthek isn't, but there's some stories about that, too."

"I heard them shouting when they carried the carcase into town," Khati said. "Heard their neighbors cheering them, too. There'll be a feast, of course, since the meat won't keep . . . but it's more than that. People are really glad there's one less crocodile. It means that in my three months in Usuit, I've done what the Great House wanted done here . . . and what I wanted. People don't bow to Sebek's children, they don't pray to them, *sacrifice—*"

Khati caught himself before the words began to tumble out. The sweat was bright on his forehead. After a moment's silence the thickset Southerner forced out a little chuckle, as if fury had not been about to don his flesh like a garment. The laugh rattled. It was as unnatural as a skeleton dancing. "Now they can set out hooks for crocodiles," Khati continued in a normal voice. "It's just another duty to the Great House. It's a little easier than chopping reeds in the irrigation canals; and besides, there's a lot of meat for you and your friends if you're lucky enough to bring one in. Bring in one of the filthy, man-slaying vermin. . . ."

Hetep cleared his throat experimentally. "Psemthek'll probably be inviting you to their feast. Do you want to go, or . . . ?"

"Umm, right," Khati said. "I used to eat crocodile, back—home. Occasionally. Didn't particularly like it, too much sulphur aftertaste even when it's fresh. But I couldn't eat it now. There's the Council meeting tonight anyway. Go on back, make amends for me, and fix me the usual supper at the house. I'll be along in good time." Khati's eye fell on the bundle of mats and jars at the edge of the bank. He added, "Oh—you might remind the fellows that they left their gear here when they carried the meat back."

Hetep nodded and began trotting along the path, bare feet flashing in the sun. A good man, Khati thought, though he'd been associated with the Temple of Sebek until Nar-mer had confiscated the lands. Perhaps Khati ought to learn more about his secretary. . . .

When Khati looked back, he blinked to see the priest Nef-neter standing beside the staked heads. The priest's gray beard was neatly trimmed and tufted beneath the wrappings of gold wire. That gold and the priest's scarab ring were the only remaining signs of the affluence he had known when the Temple of Sebek was the largest landholder in Usuit. Now the Temple had no property but that on which it stood, a room of mud bricks on a hummock in the marsh.

"You won't stop this sacrilege of your own accord, will you?" Nef-neter said. His voice was so calm as to be arrogant.

"Twelve in three months," Khati replied, letting his growing anger move words instead of the muscles bulging over his torso. "Hooked deep in the guts, then pounded on till their brains squirted out their ears." That was exaggerated, but Khati was using his tongue as a weapon—as both men understood perfectly.

"I wonder," the priest mused aloud, "just what it would take to get you to end this—foulness." He was twisting the scarab ring on his thumb, heavy silver set with a gray-green stone so lustrous that it mimicked translucence.

Khati touched his own thonged amulet, a lapis lazuli carving of Hequit, the frog goddess of his home village. "You could have a god come down and order me to stop, Nef-neter," he said. "Then I'd think about it. For now, what I've thought about is your labor duty for the Great House. From here on out, you'll man a hook and line every day—until you've killed a crocodile yourself."

Still Nef-neter refused to bust out in anger. "The others have had the choice of—" the priest's lips moved silently, then continued—"*that* sacrilege, or the usual work. Cutting reeds, repairing the dikes."

"And you don't," Khati agreed, replying to the unspoken question. "Besides that, nobody's going to bring you food any more. I know they've been doing that and I haven't stopped it; but I'll stop it now. You don't eat anything but what you scavenge from the marsh until you've brought in a crocodile—*priest*."

Nef-neter had already begun walking back to

his hut. "I'll take you at your word, councilor," he replied quietly over his shoulder.

The ex-guardsman scowled as he stalked away. He didn't have the authority to give those orders alone, only the Village Council as a whole did; but Khati had the right to name or replace the other councilors. Right of conquest, in Nar-mer's name. The right that made Khati, a Southerner with no property of his own, the superior of every other man in Usuit. Khati was sparing of his power—he knew that if he pushed too hard, well . . . any man could die on his sleeping bench with a wadded cloak pressed over his airways. But in this one thing he would not be balked.

Ahead of Khati lay Anpu's shipyard, built on fertile land near the water. The yard justified its location with its profits. Its existence slightly diminished the food supply that was the life of the whole region, but Anpu and his three sons lived very well indeed.

The yard was alive with the sound of chattering tools. On the ground sat a circle of a dozen slaves, each holding a bundle of split reeds with his feet. By stuffing additional splits into the unwrapped ends of the bundles, the workmen formed solid cones of papyrus. When the individual bundles were complete, they would be joined into fishermen's skiffs or even larger vessels to carry trade and rich men up and down the Nile.

But Anpu's endeavors were not limited to the reed boats of past ages. Using wood imported from regions where it was less scarce, he and his most skilled craftsmen were building one of a series of large, hollow-bellied vessels. Such wooden ships were able to venture safely even into the salt sea north of the Delta and come back laden with cedar and unguents and ores. They were responsible for most of Anpu's wealth and the fact that his name was well-known beyond the boundaries of the district.

The main path from the river to the village proper ran beside the boatyard. As Khati turned onto it, the pattern of stone tools thudding and clicking changed. The Steward looked up. Anpu stood at his bench, his flint adze resting on the rib he had been shaping. He was a stout, dark man with muscles formed and hardened by decades of labor no less heavy than it was skilled. His flat, beard-fringed features could never have been handsome, but they were further disfigured by a fresh scar on his nose. It had been left by the hook which had held him in Nar-mer's slave gang. Anpu's wealth had not kept him from being conscripted by Mekhit, his king, for the army which first faced the Southerners' slashing advance. In the aftermath of that campaign, Anpu's sons had ransomed their father, preserving him from ritual execution or a short, brutal life in a distant holding of the Great House. Nothing, however, could take back the humiliation of the hook.

From other parts of the yard, the faces of Anpu's sons now mirrored their father's scowl. The slaves kept to their tasks, afraid to call a greeting but unwilling to glower at the enemy of their owner. Khati felt the touch of the god tense his grip on the mace he now carried only as a symbol of authority. He had met Anpu's sort, perhaps the shipwright himself, in the blood-blinding haze of that afternoon. Mekhit's line had been bright with standards and metal-edged weapons. For all that, it had shattered like chaff from the millet when Khati's mace flailed into it.

He was no longer guardsman of the Great House, but rather the Steward in Usuit; and Anpu was Second Councilor and richest man in the village entrusted to Khati's care. There was no point in wishing for the return of the old, simple days of force and slaughter, for they would not return here if Khati did his duty as he was expected to.

Besides, it could be that Anpu had better and more personal reasons to hate Khati than anything that had happened in the past.

The fields spread to either side of the narrow path. They were dusted green with the first shoots of millet and studded with the stooped bodies of the men and women cultivating the grain. The raised walls of irrigation ditches laid the cropland out into narrow strips and allowed the owners to survey the fields during the floods without wading. The folk called cheerful greetings which Khati returned as he walked toward the village itself. The houses were built on the higher ground to the west, beyond the floods' reach and thus infertile. The Steward realized how fortunate he was that Usuit's first season under his leadership promised to be a good one for crops.

Most of the villagers were still in the fields, so the single row of houses beyond seemed quiet. Psemthek and Ro, however, had gathered a coterie of idlers and servants around them in the low-walled forecourt of Councilor Besh's house. The councilor's wife ran a tavern there as a sideline to her husband's landholdings. Khati waved as he passed the group. Ro, taller and a few minutes older than his brother, broke off in the middle of a song and tried to stand. When he slumped back on the adobe bench, his cup sloshed a swallow or two of the fresh, potent barley beer.

Psemthek cursed his brother blearily. Ro called in good humor, "Come on over tonight, Khati. Have a drink and help us eat Sebek."

Khati only waved again, smiled, and walked on.

"If you won't drink beer with Ro, perhaps you'll have a cup of water here?" called a musical voice from Anpu's house.

Khati looked up, a smile forming of its own accord. The courtyard walls were six feet high, but the gate only came up to Anit's shoulders and framed her head in the opening. Anpu's second wife was younger than his sons by the first. Her father had been an official in the court of Mekhit. Nar-mer's conquest had beggared the family, so the shipwright had picked up Anit as a bargain. And then again. . . .

"My husband just sent up a jar drawn from the center of the channel," Anit added, nodding her head to emphasize its coiffure of ringlets and pins. "Cold and clear."

"Umm," Khati mumbled, glancing westward as if to judge the sun's height.

Anit swung the gate toward her to open it. She was wearing a richly-embroidered kilt instead of the plain linen Khati would have expected. Also, she had rouged her bare nipples. She smiled. "You're sure you wouldn't prefer beer anyway?" she asked.

"Ah, no. . . ." Khati was frozen, one foot raised to step through the gateway.

"What's the matter?" Anit asked. Then, no longer coy, she added, "Are you afraid?"

"Of failing," Khati said. He was suddenly calmer. The question had clarified what was going on in his mind. "The Great House thought I could run a village for him. I've got to work with a lot of other people if I'm going to succeed. Your husband doesn't like me, but we can work together. Now." He reached out gently and pulled the door shut. "I'll come drink with you some evening when the rest of your family's home," he said.

It was hard to tell what thoughts were going on behind Anit's calm face. Her right index finger was drawing a small X in the rouge on her cheek.

As he walked off, Khati said, "I'll see you tonight at the council meeting."

It was already getting late. Women were scurrying down the street with last-minute purchases for the meals they would shortly cook. Occasionally a laborer with shouldered hoe trudged toward house or tavern. Those who passed Khati exchanged friendly waves with him. The Steward's house was on the far south end of the village. Two stone pillars framed the gate. They had been systematically defaced, but Khati spat at the nearer one anyway. When Khati replaced Nef-neter as the dwelling's resident, the gateposts had been carven crocodiles.

"Good, good, I was beginning to think I should have told the cook to wait," called Hetep from within the house. "Will you eat inside or out?"

"Oh, bring me a plate out here, I suppose," Khati replied. "But bring me a wash-bowl first. My skin always crawls after I talk to Nef-neter."

Hetep chuckled as he brought out a flat bowl of water and, across his forearm, a linen towel. "I don't know that you're fair to him," the younger man said. "Want wine with the meal?"

"Yeah—no, wait, not with the council meeting tonight. Just water, I suppose." Khati was dipping his mug full from the wide-mouthed jar in the shade when his servant returned with fresh bread and a savory dish of pork and leeks. "You were a servant in this house before I came, weren't you?" the steward asked abruptly.

Hetep set his platter carefully on the table. "That's right. Though originally the house was mine. Well, my mother's." The younger man looked at his master. "But perhaps you already know that story?"

Khati squatted down at the low table and began eating. "Not a word of it. Have a seat and tell me. And draw yourself some beer—*you* don't have a cursed meeting to go to."

Hetep dipped a mug of water and squatted across the table from Khati. "My father died before I was born," he said. "Mother turned to the temple for help, for running the estate, for raising me. She made me a ward of the temple if anything should happen to her."

"The temple. Sebek."

"The god Sebek," Hetep agreed. "And so, since . . . a crocodile took her in the river when I was five, Nef-neter raised me. He would have liked me to become his acolyte, I think, but he never forced me. When he saw that I really didn't have the vocation, he had me trained as his steward instead." The young man smiled. "So now I'm the steward of the Steward of the Great House. A rather diluted majesty, but a pleasant life for all that."

Khati paused and looked at his servant. "You could—live in the house of the beast that killed your mother?"

"For fifteen years Nef-neter was a friend to me," Hetep answered quietly. "I don't turn on friends because I—dislike their gods."

Khati let his anger pass slowly. "That's a good

way to be," he said, and he spooned more of the pork into his mouth.

Hetep brought out a small harp. He began singing the melancholy songs of farmers and boatmen and lovers. War and human conflicts eased from the courtyard. Khati smiled at the younger man in appreciation, but he said nothing until Hetep began to croon about a girl whose love crowned her like the flowers do the reeds.

"Not that," Khati snapped.

Hetep's fingers melded the chords into others as gracefully as if he had planned to do so. "Why not?" he asked.

Khati stared at the calm young face across the table from him. "Because my wife used to sing that to me," he said at last. "It was her favorite, I guess."

The secretary continued to stroke a soothing background from his harp. His lips were silent, but his eyes probed mildly until Khati said, "She died while I was on campaign. She wasn't too pregnant yet that she couldn't help set the fishing weirs. A crocodile got her." The scarred guardsman took a deep breath. "They caught the beast a few days later and beat it to death. But it's a big river. There's enough of the vermin in it to keep me busy the rest of my life."

"Men aren't supposed to understand the gods," Hetep said, "but it may be that gods do the most good when they least seem to." Then he swung into a Delta lyric about ducks in the reeds and the mist that rises from the river at dawn. Hetep was still singing when Khati reached over and squeezed his shoulder in comradeship. Then the steward walked out of the courtyard, down the nighted street toward Anpu's house and the council meeting.

Psemthek and Ro, the latter still trying to sing as the pair of them stumbled toward their gate, met Khati in the street. "Councilor!" Psemthek shouted, "come have a drink now!"

Khati saw the gate quiver ajar, displaying the worried face of Psemthek's wife—or was she Ro's? The panel closed again. A servant, too drunk to carry his lamp lighted, straggled behind the brothers.

"Psemthek!" Ro gasped before Khati could beg off again. "We didn't fetch the gear from the riverbank!"

"So?"

"There was beer left!"

Without a further word, the two men turned and began pacing determinedly back toward the track to the river.

"Hey!" Khati called, "You'll fall in a ditch and drown!"

The brothers ignored him. One of them had started to sing again. The steward shook his head and continued on his way. A moment after he had passed Ro's house, the gate opened. The woman he had seen before slipped out, cloaked and cowled. She did not look at Khati as she followed after her man—or men—at a discrete distance. Khati smiled. It was not only the gods who looked after drunken men.

Because of the numbers sometimes attending, Village Council meetings were held in the courtyards of councilors' houses. Councilors Senti and Besh, both of them large landholders, were already talking to Anpu when Khati entered. A scattering of citizens with petitions huddled against the inner walls, waiting to be called on at the council's pleasure. As Khati swung the gate closed behind him it was caught with a querulous squeal by Sanekht the brickmaker. Sanekht, the fifth member of Council, was an ancient man with a twisted body and a mind far gone in mushy senility as well.

Khati apologized to Sanekht, then nodded to the others present. He took his seat at the center of the low bench across the courtyard from the gate. The other four councilors sat down without delay. Hornef, the scribe, cleaned his pen and poised it over a fresh roll of papyrus.

"The third channel's important to more than just *my* farm," Senti continued to Anpu in a lower voice than before, "and as grown up as it is, only about half the water that should be is getting through it. We need—"

"Call to order," Khati grunted. He raised the millet cake and beer mug set out for the purpose. "First," he prayed, "we thank the gods for the past well-being of our village, and we pray for their continued indulgence."

The gate creaked open. All eyes in the courtyard turned from Khati to the thin figure of Nefneter, framed by the posts. "Do you thank *all* the gods, councilor?" the old priest demanded. "Are you willing to end your blasphemy, then?"

The rage poured into Khati and shackled his tongue. The beer began to tremble in the libation mug. From a long distance away he heard Anpu saying, "You're out of order! Sit down until you're called!" Two of the shipwright's husky sons were moving toward the intruder.

"One moment further!" Nef-neter said. "You think to offend Sebek, and of course you do. But remember that Chaos itself sometimes takes the form of a crocodile. Repent while you still have time and—"

The mug shattered in Khati's hand, beer spurting in a high arc as the steward's grip pulverized the earthenware. Khati stood. "Get him out," he croaked, pointing with fingers that wanted to twist around a mace hilt, "or—"

Anpu's sons grasped Nef-neter by both arms. They hustled him back into the street. The priest's scarab ring winked in the lamplight. The old man looked neither surprised nor discomposed, merely patient as if he were a statue in the hands of workmen.

"I've warned you," he said. His body stiffened.

The double scream was loud, even though it came all the way from the riverbank. No one in the courtyard moved. A hacking bellow deep as distant thunder swelled over the screams, drowning them and leaving only silence when it passed on.

Khati was the first man through the gate, shouldering the priest aside as he moved. The steward had carried his mace to the meeting as a symbol of authority. Now it was in his hands and a weapon again, polished and quick to crush the skulls of the enemies of the Great House. Khati's feet found the path to the river as much by memory as by the light of the thin moon. Behind him he could hear others coming, cumbered by fear and whatever arms they could snatch up in an instant.

Someone was stumbling toward him from the river. Khati braced himself in the center of the narrow path and cried, "Hold it right there!"

The figure sank down. "Sebek," a woman's voice moaned. "The god took them both!" It was Ro's wife, utterly distraught. She had lost the cape she had worn as she left her house.

Khati pushed on by her, running the rest of the way to the river. It had happened on the bank very near the shipyard. One of the brothers—the light was too dim for identification, even though the face was undamaged—lay scattered across the path and reeds. Huge clawed foot-prints—how large they were Khati refused for the moment to recognize—had trampled the ground and crushed the victim's torso. The head and limbs lay each at a little distance from the body, joined by pseudopods of the great central blood-splash. All the pieces seemed to be present.

There was no sign of the other brother.

Khati knelt, looking at the track scraped through the reeds. Men came running up behind him. Anpu was among the first. He carried the only metal weapon in the village, a copper-bladed spear with sharp edges and a point like an asp's tongue.

"What happened?" the shipwright demanded.

"The god came!" wept the woman in the background. "The god took my men!"

Khati morosely traced a footprint with his index finger. Even the webbing between the digits had been impressed in the blood-softened earth. He said nothing.

From the darkness Ro's wife continued to cry, "The crocodile god took them!"

The murmur of the crowd had begun before dawn as villagers began to gather in front of Khati's house. The sound had grown with the number of those waiting. Now it had the sibilance and power of the air before a windstorm rips out of the western desert. Only once before had Khati seen the whole population of Usuit assembled: on the day he had arrived and announced Nar-mer's initial edicts for the village.

That day Khati had been backed by a company of the Bodyguards of the Great House. Now he was alone except for Hetep, who brought his master a breakfast of milk and figs—and did not mention that the other servants had left the house.

Khati eyed the wall. It would be wide enough to stand on. He thumbed toward it and said, "Give me a lift, Hetep. If I've got to talk to them all, I want them to hear me."

The younger man nodded solemnly and locked his hands into a yoke for his master's foot. Khati stepped onto the hands and lurched upward, drawing himself erect atop the wall in a single motion.

"People of Usuit!" he roared. Gods, there were thousands of eyes on him. But they weren't hostile, not yet. It was just that they'd come to him for an answer to the spiritual catastrophe which had struck the village. And he'd damned well better have an answer. . . . "Today, I'm going to lead a party out on the river. We'll hunt the crocodile that attacked Psemthek and Ro last night."

The crowd sucked in its collective breath, an awe-struck antistrophe to Khati's words. From his vantage point, the steward could see Anpu and his family near the front of the plain of faces. Senti, Besh, and even old Sanekht were close by too. Khati's shadow carpeted a long track across his audience in the light of the rising sun.

"That's if it hasn't run away and hid already," Khati continued. "They're slimy cowards, those beasts, and they'll run from a village of brave folk like this one. But if it's still here, we'll smash its skull and drag it ashore to spit on, me and your other councilors." *That* brought some unexpected interest, Khati thought grimly. "The Council will meet here to make final plans. We'll send for a few volunteers to fill out the crew. I want all the rest of you to go home, now, go back to work. Otherwise you'll be in the way of our taking care of this skulking vermin."

"My people," another voice cried, "repent of this madness!"

There was a sudden space in the dense crowd, setting Nef-neter apart like a negative halo. Fear marked the surrounding faces, but not the hatred Khati knew was warping his own countenance into something hellish as he gazed down at the priest.

"Your sins have brought Chaos down on you," the priest said, his arms high, his scarab blinking, "but there is still hope if you—"

"Vermin!" Khati shouted, feeling the god starting to don his form. He gestured with his clenched fist, roped to his body with sinews that ridged and rippled the dark skin. "A word, a word more and your head will be on a pole while we use your body for bait!"

Nef-neter fell silent. He was a priest, after all. Perhaps he could see that it was no man but a god of fury that stood splay-legged addressing him.

"Now go!" Khati ordered the crowd. "All but the Council."

They were streaming away even as Khati leaped back within his courtyard. His flesh was trembling so that Hetep, who had just opened the gate to a giggling Sanekht, reached out an arm to steady his master.

Anpu was close behind the brickmaker. "What sort of a joke is this?" he demanded. His white nose scar stood out the brighter when his face was flushed. "How is paddling up and down the river going to help rid us of that crocodile?"

"Wait till the others are here," Khati answered, too weak to be other than calm.

The shipwright's family had entered with him, his three lowering sons and his wife who was younger than the youngest of the sons. Anit's hair-do was simpler than before, though pins of horn and ivory still set off the rich black of it. She wore no make-up this morning. Her naked eyes were more intimate, her breasts more tender.

Senti and Besh were together but otherwise unaccompanied. Hetep closed the gate behind them and barred it.

"Anpu, we'll need a boat," Khati said without preliminaries. He was master of his body again and master, he thought, of the problem as well. "A good-sized one, something impressive. We'll take nets, spears; maybe twenty men, that'll be enough for the show."

"The crocodile isn't going to come and meet us, you fool!" Anpu burst out. "We'll only be wasting our time and stirring up a little of the bottom mud."

"That's right," Khati agreed easily, "but it's not a waste of time." Surprise tinged the faces turned toward him.

"The crocodile is real," he explained, "but it wasn't here before. You all saw the size of the prints, that wasn't something we'd have overlooked if it'd been any while in the district." He'd phrased that wrong. The expressions of the others proved they had indeed seen the blood-soaked prints and that they would rather not have been reminded of them. "If it came here, it'll leave again. It's just like a flood, it comes but it doesn't stay. What we're going to do is go out on the water and prove that it's safe to the others who don't understand these things. Otherwise nobody'll go fishing, nobody'll work the fields for months, and we'll lose half the crop for nothing."

"It'll have dragged old Ro down into its den," Sanekht chuckled. He slobbered a little, then wiped the spittle into a smear of mud with his unwashed hands. "Let him get good and ripe for a while before it eats him. Maybe a week before it needs to go hunting again. Course, to fill a belly *that* big it might take—"

"When it comes out again, it'll leave!" Khati said loudly to silence the old man. "Now, who else do we take in the boat?"

"It's already too hot," Besh grumbled, putting his shoulder against the boat. The vessel slid a foot further down the bank and hung up again. "We should've waited till afternoon."

"A pass up and down the river now'll convince people to get themselves back to the fields," Khati grunted behind him. Only half the twenty crewmen were wading through the muddy shallows to launch the craft. Nar-mer's steward did not care to make an issue of the others' reluctance. The men had agreed to join what they thought was a dangerous enterprise, and that was an offer he would not have been able to compel in peacetime. Anpu and his sons were on the shore too; but that was arrogance and not fear.

And after all, Anpu had provided the boat. Its bow was now bobbing free on the brown water. The hull was papyrus. Sanekht had repeated with senile insistance that, "Crocodiles won't touch a papyrus boat," and no one else had seen a reason to argue with the old man. The frapped ends of the vessel spired up higher than a man could stand, and there was a reed deck-house just forward of the steering oar. Apart from those embellishments, the vessel was thirty feet of clumsy artifice with thicker bulwarks than its hull cavity justified. Even Anpu seemed to look with scorn at his creation. The shipwright stood like a toad erect, his bright-bladed spear a slim tower beside him.

The stern of the boat floated free. "Start loading," Khati called. "Some of you on shore bring the nets and spears, will you?"

While those who had launched the craft held it steady, the most fearful of the men on shore scampered through the shadowed water and rolled aboard. Anpu and his sons followed more deliberately, the muddy Nile slapping their calves but not the kilts bound high on their loins. As the shipwright braced himself to board, Khati said, "Let me borrow your spear while we're at this. It'll look more impressive than my flint will."

Anpu's scar blazed. "Let your king give you a metal blade—if he thinks that you're worth it. Or buy the copper yourself. You won't touch what's mine. Not a *thing* that's mine!" He climbed the fat gunwale.

"Then you'll plant your ass in the bow and use your damned toy if we *do* find something!" Khati snapped.

Anpu looked down coldly at the steward. He shuffled forward without a reply.

Leather thongs had been woven into the papyrus bundles to serve as oarlocks. Khati took one of the bow oars. Hetep knelt beside him at the other. The sycamore thwart was not wide enough for the steward's broad shoulders and those of another man as well, but Khati had been in the Bodyguard too long to take a place farther back where the belly swelled and gave more room. Even though it was no battle they were about to enter. . . .

"Pull!" called Huni, a fisherman chosen as steersman in the hope that he would not ground them ignominiously on a mudbank. Khati pulled, fouling his oar with that of the man kneeling before him. He started to curse but realized there was no point in it; they were not a trained crew, only a symbol.

Huni sent them downriver a quarter mile or so, smoothly enough. Then he ordered the boat about. They began to stagger south again against the current. The oars rubbed in places that agricultural implements did not. Men began to mutter as their skin sloughed.

"Bring her up to the end of the fields and then head'er in," Khati ordered. The morning mist had been burned from the water, leaving the surface that remained a bronze mirror reflecting the sun. Besh had been right: they should have waited for a cooler hour. But from the houses above the cropland, people were watching. Now and again a figure carrying a hoe or bird-switch walked carefully down into the fields.

Khati glanced over his left shoulder, catching in the corner of his eye the determined sternness of Anpu posing in the bow. Jutting from the reeds was the hillock bearing the linen-swathed Altar of Sebek, a triangular block as high as a man's thighs. The rude hut in which Nef-neter lived had been thrown up beside the altar after Nar-mer confiscated the house in the village. Worship had always been at the altar site, however, despite the mud and insects there, despite the wealth that had been available to raise a temple west of the fields—or at least clear of the marsh.

"All right, let's swing her," Khati called.

Anpu shouted, "Wait!"

All the oarsmen paused. Khati muttered under his breath and twisted. His shoulder bumped Hetep's. The younger man leaned aside. Ahead of them the opaque water was shadowed from beneath in a blur as long as the boat, and the shadow was coming nearer. The tendons of Anpu's legs swelled beneath the skin as the shipwright poised his spear to thrust with both hands.

One of Anpu's sons stood up amidships, rocking the craft dangerously. "Sit down, you soul-burned fool!" Khati snarled back at him. The guardsman was groping beside him for the shaft of his spear. He did not take his eyes off the huge blotch in the river. "Hetep," he said, "slide back out of my—"

The water sluiced over the bony scutes of a head more than a yard long. Behind it, the whole length of the crocodile was breaking surface. Its tail was bent in a flat S which shot the body forward faster than the boat could have been rowed to escape. Khati saw the flaps which had closed the nostrils flare open as the snout raised. The beast's gums were white except for the dark mottlings where leeches writhed among the great teeth.

Anpu squawked like a hen in a civet's jaws. He drove his spear downward. The burnished copper struck the reptile between its dilated nostrils. The metal bent back like a plaintain leaf. The shipwright dropped his weapon and cried out again, this time in certain fear and no defiance. Khati grabbed Anpu's sash in his left hand to keep the squat man from falling backwards.

The armored head glided over the bulwark and

a black-clawed foreleg slashed at Anpu. The veins were bright in the webbing where the skin stretched wide between the digits. Khati balanced his spear to jab at the eye glowing like mother-of-pearl beneath its membrane. The other forelimb reached into the boat and the bow plunged under tons of the reptile's weight. Something green flashed among the horny claws and the blood spraying from Anpu's thigh. The sash tore and the shipwright pitched forward, over the monster that was tearing at him.

When the crocodile slipped back, the boat broached like a leaping dolphin. It threw Khati into a tangle of Hetep and four other oarsmen. An anchor-stone clacked against the base of his skull, dimming into pale pastels the colors of everything he saw. The guardsman struggled to his knees, regardless of the shouting men around him. He still gripped his spear.

Anpu was floundering naked in the water. The jaws rose straight up on either side of his waist. They were twin wedges armed with three-inch teeth. The shipwright screamed. His scarred nostrils were as white as the gums closing about him. Soundlessly, the crocodile sank back into the river. Anpu continued to scream until the brown water frothed across his face. It bubbled once more, turning red as it quieted.

A harp had been playing, cool and thin in the evening breeze. Now it seemed to have stopped. Khati raised up carefully from the reed mattress on which he had flung himself as soon as he reached his house. His head still buzzed with gall and the blow it had taken from the anchor.

"Hetep!" the steward called. His voice cracked. The house was dark and close and still. "Gods grind his bones," Khati murmured as he stood and walked out into the lamplit courtyard.

Hetep was there on a bench by the gate. His harp was in his hands, but he fingered it so gently that the strings were silent. When he felt Khati's eyes, he jumped up. "Master?" he said.

The night beyond the walls breathed.

"Where are they?" Khati demanded.

Hetep dipped up a gourd full of water and waited for Khati to drink. Then he said, "They're out at the altar, I suppose."

Khati flung the gourd. It clacked on the hard soil, leaving a dark zig-zag in the dust. "Suppose! Suppose! You know they're out there, praying to that foulness!"

The close-coupled guardsman stalked to the gate and into the street beyond. He did not bother to close the panel behind him. The back of his head prickled as hairs twitched in the dried blood which Hetep had been unable to sponge wholly away while Khati slept.

"Khati," the younger man said urgently, "let them be. They won't bother you, they don't dare to. If you . . . disappeared, the Great House would just send another steward and crush a dozen skulls while he was at it."

The narrow track that wound from the house that had been Nef-neter's to the altar in the reeds was steeply slanted. Behind Khati, his servant's voice continued, "They need you for appearances. And it doesn't matter what people want to pray to, not if the taxes come in and the king gets his labor quotas—"

"Shut up!"

"Master, they won't kill you, you're killing your—"

"*Shut up*!" Khati snarled, turning toward Hetep for the first time since he left the house. "*You* can watch babies wrapped in flowers and laid out in the reeds for Sebek—if you want. *You* can watch parents kiss the snouts of the creatures fat and stinking with the flesh of their children, watch them pray, 'Greatest god, spare me again this coming year; but if you chose me from your waters, what ecstasy!' I'm going to die some day no matter what; and I'll die before I watch that happen!"

"Master," Hetep said to the guardsman's back. "I didn't go with the rest of them."

Khati paused in mid-stride. He turned again. "Maybe you should have," he said. "My friend."

The only illumination was the moon and a pair of rushlights on the covered altar. The flickering tallow was more to mark Nef-neter than to brighten the scene. The priest was speaking in thin-lipped triumph from the mound. The silent mob that had greeted Khati at his house in the morning now faced the slim priest of Sebek in a great half-circle. Those at the back could not hear the words, but they moaned responsively with the ones nearer the front. Many were in mud to their knees, holding their smallest children and oblivious to the bites of insects still unsated with their blood.

There were a few scowls, a few curses as Khati began to shoulder his way through the crowd. Then people looked at his face and swept back, still-voiced, from the steward's advance. In his wake the villagers eddied, unwilling to close too swiftly the gap Khati had plowed among them. It was as if a pasture had been sundered by the advance of a young challenger, striding straight and fiery-eyed toward the eminence on which the herd bull awaited him.

Nef-neter pointed at his rival. "God's will *shall* be done, whatever the wishes of men!" the priest roared to the crowd. They moaned worshipfully.

Khati pushed up to the firmer ground of the hillock. He stepped through the last row of villagers, two paces from the altar. One of the inner circuit of listeners was Anit, her coiffure ragged with inattention. Anpu's sons flanked her.

Nef-neter glared from behind the altar as if it were a breastwork against Khati's charge. The flames were mushy daggers to either side of the old man's face. "Why do you defy a god?" he demanded loudly.

The steward turned his back on the priest and his covered altar. It was no physical attack he feared. The villagers were spread in a broad fan, a moraine of humanity spilling down the mound. None of them was any closer to the river than the altar-stone itself was. "My people!" Khati shouted, "what madness drives you to worship this belly-crawling filth?"

There was no sound from the crowd. Then, from behind Khati, came a bellow that was not of man or of men.

Khati turned without speaking, already aware that he had lost. A dull, boat-huge torso rose from the surface of the river fifty yards away. Reeds and their fellows kept most of the villagers from seeing the crocodile, but no one could be in any doubt as to what had appeared. It was the dark epiphany of a god.

Nef-neter was silent and so motionless that only the reflected flames moved on his eyeballs. The crocodile made another sound, more of a grunt this time than a roar because its jaws were gripping something. Water sprayed high as the beast thrashed.

"Oh, aye, they don't have teeth that can cut like a dog's," mumbled somebody nearby in the crowd—was it old Sanekht? "That's why they like meat to get ripe, so when they twist it— "

The crocodile's wedge-shaped skull slashed sideways and up like a slinger's arm. The river exploded in white foam. Something sailed up and away from the burden still gripped in the terrible jaws. The missile plunged past the frozen priest. It slammed one of the rushlights from the altar before spinning into the crowd.

In the river, the crocodile had sunk again. Anit was struggling to her knees, her left hand gripping by the hair the object that had knocked her to the ground. Only the scarred nostrils served to identify Anpu's head. The neck, savaged by great conical teeth, had parted under the whiplash shock of the crocodile's jaws. As if he were dreaming, Khati saw the young woman reach back into her hair-do and come out of it with an ivory pin in her hand, six inches long and pointed. It had been carven in the shape of a crocodile. Anit's dainty hand covered the grinning jaws, but the jutting tail glinted as she drove it toward the steward's throat with a scream.

Hetep stepped in front of her, his body locking hers as his right hand drew her arm back and loosened its grip on the weapon. Untouched, Khati fell full-length on the ground. Beyond him, he heard Nef-neter cry, "Lord Sebek!" and the crowd give back the cry a thousandfold, "Lord Sebek! Lord Sebek!"

Then there was nothing but the dark.

* * *

Sunlight and Hetep's worried face greeted Khati when he opened his eyes. The servant's air of concern amused Khati, because he himself was calm. He had thought he could rule this village for the Great House; events had proved him wrong. But Khati was still of the Royal Bodyguard. He could find a way to die with honor.

"Any breakfast handy?" Khati asked with a smile.

Hetep blinked in amazement. "Something, sure. Shall I bring it now?"

"Right. And then set out my best clothes. I want to make a good impression."

After his bowl of barley-and-cheese porridge, Khati went back into his bedroom. There, in a narrow alcove covered by a hanging of embroidered linen, Khati kept his weapons. Although the smooth-headed mace had always been the tool he best wielded when the god wore his flesh, there were also six javelins in the alcove. Khati chose a pair of them, short-shafted throwing weapons with three-inch flint points. He carried the weapons into the courtyard with him. Using his strength and a saw whose stone blade was set in a wooden back, Khati cut each shaft six inches behind the head. When Hetep, still frowning, had brought a bobbin of stout flaxen cord, Khati bound the shafts side by side with the wicked flint points jutting out to either end.

"You're going to bait that and hope the crocodile catches it in its throat?" Hetep ventured.

"Something like that."

"I don't see how it can work," the younger man added after a pause.

"Well, it may not," the guardsman agreed. He had buffed his limbs with a mixture of oil and sand. A slight sheen from the oil danced over his skin even after he scraped himself off with an ebony strigil.

"Well, what're you going to bait it with?" Hetep asked.

"Me." Khati began dressing. His best kilt that he would not leave for another man. The fillet with three red-dyed kite feathers marking him a champion of champions, death in human guise.

"Khati, you can't do this to yourself! Just by being here you've made people aware that—" Hetep looked at his master's eyes, his friend's, and the words stopped.

Khati left his papyrus sandals—they would be in the way of his paddling—and his mace. He thrust his knife through the sash of his kilt, however. Like the strigil, it was of ebony. Even so dense a wood would not take a useful edge, but neither would the blade shatter as flint might against a skull or a chief's bangles of shell and turquoise. In his time, Khati had slammed the point through ribs, withdrawn it, and thrust it in again. The memory turned his thoughts red, and he began to tremble slightly.

Hetep followed him out of the house. "At least tell me what I can do to help," he begged.

Khati smiled wryly. "You can tell the next man the Great House sends here what happened to me." The servant opened his mouth to protest, but Khati cut him off. "Believe me, if there were another way I could see for you to help, I'd ask you. I'm not a saint, and I want that—creature—dead more than anything else in this life or the next." He looked at Hetep. "More even than I want to die now myself. But this is going to work alone if it works at all. You'll be a lot more useful in the future."

"If they let me," Hetep said.

"Then run, get out now!" snapped Khati. "I'm sorry, but if I knew a way to change things I'd already have done it!"

Hetep sighed. "I'll be back at the house," he said quietly. "I'll have dinner ready when you get home."

The shipyard was closed, but Anpu's three sons were there in heated conclave under a split-reed canopy. Khati stepped through the gate. One of the big men growled and stood, his hand snaking for a nearby maul. His two brothers pulled him back.

"What do *you* want?" one of them demanded.

"That," Khati replied. He pointed at one of a half-dozen net-stringer's floats leaning against the back fence. They were the simplest of craft, single bundles of reeds bent and flattened a little so as not to roll in the water. The user rode the bundle, either kicking with his feet or stroking to alternate sides with a short paddle. Khati's hands would be full, so he must needs kick. . . . "I want to go out in the water alone."

The one who had reached for the maul flushed and shouted, "You'll have nothing from here, you goat-licker, except—"

"Hapi!" snapped his eldest brother. Hapi fell blankly silent. The brother who had stood in the boat when the crocodile first surfaced said, "Take it and get out. The House of Anpu is shut of you and your king."

Khati nodded. He shouldered the float and strode away. It was an awkward burden but light enough to be handled alone by a strong man.

As the guardsman stepped out through the gate again, one of the brothers called, "Do you think the crocodile will send you back with your nose pierced, councilor?"

Khati did not answer.

The track torn through the reeds when the crocodile attacked Ro and Psemthek made a smooth, brown entrance to the stream. Khati stepped into it, feeling the crushed stems twist under his weight. Mud spurted between his toes like a thing alive. When the ripples began to slap his kilt, he set the float in the water and climbed gingerly aboard. Holding his double-pointed weapon flat against the bundle in front of him, he kicked out beyond the reeds. The hammering sun dried the linen of his kilt stiffly against his hips.

Khati's feet no longer touched the bottom, but the water was still fairly shallow and its current mild. He thrust steadily upstream, aided by the breeze that blew against his back. Eyes followed Khati's slow progress. The whole village was at work today. Usuit had made its peace with the new king, as it had with Nar-mer before. It is not for men to concern themselves with the struggles of the gods.

And if now and then a child would wail on Sebek's altar as the new king waddled up from the Nile—it is not for men to quarrel with the ways of gods.

Nef-neter stood now at that altar, still and erect as he stared eastward. Khati glared up at the priest who had defeated him, but the sun was bright and the distance too great for eye contact. Nef-neter could have been carven from sandstone for all he seemed to move.

Ahead of Khati the surface fluxed, but the tops

of the nearest reeds bent also. A stray gust had troubled the water, not something below it.

Water riffled again. This time there could be no doubt of the eyes that rose from beneath. Bulbous and high-set, they could have been a frog's but for their size. With his left hand Khati fingered the charm of frog-faced Hequit that hung against his own breast. The cord parted. Before Khati could grab it, the amulet had splashed into the water.

The body shadowing the tawny surface could have been no thing on earth but one, and it was approaching very swiftly. The crocodile had slid from its den somewhere under the bank and was moving to take the bait.

Khati began whispering a prayer, not for victory but of thanks. Nothing mattered but that he had another chance to kill. The float bobbled sideways skittishly as Khati shifted. He kept his weapon hidden as far as possible against the papyrus.

The crocodile twisted its length into an S through which all the monstrous bulk was driven forward. The blunt snout cut the surface in a V of spray. The jaws opened and the forelegs flattened back against the pale belly plates.

Khati shouted and thrust his weapon out vertically to the rush, but the jaws closed short of his hand and the double points. The bundled reeds of the float shredded as the teeth crushed through them. The float had been driven backward by the beast's charge, but the reptile was sinking now with the tiny vessel in its jaws. The papyrus did not have enough buoyancy to keep the great creature on the surface.

Khati tried to jump free. His kilt was tangled in the separating float. As his torso slid under water, the guardsman drove one end of his weapon at the crocodile's jaws as if he held an ordinary knife. The blade slashed deeply across the white gums. The float wobbled. A membrane drew across and back over the eye focused on Khati. He struck again but the jaws shifted, opening slightly, and then closed even tighter in a double palisade of teeth. Half of the weapon was within the crocodile's mouth, but it lay horizontal and harmless like a bit to which no reins were attached.

Khati's right wrist was held by the interlocking rows of teeth. They were cones, pointed to grip but without shearing edges to meet and dismember prey. Because wadded papyrus still jammed the creature's gape, the tooth in the upper jaw that pinned Khati's wrist to the gum below did not even break his skin; but the steward could not escape without cutting off his right hand. That he had neither the time nor the tools to accomplish.

The crocodile was still sinking. The float had broken apart. Shreds and sticks of papyrus mottled the golden surface as Khati went under. He reached out with his left hand, skidding a thumb across bone and scales as hard as bone as he struggled to find the creature's eye.

It was getting darker, getting cold. Khati should have filled his lungs before the crocodile pulled him under the Nile, but there had not been time to think. There was never enough time. Perhaps the knife would reach what his bare hand could not.

But suddenly it was too cold for even that. There was time now, however, all the time in the world—until the last spot of light went out.

Khati awoke, but for a moment or more he did not realize it. Then, though his eyes and ears told him nothing, the fetor and sharp objects in the muck brought him to an awareness that he lived. He thrust out his hands, touching earthen walls on either side. When he tried to stand, the roof caught him at once and threw him prostrate. Khati's eyes were dancing with lights now, visual echoes of the pulse behind his retinas. He vomited, only a little water with the taste of mud and bile. While unconscious he must have lost his breakfast and most of the water he had swallowed on the way to drowning.

When Khati reached forward, he touched scales and the great teeth which had dragged him beneath the surface. He knew where he was and why. Some time this night or the next, the crocodile would awaken and tug its prey back from its den into the Nile for dismemberment.

The beast did not appear to be breathing; its nostril flaps were closed. Khati's own breath was quick and ragged until he slowed it deliberately. He knew that the pain which sledged his temples might as easily be from the foul air as from the battering his head had taken during the past day.

Whatever was breathable in the den had to have come from the outside. Turning very slowly in the tight place, Khati retreated from the crocodile. The tunnel shrank almost immediately and ended.

Nef-neter had threatened the village with Chaos if it defied him, but the crocodile had not shown itself to be an enemy of order. Only of order which Nef-neter himself had not imposed. And the sun on the crocodile's foreclaws had picked out a green scarab ring like the one the priest wore. . . .

Khati squirmed onto his back in the slime of the

den. It was a mixture of finely-divided silt and scraps of the crocodile's previous victims. The wooden knife was still in Khati's sash. He slipped it out and jabbed at the low ceiling above him. Dirt fell on his face.

The den was a tight workplace which grew tighter each time the ebony chopped up into the clay. Crocodiles dig by thrusting their clawed forefeet deep into the mud and squirming backwards. The double armloads of muck are dumped in the river. Since the monster's bulk filled the den as fully as a sword does its sheath, there was nowhere for Khati to pile dirt save around his body.

Each upward stroke of the knife rammed a wedge of pain up Khati's sinuses as well. He did not really feel the dirt cascade over his face and chest. After half a dozen blows, he paused and brushed the accumulation back toward his feet. When he kicked it further, his toes brushed the scaly horror below him in the den. Khati froze as terror overmastered pain, but the crocodile was as motionless as a corpse. Edging forward, giving his body a little twist to clear more of the dirt from his clammy skin, Khati resumed his attack on the ceiling.

To a man in total darkness, the world is everything beyond the hairs fringing his flesh. In the den, that world was clay and the heat which crushed and corroded away all the strength that once had been Khati's. He found that he had driven a shaft as long as his arm and no wider than that. He could reach no farther. His legs to the waist were mounded over by earth, his face and chest were caked with it; and all he had done was prove that the open air was still further above him. Mumbling a curse, Khati began to widen the narrow upward track.

If it really pointed up. Khati had no direction in the blackness, no trustworthy instinct when each blood-pulse tried to split his skull with its hammering. But the dirt pattered onto his closed eyelids—that was proof enough. Besides, there was no choice. Only by cutting like a machine into the earth could Khati control the agony that wracked him.

Because of that machine-like pace, the guardsman bloodied his knuckles with a second blow bare-handed at the rock that had torn the knife from his hand. He paused, letting the new red pain wash over him. Then he reached out with both hands, touching the exposed surface. Raising the knife again—the point had splintered raggedly—Khati probed gently at the stone. It was rounded and at least as large as his head. When he had scraped the edges clear, he found they were locked by other stones, all held together by a matrix of alluvial silt. Khati was beneath a pavement—or a cairn.

The air was getting very dense.

Carefully, Khati worked the stone free. When he slid it past his body and against the pillow of dirt between him and the crocodile, an unnoticed edge flayed a patch of skin from his chest. The stone rested under the soles of his feet, giving him a better purchase as he worried out the block beside it and then a third. Khati's knees were high up against his chest, but he was through the rock stratum. He thrust his battered knife up with all his strength.

The blade wedged in a second layer of rocks. Despite the ebony's toughness, the wood snapped apart between the stress of Khati's thrust and the inflexible stone.

Khati was breathing very deeply, but there was no oxygen. His lungs filled with white fire at every breath, twisting and unraveling like burning wool. Only his chest moved, but he was not resting, not gathering strength. His strength had been dissipated. Nef-neter had defeated him, the scaly vermin behind had defeated him; and Death would soon come by to take the wager. And yet—

Fury, the god that had been with Khati all through his life, strode closer now. Fury had carried him a dozen times into blocks of opposing spearmen and brought him through, reeking of brains and blood, with no conscious memory of the blows he had struck. The red haze soaked into his tattered flesh, quenching the fire in his lungs. Fury set Khati's shoulders against the stones above him. It straightened his legs against the stones beneath. What is flesh to stone?

But stone is nothing to a god!

Slowly but with the certainty of an air bubble rising through a marsh, Khati's shoulders lifted. Stones and earth burst upward above him. The sun-blasted air sluiced over his torso like an ice bath. Khati saw nothing, heard none of the screams from the crowd that watched him lever himself upright from the ground.

When the rage lifted its blinders from his eyes, Khati saw that he stood behind the Altar of Sebek. It was uncovered now for the first time in his memory. Nef-neter beside it had again been haranguing the villagers. The priest turned and his eyes grew as blank as the glaring sun. The crowd gaped at Khati as if he were a god in truth and not merely the flesh a god had worn.

The altar was the fossilized skull of a crocodile larger than the one denned beneath it; and tied to that altar, dressed in a set of Khati's own clothes, was Hetep.

Nef-neter raised his hand. On it shone his gray-green scarab, twin to the one on the foreclaw of the great crocodile. His lips began moving soundlessly. Then his eyes glazed again and the priest's body stiffened into an immobility equal to that of the monster when Khati had shared its den.

Khati strode to the altar. His body was without feeling, save for the blissful anodyne of oxygen rushing into his lungs to burn away the pain. Two of Anpu's sons stood beside Hetep. They fell back at Khati's advance, wild terror flickering across their faces.

The fossil altar was grimly complete down to hooked teeth longer than a man's thumb. If stone had once filled the cavities of the skull, it had since been leached out by acidic waters or painstakingly drilled away by generations of priests. A papyrus cord through the fossil's eyesockets bound Hetep's wrists. Khati gripped it with both hands. His eyes looked into those of his servant.

Hetep tried to smile. Blood and bruises marred his handsome face. "I don't have a meal ready after all," he whispered. "You should dismiss me."

Khati twisted his hands and the cord between them tore as if rotten. Hetep stood. His sash sagged with the weight of Khati's mace. For his sorcery, Nef-neter had made the servant as close an analogue to the master as was possible.

Reeds shuddered in the Nile as the crocodile rose.

The crowd sighed; a dry, mindless sound like wind through the papyrus.

Hetep flexed his hands. He looked down at the river, the waves washing to either side as the creature clambered ashore. "Master," he began, "we'd better. . . ." He stopped when he realized that no one was listening to him.

The crocodile grunted as it came. There was no screaming panic, even among the villagers standing on the side-slopes of the hillock with a perfect view of the creature. A god was coming. Mudbrick houses had not even the pretense of security.

Khati's form was no longer his own. His last conscious thought was not of the crocodile beginning to mount the hill on high, splayed legs. Instead Khati was remembering his first battle, an array of black-glittering spearpoints bearing down on Nar-mer's standard. His hand had sweated on his mace haft then as he watched them. After that afternoon, even his comrades of the Guard had looked at him in awe, but Khati himself could not recall an instant of his slashing attack. His mind had been smothered in a haze of blood.

As it was now.

The villagers were keening, but the advancing crocodile gave a triple grunt louder than the thousands of human throats.

"Khati!" Hetep was shouting, "we've got to run!"

Khati shrugged off his friend's hand without really noticing it. He knelt, touching the fossil skull at the back and side of its jaw.

"Master, you can't move that, it weighs—"

Khati stood, his skin flushing black with the sudden exertion. The blood in his ears roared louder than the crocodile a dozen feet away. The beast's right foreleg extended, mirroring Nef-neter's frozen gesture. The scarab rings of priest and monster blazed at one another. The jaws were open, the ragged teeth cruel and wide enough to gulp the sun. Khati's own mouth was a rictus of flesh as tense as bone. He wheezed with mindless strain as he hurled the four-hundred pound altar down at the oncoming crocodile.

Khati fell forward as he released the missile. His mind and body were no longer the pawns of fury, but the heaping abuse of past hours had spent him totally. Through the tumult of shouting and the crocodile's explosive bellows, Khati heard the familiar *thock*! of his own mace on a skull. His eyes flashed him a tumbling kaleidoscope of impressions. One flicker was Hetep, standing over Nef-neter's body with the bloody mace in his hands. The priest's soul would never again re-enter the flesh in which it had been born; the back of the old man's skull bore a dent the size of the macehead.

And the crowd of villagers was crying, "Khati! Khati!"

The sunlight was a bath soaking poisons from the scars and bruises which still colored Khati's skin. He turned from the Nile. The two skulls on posts grinned back at him. That of the crocodile had been partly cleaned by birds and insects. The scavengers even picked at the brains where the cranium had been pulverized by the impact of the stone altar. Nef-neter, however, had been spared by everything but the sun itself. That had drawn the skin away from the priest's teeth in black ridges.

Khati stood, hands on hips, and began to laugh. In the fields, men and women heard their leader. They nodded toward the sound and trembled; and the prayers they muttered were for mercy from a god still more terrible than Sebek.

DRAKE, DAVID
Birds of Prey

The time: 262 A.D. The place: Imperial Rome. There had never been a greater empire, but now it is dying. Everywhere its armies are in retreat, and what had been civilization seethes with riots and bizarre cults. Against the imminent fall of the Long Night stands Aulus Perennius, an Imperial secret agent as tough and ruthless as the age in which he lives. But he stands alone—until a traveller from Earth's far future recruits him for a mission so strange it cannot be disclosed.

55912-5 (trade paper) $7.95
55909-5 (hardcover) $14.95

DRAKE, DAVID
Ranks of Bronze

Disguised alien traders bought captured Roman soldiers on the slave market because they needed troops who could win battles without high-tech weaponry. The leigionaires provided victories, smashing barbarian armies with the swords, javelins, and discipline that had won a world. But the worlds on which they now fought were strange ones, and the spoils of victory did not include freedom. If the legionaires went home, it would be through the use of the beam weapons and force screens of their ruthless alien owners. It's been 2000 years—and now they want to go home. **65568-X $3.50**

DRAKE, DAVID, & WAGNER, KARL EDWARD
Killer

Vonones and Lycon capture wild animals to sell for bloodsport in ancient Rome. A vicious animal sold to them by a trader turns out to be more than they bargained for—it is the sole survivor of the crash of an alien spacecraft. Possessed of intelligence nearly human, it has two goals in life: to breed and to kill.

55931-1 $2.95

Here is an excerpt from the new collection "MEN HUNTING THINGS," edited by David Drake, coming in April 1988 from Baen Books:

IT'S A LOT LIKE WAR

A hunter and a soldier on a modern battlefield contrast in more ways than they're similar.

That wasn't always the case. Captain C.H. Stigand's 1913 book of reminiscences, HUNTING THE ELEPHANT IN AFRICA, contains a chapter entitled "Stalking the African" (between "Camp Hints" and "Hunting the Bongo"). It's a straightforward series of anecdotes involving the business for which Stigand was paid by his government—punitive expeditions against native races in the British African colonies.

Readers of modern sensibilities may be pleased to learn that Stigand died six years later with a Dinka spear through his ribs; but he was a man of his times, not an aberration. Richard Meinertzhagen wrote with great satisfaction of the unique "right and left" he made during a punitive expedition against the Irryeni in 1904: he shot a native with the right barrel of his elephant gun—and then dropped the lion which his first shot had startled into view.

It would be easy enough to say that the whites who served in Africa in the 19th century considered native races to be sub-human and therefore game to be hunted under a specialized set of rules. There's some justification for viewing the colonial overlords that way. The stringency of the attendant "hunting laws" varied from British and German possessions, whose administrators took their "civilizing mission" seriously, to the Congo Free State where Leopold, King of the Belgians, gave the dregs of all the world license to do as they pleased—so long as it made him a profit.

(For what it's worth, Leopold's butchers *didn't* bring him much profit. The Congo became a Belgian—rather than a personal—possession when Leopold defaulted on the loans his country had advanced him against the colony's security.)

But the unity of hunting and war went beyond racial attitudes. Meinertzhagen was seventy years old in 1948 when his cruise ship docked in Haifa during the Israeli War of Independence. He borrowed a rifle and 200 rounds—which he fired off during what he described as "a glorious day!", increasing his personal bag by perhaps twenty Arab gunmen.

Similarly, Frederick Courteney Selous—perhaps the most famous big-game hunter of them all—enlisted at the outbreak of World War One even though he *wasn't* a professional soldier. He was sixty-five years old when a German sniper blew his brains out in what is now Tanzania.

Hunters and soldiers were nearly identical for most of the millennia since human societies became organized enough to wage war. Why isn't that still true today?

In large measure, I think, the change is due to the advance of technology. In modern warfare, a soldier who is seen by the enemy is probably doomed. Indeed, most casualties are men who *weren't* seen by the enemy. They were simply caught by bombs, shells, or automatic gunfire sweeping an area.

A glance at casualties grouped by cause of wound from World War One onward suggests that indirect artillery fire is the only significant factor in battle. All other weapons—tanks included—serve only to provide targets for the howitzers to grind up; and the gunners lobbing their shells in high arcs almost never see a living enemy.

The reality isn't quite *that* simple; but I defy anybody who's spent time in a modern war zone to tell me that they felt personally in control of their environment.

Hunters can be killed or injured by their intended prey. Still, most of them die in bed. (The most likely human victim of a hungry leopard or a peckish rhinoceros has always been an unarmed native who was in the wrong place at the wrong time.) Very few soldiers become battle casualties either—but soldiers don't have the option that hunters have, to go home any time they please.

A modern war zone is a terrifying place, if you let yourself think about it; and even at its smallest scale, guerrilla warfare, it's utterly impersonal.

A guerrilla can never be sure that the infra-red trace of his stove hasn't been spotted by an aircraft in the silent darkness, or that his footsteps aren't being picked up by sensors disguised as pebbles along the trail down which he pads. Either way, a salvo of artillery shells may be the last thing he hears—unless they've blown him out of existence before the shriek of their supersonic passage reaches his ears.

But technology doesn't free his opponent from fear—or give him personal control of the battlefield, either. When the counter-insurgent moves, he's likely to put his foot or his vehicle on top of a mine. The blast will be the only warning he has that he's being maimed. Even men protected by the four-inch steel of a tank know the guerrillas may have buried a 500-pound bomb under *this* stretch of road. If that happens, his family will be sent a hundred and fifty pounds of sand—with instructions not to open the coffin.

At rest, the counter-insurgent wears his boots because he may be attacked at any instant. Then he'll shoot out into the night—but he'll have no target except the muzzle flashes of the guns trying to kill him, and there'll be no result to point to in the morning except perhaps a smear of blood or a weapon dropped somewhere along the tree line.

If a rocket screams across the darkness, the counter-insurgent can hunch down in his slit trench and pray that the glowing green ball with a sound like a steam locomotive will land on somebody else instead. Prayer probably won't help, any more than it'll stop the rain or make the mosquitos stop biting. But nothing else will help either.

So nowadays, a soldier doesn't have much in common with a hunter. That's not to say that warfare is no longer similar to hunting, however.

On the contrary: modern soldiers and hunted beasts have a great deal in common.

APRIL 1988 * 65399-7 * 288 pp * $2.95

ENTER A NEW WORLD OF FANTASY . . .

Sometimes an author grows in stature so steadily that it seems as if he has always been a master. Such a one is David Drake, whose rise to fame has been driven equally by his archetypal creation, Colonel Alois Hammer's armored brigade of future mercenaries, and his non-series science fiction novels such as **Ranks of Bronze**, and **Fortress**.

Now Drake commences a new literary Quest, this time in the universe of fantasy. Just as he has become the acknowledged peer of such authors as Jerry Pournelle and Gordon R. Dickson in military and historically oriented science fiction, he will now take his place as a leading proponent of fantasy adventure. So enter now . . .

AUGUST 1988 65424-1 352 PP. $3.95

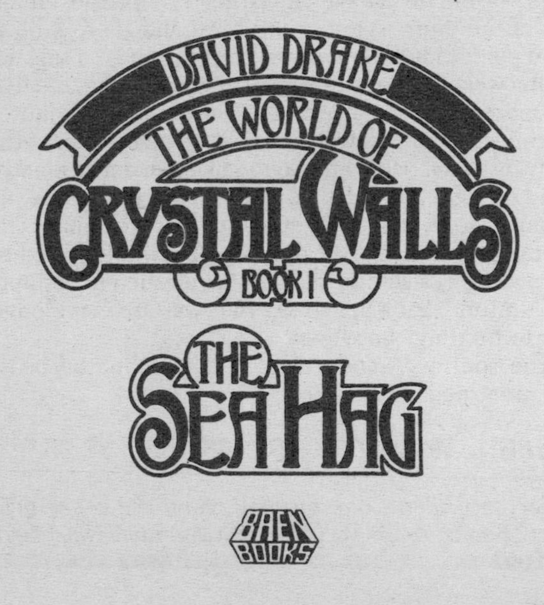